I0607211

THE SEARCH FOR Diego

A LAND IN TURMOIL: BOOK TWO

E. PAUL BERGERON

Cover Art by Sandra Bergeron

Cover Design & Formatting by Gray Publishing Services

ISBN 978-0996701310

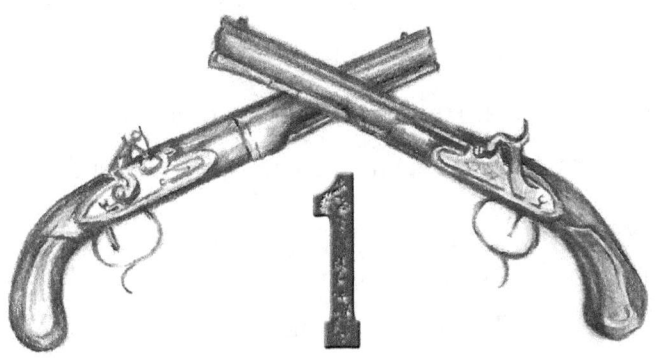

MOJAVE DESERT, ALTA CALIFORNIA
MARCH 1823

The sound of the black mule's hoof striking rock woke MacLeod. He sat up, listening for sounds not of the night. The mule shuffled its feet and stomped again. MacLeod slid out from under the blanket and tucked it back around Maria and the child, feeling for the rifle on the ground. Still no sounds came to him other than the breathing of the two at his side. A few feet away lay the dim form of the Navajo, Sebastian.

Then he heard it, a scuffling, like feet running across the sand and rock. He crawled over to where Sebastian slept. The Indian held up his hand and touched his lips. Something hid in the darkness. They listened and waited.

The mule stomped again.

MacLeod crawled back to the sleeping figures and put his hand over Maria's mouth. She sat up immediately. He shook his head and pressed a pistol into her hand, then silently moved out to where the picketed horse stood. He fingered the scarred stock of the Kentucky rifle, dropped to one knee, and watched for the first dim glow of the new day. He turned to look behind the camp where the two Indian guides had made their own camp. Nothing stirred. He reached out his hand and felt the tautness of the horse's picket, then he heard Maria's horse snort. The animals appeared to feel the same unseen presence.

The darkness began to lift as the new day came to life. MacLeod studied the dim outline of the shrubs and cacti, knowing that anyone approaching from the river would have the light at their back.

He spun around and threw himself to the ground. If anything is out there, he thought, why not attack the camp from behind while we're outlined in the light of dawn? And why had he not heard anything from the Indian camp? He yelled a warning to Sebastian as the first wave of arrows whistled through the air. He heard a cry and spun around. Maria lay on her side, attempting to reach for the arrow lodged in her back. MacLeod fell to his knees beside her as figures rose from the ground and charged the camp.

The flash of light from Sebastian's musket momentarily lit up the scene. MacLeod saw a thick body rush at Sebastian. MacLeod brought his rifle to his shoulder and fired. The Indian spun around and fell into a cactus beside Sebastian. Maria cried out as she twisted away from the wave of arrows that slammed into the ground in the center of the camp. MacLeod pulled his pistol from his belt and whirled to face another attacker, firing into the charging Indian's chest. He dropped the pistol and reached for his knife as two Indians burst from the darkness and leaped at him. He drove the knife into the belly of the first. He saw the knife in the other Indian's hand and knew he had no time to react as the Indian prepared to strike.

He felt the concussion of the ball as it passed his cheek an instant before the bark of the pistol. The Indian shuddered and fell to his knees, clutching at his side. MacLeod drove his knife into the dying Indian's throat and felt the rush of hot blood cover his hand.

MacLeod pushed the body away and swung around to search the desert landscape for other attackers. Three figures raced back toward the river, driving Maria's horse and the mules. He recharged his rifle and laid it on the ground beside Maria. He stole a glance at the cactus where Sebastian had made his stand. Two bodies lay motionless. As gently as he could, he shifted Maria to see where the arrow had struck her. On the ground lay the spent pistol she had found the strength to lift and fire to save him.

She moaned as she reached for the tiny bundle her body had protected.

"He's fine," MacLeod said, lifting the edge of the blanket to show the squirming baby, who looked ready to demand his breakfast. "I need to see how bad you're hurt."

"Will they return?" she asked through the pain.

"Doubt they will. I think they lost a few more than they expected."

"And Sebastian?"

"Don't know for sure. I'll check as soon as I take care of you. He reached for the arrow shaft. "I'm going to break it off, then we'll try to get it out." He ran his fingers through the tears on her cheek, then snapped off most of the arrow shaft. Her body shook as she attempted to muffle her cries with her hand. He rolled up a blanket and placed it behind her, then rolled her gently onto her side. The baby began crying.

Maria eased her dress off of her shoulder and gently pulled the child to her breast. He immediately sought the engorged nipple and began suckling. MacLeod bent to help her and caught his breath when he saw the point of the arrowhead protruding from below her breast. It brought back memories of Lucien Charbonneau, the man who had brought MacLeod west with him to trap beaver. After an Indian attack in the mountains north of New Mexico, MacLeod had removed an arrow from Charbonneau's chest.

He pulled the blanket up to ward off the early morning chill, not wanting her to see the concern on his face.

"William, we must talk."

The weakness in her voice startled him. "We will, but you need to save your strength. There'll be time later."

"No, there is not much time. I can feel this. We must talk now."

"You can't give up, Maria, not after everything. Diego will need you. I'll get it out, just lie still."

"No, it is no good. I have little time left. Please listen to me. You must keep going; you cannot go back. You will not have Sebastian to guide you." She stopped, her breath coming in thin gasps. "I know he is dead. He has not come to see me."

MacLeod took up the corner of the blanket and wiped the perspiration from her forehead. She closed her eyes and moaned softly. Her body shook with painful spasms, and he knew he could do nothing to alleviate her suffering.

She drew in a deep breath and continued. "Our child must live, William. We have gone through so much pain to bring him this far. Please take him to this place that Father Alvarez has spoken of."

MacLeod waited for her to continue, wanting to do something for her but knowing he could do nothing. He watched her take her hand from the child and pull something from her neck.

"Give this to him when he is old enough to understand. It is all I have," she said.

MacLeod eased the thin silver chain and cross from her fingers and wrapped it in his fist. "I promise. I'll give it to him and tell him our story, so he can understand what he's lost."

"I feel it, William, I feel it coming. Save him. He is all that is left of me." She took a deep breath. "I have always loved only you. Love Diego so."

He heard the breath leave her body. He waited, hoping and listening for another, then her body went limp in his arms and he knew he was alone.

The rising sun cast grotesque shadows across the hard, dry, desert floor. Tall, knurled cacti, bent and battered by nature's forces, along with twisted creosote and weathered mesquite spread out, seeking water far below the rocky surface. MacLeod held her to his chest and rocked, his tears dripping onto her lifeless face. Why had God taken her after allowing her to live through the terror of the last year? They had spoken of a Creator who loved his children, yet He allowed many who wrought death and havoc to live, while this woman lay dead in his arms. All because of their love, and the night she came to him in his cell.

The child began to cry. MacLeod ignored the infant's distress, wiping the tears from his own face while he fought to understand. Had they not suffered enough?

MacLeod pulled the blanket up to keep her warm while the sun climbed higher against a brilliant blue sky. He understood the difficulty in his situation. If it were only himself, he would return to the river and the Indians who lived on the banks of the Rio Colorado, who had pretended to offer their friendship. He would deal out death to as many as he could before they overwhelmed him. But his revenge would have to wait.

The whimpering of the child, their son, brought MacLeod back to reality. A stiff wind rustled the branches of the surrounding bushes, making him aware of the progressing day. He opened his fist to reveal the thin silver chain and cross she had given him in his jail cell in Santa Fe. It was all he had left of her.

As his immediate grief abated, he recalled her last words. She had loved him always, and her request to love their son Diego and continue on to that place the priest had spoken of.

MacLeod dropped the chain and cross into his pocket and gently laid her back on the ground, covering her with the blanket as tears rolled down his cheeks. He pushed himself to his feet and searched the land leading back toward the river for any sign of movement. He doubted the Indians would return for the bodies they had left behind. One thing was for certain, he couldn't remain there for any length of time.

MacLeod picked up his rifle and went to check on Sebastian. The old man had taken one of the Indians with him in death. MacLeod recognized the scars on the back of the Indian, one of the river Indians who had escaped from a California mission and made it back to his village. He had offered to guide them to the waterholes. MacLeod wondered whether the attack had been planned before he left the village.

After again searching the approaches from the river for another attack, MacLeod checked on the bodies the retreating Indians had left behind. He found the other mission Indian guide behind the camp, apparently the first one MacLeod killed. The Indians, who called themselves *Hamakhaave,* saying it meant the people who live beside the water, had welcomed them to their camp and traded beans and squash and small pumpkins, along with dried fish, for a couple of knives MacLeod had brought for the purpose. The next morning their chief ordered half a dozen of his warriors to help them cross the river. MacLeod remembered the old chief standing on the far shore and waving his goodbye. *So much for trusting Indians.*

When the baby's wail continued, MacLeod found the bag with the cloths and a handful of soft moss Maria used to clean the child and brought it back to where he lay. MacLeod picked up the baby and laid him beneath the shade of a small creosote bush. He had watched her change the soiled clothes, but found himself frustrated at the effort to clean and wrap the squirming body.

By the time he finished, the child had ceased crying and went back to sleep. MacLeod wondered how long it would be until hunger began the process again. And how would he feed a six-month-old child who had suckled at his mother's breast since the day he was born.

Thankful he had picketed his own horse close enough to camp that the Indians had not cut it loose, MacLeod began gathering what he thought he could take with him. He tossed two empty water bags into a pile, along with a small bag containing beans and a dozen squash-like gourds. A third water bag still held the precious liquid, and he placed it beside his saddle, knowing water would be his biggest concern.

MacLeod looked at his dead wife's body. He had to decide where to bury her and Sebastian. He couldn't leave her body in the shallow sandy wash where they had made camp. Their guides said the next spring could be found in small pools in a large rocky outcropping. Supposedly it wasn't far, but darkness had come on before they could reach it the previous night. He would take her there and hope to find a place to keep her body from the vultures and animals hunting food. He could do nothing for Sebastian, the old Navajo who had offered to lead them to California. MacLeod scooped out the sand and rock from beneath a large cactus and buried him, remembering two others he had done the same for. Belanger and Stewart, the two men who had mentored him during the months they spent trapping beaver in the mountains in Spanish territory. They too had died, the result of an Indian attack.

He brought the dun gelding over and placed Maria's body across the saddle. He then tied on the bags of food and the small amount of gear he felt he could take, along with the bag of silver coins, his earnings from two years of trapping. Another bag held the dozen thin bars of silver he had found deep in a cave in the Sacramento Mountains of New Mexico. He cast a last look back at the land they had come through, then picked up the child and led the horse across the barren land.

THE SPRINGS

MacLeod led the dun, with Maria's body lashed across the saddle, toward a leafy, gray-green tree growing in an arroyo at the bottom of a small mountain of rocks.

Above the arroyo he found a series of small pools fed by a hidden spring. MacLeod knelt by a pool and dribbled the water through his fingers. He tasted it. Slightly brackish but not much worse than the muddy river water they had been drinking.

He found a shaded spot for the child and eased Maria's stiffening body off the horse. He carried her body up into the rocks until he found a spot where erosion had carved a shallow cave beneath a rocky ledge. Carefully he placed her beneath the ledge and began filling the opening with loose rocks until only her blanket-wrapped head was exposed. Before completing the burial, he brought the child up, and they sat beside her body, where he said all the things he wanted to say before tucking a strand of her hair behind her ear and covering her face with the blanket.

After closing up the crypt, he retrieved a dead tree and placed it over the spot, then picked up the child and made a crude camp by the side of the pool. MacLeod gathered dry sticks and built a fire. While water heated, he went in search of a place to bury the coins and silver bars, realizing they were too heavy to carry any farther. About twenty paces away from where he had buried Maria, a lone tree grew out of a narrow crack in the rocks. MacLeod pulled several small boulders from beneath the crack and stuffed the bags into the crevice, then covered the bags with rocks.

He returned to the fire and fed the child cooked squash, then dipped a clean cloth in the water for him to suck on. It wasn't mother's milk but it would have to do.

The next morning, MacLeod went through the ritual of feeding his son while grieving the loss of Maria. He found the small bible his mother had given him before leaving his home near Boston and thought about finding a passage to read over Maria's grave. Again, he wondered why God let this happen to her after all she had been through. He tossed the bible on the pile of gear and picked up the three water bags.

He walked to the pool. There, as he attempted to fill the bags, he discovered two them had been trampled by the milling stock during the attack could no longer hold water. The night before, MacLeod had watched the sun set behind a jagged peak far out across the desert, where he figured he would find California. He would use the peak as a landmark as long as he could. But as MacLeod filled the remaining water bag, he contemplated how long he, the child, and the horse could survive with so little water.

He returned to the fire, where he let the baby suck on the water-soaked cloth before leading the horse back to the pool to drink. Then, with the child in his arms, he made a last trip to the cairn to sit by the rocky grave a moment and say goodbye, wondering if he could ever find the spot again.

After a final look at Maria's grave, MacLeod mounted his horse, turned up the dry wash, and out onto the scrub-covered land. Somewhere ahead lay this place where he and Maria had hoped to begin a new life. But MacLeod knew that before he ever got to California, his goal would be finding the next water hole.

Three days later, another barren range of mountains forced him north, along its base. He followed it the rest of the day, then made another dry camp among a cluster of mesquite bushes. The baby had cried himself out, and MacLeod opened the bag to see what food they had left. Three more squash and a small bag of maize, but not enough water left to cook it in. He let the baby suck up as much water as he wanted, while he rolled out the blankets to wait for dawn.

Two days later, in the late afternoon, MacLeod dug the sand from his eyes and squinted toward a small grove of trees nestled in a narrow defile by the side of the mountain range. He kneed the horse toward it, afraid to hope.

A spring gurgled out of the rocks into a glistening pool of clear water. A rich growth of small plants grew on the edges of the pool. MacLeod sat the child in the shade of a juniper and washed the boy's face and hands, then dripped the cool, clean water into his mouth.

After quenching his own thirst MacLeod filled the water bag and led the horse up to drink. The sparse vegetation would provide much needed food for the horse but MacLeod had to find food for himself and his son. He picketed the horse near the spring and built an enclosure with the saddle and gear to keep the child from crawling out from under the tree.

Later that day, MacLeod walked back to the spring empty handed. Not even a lizard, although the last ones he had eaten made him sick. He had to find something soon or shoot the horse, but how far could he walk? He searched the shaded area beneath the juniper for the child, hoping he hadn't crawled out and gotten his hands full of thorns again.

Ghostly tendrils of shade cast a spider web of shadow across the sand and rock where he had left the youngster. The child had managed to roll over and crawl up against the saddle before falling asleep. MacLeod wondered how he had managed to pull the thin gray strip of blanket over beside him, the one MacLeod had torn off and used to wash him with.

MacLeod froze a dozen feet away as a snake raised its triangular-shaped head. It had crawled into the shade by the child's side. MacLeod placed the rifle on the ground and eased his way to his left, hoping to draw the rattlesnake's attention. If he got too close, causing it to coil, the movement might wake the child. MacLeod kept his eye on the black-and-white striped rattle at the end of its tail. He needed to find a way to bring the snake to him or send it back up into the rocks. His moccasin caught on a dead branch as he shuffled a few feet closer. Without taking his eyes off the deadly viper he reached down and picked up the six-foot branch, noting the split in the far end.

The child whimpered in his sleep, drawing a measured response from the snake. MacLeod had to move slowly, but time was running out. He was sure the child would wake at any moment. MacLeod moved a step closer and paused. The rattlesnake followed his movements, swinging its head from side to side, its body quivering with anticipation. MacLeod shuffled his feet another foot closer, wondering what he would do if the snake refused to move. He dropped the forked end of the branch into the sand and edged it closer. The snake raised its head another inch as MacLeod scratched the dirt a few feet in front of it.

"Come on fellow," MacLeod muttered. "Move away now, just off into those rocks where you know you'll be safe."

He lifted the branch out of the dirt, moving it a few inches closer. The snake backed its head away, following the movement of the branch. MacLeod moved closer. The snake's body curled tighter, its tail whipping the air to issue its warning.

The child whimpered. The snake seemed to sense the danger behind it and rose into the air as it twisted about and drew back its head, its mouth open to expose its needle-like fangs.

MacLeod screamed, lunging at the snake. The forked branch caught the head in its downward arc. MacLeod's follow through pinned the snake in the sand, inches from the child's head. The snake wrapped its body around the branch, fighting to release itself. MacLeod pulled his knife and sliced off the head, kicking it into the rocks before kneeling down and taking the child in his arms.

Later, he skinned the snake and roasted it. The meat lasted for two days. Meanwhile, he had fed Diego the last of the squash that morning, and the food bag hung empty from the saddle.

MacLeod sat and watched the big black mule pawing at a tuft of desert grass, looking for food. MacLeod had awoken that morning to find the mule trailing the end of a woven reed rope,. Somehow it had broken away from the Indian attackers and following MacLeod's trail across the miles of dry desert.

MacLeod wasn't sure he could kill the animal. Their love-hate relationship went back to the first time he had seen it, standing beside the short, squat figure of a French Canadian fur trapper named Belanger. But if he couldn't find anything to eat soon he would have to.

The child whimpered. MacLeod picked him up and placed him in the blanket sling he had made, and pulled the edges up to shield his face from the sun and wind. He led the horse out from the shade of a creosote bush and worked his way through a thick band of prickly pear cactus, watching out for the small cholla cactus that seemed to leap out and impale his toes with their needle-like thorns.

Late that afternoon MacLeod couldn't go much farther, having stumbled and fallen twice, once dumping the baby onto the rock-embedded sand. The last of the water wet the bottom of the canvas bag, not much more than a mouthful. He pulled the brim of his hat lower to ward off the stinging wind. driven grains of sand and debris, and followed the dry wash toward a brilliant sun slowly dropping down behind yet another range of unforgiving mountains.A gust of wind whipped at the brim of his felt hat. MacLeod jammed it back on his head, for the moment lifting his eyes to check the direction of the wash. He caught the flicker of movement a half mile ahead. A coyote, possibly. He had seen nothing else, not for human eating but possibly tracks leading to water. Then two figures rose from the ground and walked behind a line of willows. One figure emerged leading a horse.

MacLeod slid the rifle out from beneath his leg and laid it across the front of the saddle. He worked the horse out of the wash toward the two figures.

Another hundred yards closer and they saw him. Indians, a man and a woman with one horse between them. The woman turned as if to run as he approached. She held a bundle in her arms. At their feet the sun glistened on a small pool of water nestled among a shallow ring of rocks. MacLeod's throat constricted at the sight. The child on his back had ceased its wailing and only an occasional shifting in his blanket cocoon signaled that he still lived. MacLeod had given up removing him from his back and carrying him in his arms. He feared the thought of watching his son take his last breath.

The man pushed the woman aside and brandished a long-shafted spear, indicating his rights to the water hole. MacLeod closed the distance, his rifle hanging heavily from his exhausted arm. He wasn't sure he had the strength to lift it, let alone the will to recharge it.

The man, wearing a cotton shirt and loincloth, stepped in front of the pool, his arms and legs heavily tattooed, his black hair chopped at the shoulder.

MacLeod noted the crude saddle on a well-fed horse and halted a dozen paces away. The mind-numbing desire for the water only a few feet away deadened his ability to react as the black mule made for the water. MacLeod slid from the saddle and leaned against the horse until he felt steady enough to stagger forward.

The Indian raised his spear and braced himself as the child on MacLeod's back began to cry.

A mother's look of concern creased the woman's face. She spoke a few words to the man and handed him the bundle she had in her arms, cutting off his protests, and held her arms out to MacLeod.

His mouth hung open in disbelief. He knelt and laid the rifle in the sand, easing the blanket from his back and struggling back to his feet. The woman took the child and went to sit in the shade of the willows, lowering her dress to expose a milk-filled breast. Soon the sound of the baby suckling brought dry tears to MacLeod's eyes. He dropped to his knees, crawled past the man, and buried his face in the water.

Dusk brought a coolness to the high desert; the shadows lengthened and the air cooled. The stock roamed free to search for food, never wandering far from the shallow pool of water seeping out of the ground.

MacLeod took one of the trade knives from his pack and forced it on the Indian, who stood in awe of the weapon. Both children slept soundly with full stomachs as MacLeod watched the falling sun sink behind a row of far-off mountains. He wondered if this California he sought could be much farther. He bowed his head and thanked Maria for the promise she had solicited from him. He would continue on the next day.

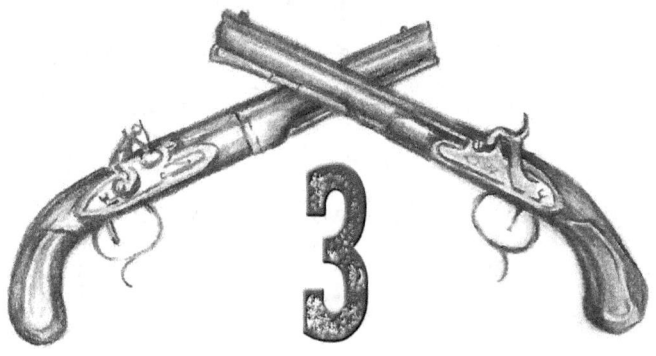

MacLeod woke with the morning sunlight filtering through the scaly branches of an ancient creosote. Both the dun and the mule stood passively by the shallow pool of water. He rolled over and instinctively reached for the rifle, fearing for an instant its possible loss. He wrapped his hand around the familiar stock and sat up, brushing away the accumulation of wind-driven sand and dry matter from his face. Diego lay at his side, snug in his blanket. But the Indians who had shared their food with him, and the woman who fed his child, were gone. A melon and a small bag of beans sat beside his saddle.

MacLeod filled the water bag and saddled the dun. Then he washed the child's face, fed him, placed him in the blanket, and swung the child onto his back. He climbed into the saddle and urged the horse forward; the black mule followed on its own.

The night before, the Indian man had drawn a crude map in the sand. He had pointed to the seemingly unbroken range of purple-tinted mountains to the west and to a narrow notch just to the south of a high peak. He drew a line to represent the dry riverbed where they sat, and where MacLeod would find water, and also where to leave the riverbed and travel toward the notch. When asked how far the mission was, the Indian indicated it was still many days away, leaving MacLeod to wonder how the man knew.

As the sun climbed out of the desert floor, he urged the horse into a fast walk. The food the Indians shared was not enough to overcome the gnawing hunger in his belly. He knew the child needed proper food and care soon to survive.

Just before dusk, MacLeod caught a flicker of movement at the base of a willow thicket about two hundred yards away. He slid off the dun and whistled. A young antelope's head turned to investigate the unfamiliar sound and MacLeod's ball struck it behind the shoulder.

The meat lasted until he rode up out of the river bed three days later and kneed the horse toward the notch in the mountain range, which he could easily discern as he drew nearer to it.

MacLeod's hopes began to rise as he worked his way down the narrowing canyon. Perhaps he and Diego would make it to this place Father Alvarez had tried to describe from the little information he possessed. MacLeod touched the pocket holding the letter to a Father Fernández, who resided in a place called San Gabriel. The passport given to him by New Mexico Governor Melgares had been lost in the Indian attack, making MacLeod uneasy about the reception that awaited him.

Sometime after the shadows began to shorten, he spotted a thin pillar of smoke rising from a grove of trees a mile or so ahead. As he rode toward it, an increasing number of cattle and horses grazed in lush fields on either side of the road, then a dwelling, a low adobe hut with an outside fire pit. The two Indians tending the fire froze as he passed, then they hustled inside.

MacLeod knew the three riders he saw on the road ahead were military. He felt a tightened in his chest as they closed. He raised the muzzle of the rifle a few inches.

Two of the men held long lances similar to what MacLeod had seen in New Mexico. The third wore a blue jacket and pants, with a wide-brimmed hat, and sat stiffly with his hand resting on the hilt of a sword. MacLeod took him for an officer, or at least the one in charge.

The dun halted without a word from Macleod, who kept his eyes on the one with the sword. The man kneed his horse onto the road in front of Macleod and held up his hand. He looked to be about five feet tall, more boy than man until MacLeod saw the thread of a mustache on the upper lip of the round face. The two with him wore pieces of the same type of uniform, well frayed and not overly clean. All rode solid, well-fed horses.

Macleod licked his dry lips and spoke to them in Spanish. "You fellows are sure a sight for sore eyes. I'm looking for a mission they call San Gabriel. Hope it's not too far."

The black mule walked past MacLeod, searching for grass along the side of the road. The young man's horse side hopped out of the mule's path, causing the man to swear and rake his horse's flanks with his spurs. The horse leapt forward before being wrenched back on its haunches. MacLeod noted the recent scaring on the horse's side from the use of punishing spurs.

The man jerked his horse around to face MacLeod, held out his hand. "Your passport," he demanded.

MacLeod had spent the winter months practicing his Spanish with Maria's father, Don Augustin de Cordero, but had still depended on Maria taking the greater part of any discussion. He shook his head, saying, "No passport. Lost it at the river. You'll have to take my word for it for now."

A look of confusion on the officer's face turned to one of anger. "You will produce your passport now, yes?"

MacLeod held his hands up and shrugged. "Sorry, no passport. I'll explain to your comandante."

The man's hand clasped the butt of his sword.

"I wouldn't do that," MacLeod said, reverting to English, then said in Spanish, "Please, take me to your superior."

The man shook his head and pointed toward the way MacLeod had come.

A heavy weariness draped over MacLeod's shoulders. He felt the child squirming in the blanket slung across his back and wanted no part of an argument with this man. He shook his head and used his rifle to point in the direction the three had come from. *"Allez,"* MacLeod ordered, too tired to realize he had spoken in French.

The young man spoke to the other two, then addressed MacLeod. "I am Corporal José Sepúlveda Rodríguez, and I have the authority to place you under arrest for not having Our Excellency the Governor's permission to be on his roads. You must hand over to me immediately your guns."

"Look, you arrogant little ass. I got no time for nonsense," he muttered. "Why don't you just lead off and take me to whoever it is that has more authority than you. I'll explain it to him. But I can't go back the way I came."

Corporal Rodríguez grunted and held his hand out for MacLeod's rifle.

"Afraid not that either. I'll just hang onto it a spell," he said. "You best head on down that way toward that big building I think I see in the distance and we'll settle things there." He supposed he should have removed their weapons but thought better of it. Not that he was thinking any too clearly at that moment. The three fell into a line and started down the road with MacLeod bringing up the rear. He couldn't believe he had probably made enemies out of the first people he had met in this country.

They followed the rough track, passing a squealing *carreta* drawn by a pair of oxen and driven by an old Indian bearing a switch. The lofty, pine-covered mountains, some summits still bearing their winter snow, led them north through fields of young grain and crops tended by slow-moving Indians.

Two horsemen trotted over to watch the small cavalcade pass, then galloped away to push cattle into another pasture. Another horseman sat hunched over his saddle until the young officer barked out an order that sent the man on ahead to inform those at the mission of their approach.

The young man repeated his hand motion to follow. MacLeod shook his head. But if the man wanted to act like a general that was fine, MacLeod was too dammed tired, hungry, and worried about the child to care. Let the idiot pose and strut if that's what he wanted to do.

They rode through an area of orchards and more fields of early spring crops, and wadded a slow-flowing river. Ahead, a large structure caught the rays of the sun, giving the adobe walls a golden-like hue. A false front held a series of large bells. As MacLeod studied the building, comparing it to the churches he had seen in New Mexico, the bells began to ring.

At the first peal of the bells, the Indian workers dropped their tools and trudged toward the building, which MacLeod took to be the mission. The corporal touched his horse with the needle-like rowels on his spurs, causing the horse to do a jig. He urged the horse into a cluster of young Indian girls, cutting one out of the group. The girl tried to elude the horse and return to the others, but the officer continued to herd her off to the side of the road. When he bent down to reach for her, she dodged under the horse's neck and scampered back to join the others.

A gate opened in the high adobe wall behind the mission and a robed figure emerged, holding an Indian child by the hand.

Corporal Rodríguez reined his horse over to the side of the road and squared his shoulders. He pointed toward the figure at the gate, then dropped his hand to the hilt of his sword.

MacLeod saw the anger still present in the young eyes as he came alongside the man. Apparently this one wasn't used to being challenged, or contradicted. MacLeod figured he might remember that in the future, should their paths cross again.

The man puffed out his chest and gripped the sword handle. "You are under my arrest until you go with me to see my comandante. Do not leave this place until I come for you."

MacLeod tipped his hat. "Yeah, you go ahead and do that boy," he muttered. He touched the dun and walked the horse toward the mission gate.

A short, heavy-set figure stood at the gate, his hands clasped at his waist. He shooed away a handful of Indian children who ran to encircle him.

MacLeod knew he wasn't presenting much of an appearance, being dirty, wind burnt, his beard and hair long and matted. His clothes hung loose on his gaunt frame as he swung off the dun and steadied himself. "I am looking for Father Fernández," he said. His hand sought the letter from Alvarez.

The man tilted his head in acknowledgement. "I am Father Francisco Fernández. You have come a long way I can see. You are welcome."

MacLeod felt the emotions well up within him. "I have brought you a letter from an old friend. He wishes you well."

Then Diego began to cry.

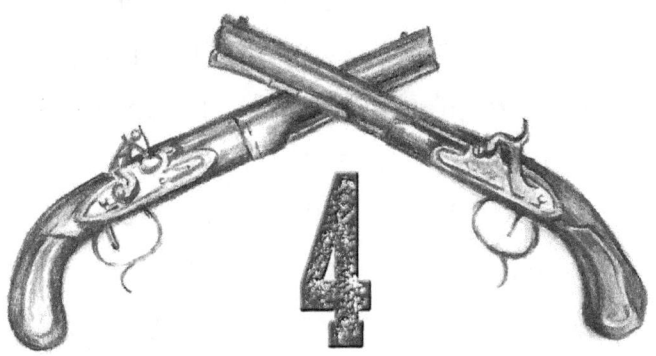

MISSION OF SAN GABRIEL ARCÁNGEL

MacLeod eased the blanket off his back and took the child in his arms. "Father, please, my son needs food and care. Do you have a woman who can help?"

Father Fernández's face showed his concern as he took the child in his arms and spoke to the boy at his side. The youngster sprinted back through the gate into the courtyard.

"Come, you also need food for yourself. I have sent the boy for someone who will care for the child."

Father Fernández led MacLeod into a long narrow room that had a series of wooden tables and benches. Indian women cleared bowls and cups from the tables and carried them to a large steaming tub.

"This is the *pozolero* where the meals are prepared and served. Sit, I will have food and drink brought," Fernández said.

MacLeod lowered himself onto one of the benches and rested his head on his arms. The worry for the child had taken its toll on him and he wondered if it was too late. The last couple of days the child's cries were rare.

MacLeod raised his head at the sound of scurrying feet on the hard-packed floor. A tall, thin woman, with long braided gray hair followed the boy over to where Fernández waited. She took the child and peeled away the soiled clothing. Without a word she hurried from the room with the child.

Father Fernández placed his hand on MacLeod's shoulder. "Her name is Rosalie Lorenzana. She will take him and care for him. If God should will it, your son will live. I will pray for him."

MacLeod wasn't about to question why God had stood aside and let Maria die, at least not at that moment. Someone placed a bowl of broth before him, swimming with vegetables and pieces of meat. It was accompanied with a stack of tortillas and a wooden spoon.

"It is called *puchero,* it is a meal we serve at this time of day. When you have eaten, the boy will show you where you can rest. We will talk later."

"Thank you, Father," MacLeod said. He spooned food into his mouth, wanting to say more but hunger overruled further talk. He ate two bowls of the stew and fell asleep at the table.

When MacLeod woke, he had no recollection of being led to the small room where he lay. A narrow bed occupied one wall, a wooden chest, over which hung a crude carving, sat against another wall. Someone had covered him with a thin woolen blanket.

"You have rested, that is well. Perhaps you can tell me now what it is I can do for you."

MacLeod sat up and rubbed the sleep from his eyes, then attempted to comb his beard with his fingers. The soft light filtering in through the narrow slit above his head told him he had slept through the rest of the afternoon and the night.

"Have you seen my son this morning? Is he all right?"

"He is doing as well as can be expected, I am told. I will take you to him following morning prayers."

"The letter from Father Alvarez, you have read it?"

The old Franciscan smiled. "Yes, it has been many years since we have communicated. Our paths have gone in such different directions. Perhaps we will have time to talk about my friend later. We were much alike."

MacLeod smiled, inwardly comparing the two men. Whereas Alvarez was tall and gaunt, with graying hair, Father Fernández had the same light-colored skin but looked as if he had not missed a meal in some time, and would hardly reach Alvarez's shoulder.

A thought came to MacLeod. Something that had not troubled him the last couple of weeks, simply because the need for food and water consumed his every hour. Before he had a chance to formulate it, the old man sat on the edge of the cot and stared up at the crude wooden crucifix on the whitewashed wall.

"This room is the one the good Father Zalvidea slept in. He loved the way the morning sun falls on our Christ, giving him the golden glow you see now."

"I'm sorry if I put him out of his room," MacLeod said.

"No, no, he has gone to another mission until he is well enough to return to his college in Mexico. But that is not why I have come. I must warn you, you have stirred the fire in our Corporal Rodríguez. He has come to me already this morning, demanding to take you to San Diego."

MacLeod let his breath out slowly as he reflected on his prior experience with Mexican authorities. "That little man should be reined in some. It appears he's too taken with his own position."

Father Fernández took a moment to answer. "You must be aware. Corporal Rodríguez carries much authority. Do not diminish his importance by his stature. His father is a former governor, before our independence. He has many friends."

MacLeod weighed the information for a moment, realizing he had probably made a big mistake by embarrassing the strutting little peacock, but he had pretty much come to the conclusion he wasn't going to stay in California any longer than he had to.

The priest continued, although he appeared troubled. "The letter speaks of a woman."

MacLeod nodded. "I buried her back a ways. She was killed by Indians from the river."

"Father Alvarez has noted in his letter that you are not of the Church, and you and this woman were not married." It came across as a question needing affirmation.

"It's in his letter. He told me he would explain this to you."

"Yes, he has told me the story of her abduction."

"There was no abduction by Indians." MacLeod wanted that idea blunted immediately. "She was taken by someone in authority, a friend of the governor, by the way, and sold to the Indians."

"Yes, but there is the question of the child, and of you and her," Fernández said, his eyes still focused on the figure on the wall.

MacLeod thought about his answer. They had talked about it, he and Maria. "You should know, Father, we were going to take care of it as soon as we could."

"Ah, you wished to come here and become one of us. Then you could have married?"

"Something like that," MacLeod said. He wondered how many black marks he was putting up beside his name. They had spoken of it, but not like the good father supposed. They thought they might find an American ship's captain to marry them, if one could be found. But there was something else he needed to ask while he had the opportunity. "When she died, we were alone and I know she would have wanted a priest to say something for her. Is that still possible?"

"Yes, I will pray about this and look for an answer. She had many things for which she should have confessed."

MacLeod fought to control the outburst welling up inside him. "Father, if you had known Maria, you would feel different. Yes, what we did you consider sinful, but how can you justify holding her responsible for that one indiscretion, when you have so many confess their sins and then they walk outside and do the same things again. They know you'll forgive them if they come in and confess again. Seems a might hypocritical, doesn't it? Besides, she spoke with Father Alvarez."

Father Fernández nodded slowly and rose from the bed. MacLeod followed him outside into the warmth of the late morning. Across the plaza, two soldiers slouched against the wall of a small building and watched a group of Indian women work, while other soldiers sat smoking in the shade of a fruit tree.

A robed figure emerged from the door in the church and shuffled across the plaza. He passed a group of small children who scurried out of his way. The thin, hunched figure carried a short whip-like shaft in his hand, muttering to himself and occasionally striking his back with the whip.

MacLeod had seen it before, in churches in New Mexico, a group called *penitentes.*

"That is Father Pérez. He is with us for a while, to rest himself."

"Appears somewhat troubled."

"Yes, I do not believe in the use of the discipline, although the blessed founder and father of our missions here in California, Father Junipero Serra, believed abusing himself as punishment heightened his acceptance by Our Father."

"Doesn't look like any of the Indians are too happy to see him," MacLeod said.

"No. Father Pérez questions their belief in our teachings. It is thought perhaps he is too severe in his punishment for their failures. In many ways they are like children. But, we must address your position here. I have guaranteed your behavior while you are with us, and convinced Corporal Rodríguez that you need a few days to regain your strength. Then it will be necessary for you to go with him and seek permission to remain."

"Where do I do this?"

"In San Diego. He will escort you there."

MacLeod recalled the last time he had been escorted to a town to obtain papers. He promised himself he would keep his opinions to himself this time if asked.

The tolling of the bells announced the approach of morning prayers. MacLeod stood up and walked to the open door. He watched the Indian workers lay down their tools and make their way toward the church. "I want to see my son."

"Of course," Father Fernández said. "I will take you to him when I return."

"Can you not tell me where he is? I can find my way."

"There are things I must tell you first, about the woman who is caring for him."

MacLeod rubbed his hands over his face and head. "Then I'm going down to the river and clean up some. Not much I can do for these clothes till I can find others. Least I'll feel a sight more presentable."

He found a spot along the bank of the river away from the women washing clothes under the watchful eye of an old Indian woman. MacLeod looked both ways, then quickly stripped off his clothes. He waded in until the water rose to his knees, then sat down and ducked his head under. He groaned with delight as the cool water rushed over him, leaching the accumulated grime from his body. After scrubbing his clothes as best he could, he used his knife to shave off the matted beard.

MacLeod wrung as much water as he could out of the hide clothing before struggling back into the still-damp shirt and pants, and returning to the mission. He found Father Fernández by the door of the room, conversing with a weathered old man.

"This is Juan, our majordomo," the priest said. "He is in charge of those that care for our gardens. He is telling me of his concern for the treatment of some of his workers by the soldiers."

"What do the soldiers have to do with the Indians?" MacLeod asked. "Seems they don't do much of anything from what I've seen."

"Yes, it is a problem. All the missions are assigned soldiers to protect us from attack, and to bring back our neophytes who leave without permission." Fernández dismissed the man and took MacLeod by the arm, leading him along the roofed corridor-like structure that fronted the rooms. "But the soldiers do not always follow our teachings the way they should. They set a bad example for our neophytes."

"Neophytes?"

"Of course, you would not understand," Father Fernández said. "We are different from the churches in Nuevo Mexico. First you would have to understand the reason we are here to begin with. It is something we can discuss at another time. Neophytes are the Indians who have come to the Church and have been baptized. Now they are our children, and we must protect them. There are times when they stray and perhaps wish to go back to their heathen ways in the villages they came from. The duty of the soldiers is to bring them back to their home here."

"What if they don't want to come back?" MacLeod asked.

"We cannot allow this to happen. They are our children."

MacLeod looked at the activity in the plaza and the number of Indians he had seen tending the crops. "How many of these Indians belong to this mission?"

Father Fernández's brow furrowed. "I believe there are near a thousand neophytes here at San Gabriel. The number changes constantly, with baptisms and deaths."

They walked down the shaded corridor to the end of a row of small adobe buildings. Across the courtyard a steady stream of smoke rose into the air, carrying a rancid smell. MacLeod pointed. "What are those large pots for?"

"Those are the vats we use to render the tallow from the beef. Some of it is used here at the mission; the rest is bagged and sold. We have a need to slaughter beef every day. You passed many of our orchards when you came from the mountains. We have apple and cherry trees, as well as fig and others. Our vineyards are further out, but we also grow all the vegetables we need to feed these people, and we are teaching them how to grow these crops for when they take over these lands."

"You're going to give the Indians all of this, and the lands?" MacLeod asked.

"That is why we were sent here. To bring these children into the Church and show them how to live as Christianized people."

Two soldiers sat on a bench smoking thin cigarettes. They rose as the good father passed. MacLeod noted the thin, tattered uniforms and the smell emanating from their bodies, making him wonder what he had smelled like before his bath.

They turned the corner at the far end of the buildings as the sound of deep, melodic chanting flowed from the sanctuary. Fernández's face broke into a grin. "We have our own choir. They are practicing for Sunday's service."

"Those are Indians singing?" MacLeod had never heard of it in New Mexico.

"Yes, some are quite accomplished. There are many things they can do once we teach them. Unfortunately many do not care to learn any new ways."

They walked across a wide path to a row of smaller adobe huts. Father Fernández pulled MacLeod aside before they reached the first hut and led him to a wooden bench beneath a shade tree.

"There are things you should know before you meet this woman," Fernández said. He lowered himself onto the bench, indicating for MacLeod to sit beside him. "Her name is Francesca, this woman you will meet. It is a sad story of why she is here, but she is a good woman and has a child of her own, so is able to care for your son. Like you, she has lost someone. Her husband was assigned to another mission in the north and was killed while searching for runaway neophytes. He died before the child was born."

MacLeod shifted on the bench. "But why is she here and not at the other place?"

Father Fernández remained silent for a moment. "Some things I do not know, but her family has cast her out. The woman who I gave your child to is Rosalie, and the Señora Francesca shares this room with her. Rosalie is also a great help in our kitchen. But Señora Francesca rarely speaks. She has yet to put her full trust in me.

"There is one more thing I must warn you of," the priest added. "Your story of crossing this desert from the river will be viewed as untruthful. No one has ever done this from your country. I do not wish to say this is untruthful, but you might consider having come here another way."

Rosalie, the tall woman from the day before, met them at the door and bowed her head to the priest. She studied MacLeod for a moment before stepping aside to let them enter, then walked to the other side of the room and stood beside a woman sitting on a stool near a sleeping pallet.

MacLeod entered the dark room and waited for his eyes to adjust. The room was narrow, with raw adobe walls and a slit in the wall to let in light. He saw that the dirt floor had been swept clean and the blanket on the end of the bed folded neatly. A low stand held a jug and washbowl.

Father Fernández spoke softly to the woman on the stool, whose head was bowed, a shawl-like blanket over her shoulder. When she raised her head, the blanket slid off her shoulder to reveal her breast and a child suckling. The woman lowered her head again and handed the child to Rosalie, then covered herself.

MacLeod caught a brief glimpse of a thin, shy smile on the young woman's face. She looked about Maria's age, possibly a few years younger, though he couldn't tell with such a short glimpse. But the smile seemed to hold a deep sadness, as if remembering something that brought conflicting feelings.

Rosalie and passed the child to MacLeod. He held his son in his hands, noting the clean clothes they had wrapped him in. "How is he today?"

"He is weak, but he has eaten and slept," Rosalie said. "He will need time to become stronger. You are fortunate he still lives."

MacLeod nodded, knowing how true her words were. His own body cried out for rest and proper food. "There's no way I can thank you enough for what you have done. I was afraid for him."

"And what is he called?" the young woman asked.

"His name is Diego, Diego MacLeod, *señorita*."

She appeared to think for a moment, then asked, "And you?"

"My name is William Wallace MacLeod."

The young woman said a few words to Rosalie, who walked to the other side of the room and reached into a small box on the floor. She returned carrying another child. "This is Señora Francesca's child," Rosalie said. You are fortunate she has enough milk to feed both."

MacLeod watched as she placed the baby under her blouse and covered herself again. He handed his son back to Rosalie and started to leave, then turned back and spoke to the young woman sitting on the stool. "Thank you, for Diego, and for me."

She nodded without raising her head. MacLeod felt disappointment. He wanted to see again that strange sad smile that spoke without words.

Father Fernández waited outside the door. Across the courtyard MacLeod saw the stooped figure of Father Pérez talking to Corporal Rodríguez.

"I must leave today for a time. I have to see to problems at another place," Father Fernández said. "Father Pérez will be in charge until I return. Perhaps then you will tell me more of our mutual friend, Father Alvarez."

The old Franciscan shuffled across the dirt and entered a gate in the mission wall. MacLeod watched him until becoming aware of an approaching rider.

Rodríguez reined his horse to a halt and stared at MacLeod before speaking. "You will prepare yourself to leave in two days. I will escort you to my comandante for him to make the decision about your illegal entrance into Alta California."

"I need more time," MacLeod replied. "My son is too weak to travel. The journey may kill him."

"Two days. I will return at this hour after morning prayers." Rodríguez spun his horse about and drove his spurs into its flanks.

MacLeod felt the cold fury begin to creep up through his body. He knew he had to temper its effect or bring on an inevitable clash that he couldn't win. He had a full day to make his decision about what to do.

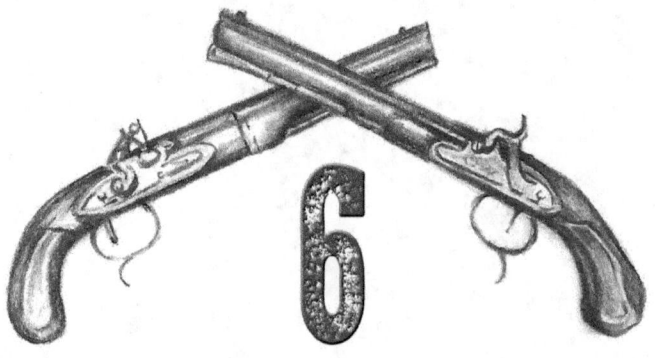

F rancesca rocked gently, the child in her arms fighting to remain awake and continue suckling at her breast. She had not asked his age, but she thought he was older than her Catalina, who had rolled over onto her stomach and attempted to crawl to the side of her crib.

Loud voices rose in heated discussion outside their room. She recognized the voice of the little corporal, and that of this one who had come from somewhere across the river. She could not help thinking about him. *Who is he? And how did he come to be here? And the mother of this child in her arms. Where is she?*

Rosalie shuffled over and took the sleeping baby from her.

"Have you seen his eyes, the color?" Francesca said. "I have never seen this. They are like the sky in summer."

"The one Father brought has eyes like this. I see trouble in them."

"Not this poor child, Rosalie. Perhaps this time you are wrong."

Francesca thought about the strange man again, remembering the stories she had heard of foreigners coming to their land who had blue eyes and white skin. Some of her friends wanted one for a husband, but there were few who stayed. Most returned to their ships and sailed away.

The old woman placed the sleeping child on a blanket in the corner of the room and carefully covered him.

Francesca watched her for a moment. "What did Father Fernández tell you about them? He must have told you why the child is so weak. And what about the mother?"

"They travelled far to reach here. They left a place called Santa Fe, he said, in Nuevo Mexico. He said they were attacked at a river and the woman was killed. He said the man carried the baby for fifteen days with little to eat."

"From the river? I have heard we send soldiers there and they sometimes cannot find their way. How is it this man survived?" Francesca remembered the hurt in the man's eyes and then understood the reason for it. She thought of her own hurt, and wondered if he felt it in the same way, and when would it end? She knew Rosalie would say *He* would decide when to end this hurt.

She walked to the open door and said, "I saw great strength in him. It made me fear him. I do not know why, but he is a man to be feared, I think, if he did not like you."

Francesca watched as the strange foreigner and the little corporal appeared to argue and shuddered. "What will they do with him? Will they let him stay?"

Rosalie put her arms on the young woman's shoulders. "He must get permission to remain. The authorities seldom allow this."

Francesca waited for him to turn around to see him again. She had only looked up briefly when he was in their room. Could he see her disgrace? *Will he return again tomorrow to see his son?*

"Father Fernández is to leave for some days," Rosalie said. "I am told the other one will take his place."

Francesca's shoulders tightened involuntarily. "I know it is a sin, but I do not like this Father Pérez. I do not like the way he looks at me. Do you think he knows? Do you think Father Fernández told him, about us?"

"He has only the Church in his thoughts. He does not care for the people," Rosalie said. "But I do not think Father Fernández would say anything to him."

"I do not like the way he beats himself. It is as if he hates himself, and that is why he seems to hate others."

"The good Father Serra did also, but he loved everyone. It depends on the man, I believe. This one seeks to drive out the devil, I think."

Francesca turned and walked to the box that held Catalina. She picked up her daughter and placed her on the floor, watching the child crawled over to the sleeping Diego.

And what will happen to you my child?

El Presidio Reál de San Diego

They rode for three days along a road cut deep from the hewn wooden wheels of many *carretas* and passed rolling pastures dotted with more cattle than MacLeod thought existed. Horses roamed wild over the green hills and found shade beneath the lofty branches of large oaks, or ran from the Indians on horseback whom Father Fernández referred to as *vaqueros*. He had pointed them out to MacLeod, explaining that the only Indians allowed to ride horses were these *vaqueros*. MacLeod remembered the Indian man and woman who had saved his and Diego's life and wondered if he was a *vaquero* who decided there might be a better life beyond the mission.

The first night had been spent at the Mission of San Juan Capistrano. Great iron bells hung in a row and rang out a welcome as they had entered the courtyard, Rodríguez always in front, like a conquering general leading the cavalcade of three. That evening, MacLeod learned about the massive earthquake a number of years before that had claimed the lives of forty Indians worshippers. The piles of loose stone and adobe bricks still lay against the collapsed wall of the church.

The next day, travelling slowly southward, the sounds of the sea and smell of the salt air offered a constant reminder that the great Pacific Ocean lay a short distance beyond a series of low hills. That night they stopped at San Luis Rey de Francia, where once again fresh horses awaited them in the morning.

MacLeod felt refreshed, breathing in the pure, clean ocean air that prevailed, and after the morning haze burned off, the green hills gave the land a pastoral beauty he had not seen since he left New England.

The soldiers ignored him, laughing among themselves and occasionally casting a derisive glance at their prisoner. With no one to talk to, MacLeod relived the past few days, not allowing his thoughts to drift back to the river and Maria's death. He would learn to deal with it later. Instead, he concentrated on Diego, and how he looked the morning Rodríguez and his two soldiers came for him. Father Fernández had left for a pueblo some miles away and could not be called on to intercede. Rodríguez had demanded the old woman hand over the child so he could be taken to San Diego, but Francesca had confronted the corporal with a steadfastness that MacLeod had not thought was in her.

"You must leave him here with me," she said. "I will look after him as if he were my own."

Macleod recalled the same shy smile that momentarily replaced the sadness in her eyes. He had nodded to her, not knowing how to accept this gift, which would certainly save his son's life. He had wiped away the tears that formed and mouthed a simple thank you. Father Fernández had mentioned the woman had recently lost her husband. She faced an uncertain future with a young child until she found someone else to marry. From what MacLeod had seen of the local male population, he thought her future appeared dim.

Rodríguez broke MacLeod's reverie as he led them past fields of new mustard that covered much of the surrounding hills and fields before cutting back to the coast. There MacLeod first glimpsed the San Diego Presidio. In contrast to the well-kept grounds of the missions, the presidio sat on the side of a barren hill that sloped toward the harbor. Below the walled military post, badly constructed houses sat on both sides of a thin creek. Gardens scraped out of the thin soil grew alongside several dwellings.

A sloop lay at anchor in the harbor, rocking gently in the afternoon breeze. No flag flew at the fantail. MacLeod had heard Father Fernández speak of the foreign ships that were coming to trade since Mexico won its independence from Spain, bringing goods that could not be obtained in the region.

Corporal Rodríguez squared his shoulders and placed his hand on the hilt of his sword as he walked his horse through the gate in the walled compound, ordering the two guards to stand to attention. Both rose slowly to their feet, their muskets lying in the dirt, and offered a clumsy salute. Rodríguez's hand snapped to his head in return and rode toward a small adobe house in the center of the square.

Before dismounting, MacLeod took an inventory of the grounds. A row of rusting cannons faced the harbor, the carriages of two were cracked, the wheels on another lay alongside the tilted hunk of iron. A broken ramrod sprouted out of the muzzle of another.

Rodríguez hesitated at the door to the house and took off his hat as a barefoot young girl walked past, a basket clasped to one hip. She wore a loose-fitting white blouse that failed to conceal much of her well-developed body. Rodríguez bowed his head and spoke to her, then pointed over his shoulder toward MacLeod. The girl walked a couple of steps in MacLeod's direction and tilted her head, her eyes wide with approval.

"If he is your prisoner," she asked, "how is it he has his big gun and you have nothing but that little sword?" She threw back her head and walked off, smiling at Macleod as she passed.

MacLeod's ducked his head and followed Rodríguez into the dank room, the smell of unwashed bodies and stale food competed with the heavy odor of wine. Rodríguez halted before a thick-bodied man behind the scarred wooden table and saluted. The man ignored Rodríguez and dipped a quill into a small bottle of ink, then painstakingly signed his name to the paper in front of him. When he finished, he waved the paper in the air to dry it and smiled at his accomplishment. Rodríguez still held his salute, standing at rigid attention while waiting for the man behind the desk to acknowledge his presence.

A colony of flies buzzed around a plate of food sitting on the side of the table. The seated man muttered as he picked up another piece of paper with one hand and a mug with the other. He took a drink, spilling some of the red liquid on the paper he had just signed. Still holding the mug, he leaned over and blotted off the liquid with his sleeve.

MacLeod watched the interplay between the two men, grinning at Rodríguez's formal display of soldierly conduct while the man behind the desk refused to acknowledge the corporal.

Finally, the man pushed himself half out of his chair and touched his head in a mock salute. "Corporal Rodríguez, I hope your esteemed father is well. Please pass along to him my wishes for his continued good health." He then sat down and cleared his throat.

Rodríguez snapped his arm back to his side while focusing on the wall behind the man's head. "My Comandante, I most certainly will. He always speaks of you with the highest esteem."

"Good, good," the man replied. "Now what is this you have brought to me that you have left your assigned station for?"

Rodríguez pointed at MacLeod, who stood leaning on his rifle. "I found this man who has entered our country without a passport. He claims he lost papers of some sort issued to him by the governor of *Nuevo Mexico*, or some place. He cannot prove any of this so I have arrested him and brought him to you. He would not admit anything but it is my belief he also helped some neophytes escape that I and my men were chasing."

This new accusation startled MacLeod. Nothing had been said about escaping Indians, although from what MacLeod had seen at the missions, he couldn't blame any of them for wanting to leave.

The man behind the table rose and held out his hands, wide apart. "You have no passport, how is this?"

MacLeod took a step forward. "The corporal here just explained to you that I don't have any. My party was attacked by Indians after we crossed that river east of here. Everything was taken."

"I am Captain Manuel Martín from Company Five. I have been appointed Comandante of the presidio here in San Diego. I have the authority to arrest anyone who does not have the proper passport. Now, you say you have nothing to show me why you are here. Where is this place you come from?"

"Well now..." MacLeod paused to clear his throat. "Captain Martín, I come from Boston, in the United States of America, but I was in New Mexico awhile until I came here. I figured as soon as we got to this country we'd see about getting the proper papers, but your man here decided to make it his concern. Seems a waste of people's time having them ride all the way here for something I was going to do anyway." MacLeod watched the look of disbelief build on the man's face.

The comandante shook his head. "That is impossible. No one has ever entered this country from these United States place you speak of unless they come here on a ship. I do not believe you. My own trained soldiers have tried to find a route to this river.

Sometimes they are successful and sometimes they fail and return, and sometimes they do not return. So, I do not wish to hear any more of your lies. How did you come here? You are from a ship, am I right?"

"No, sir, we didn't come on a ship."

The comandante slammed his hand on the desk. "No, if you continue this lie, I will not be able to help you. It is good you came by a ship. More and more people are coming here by ships."

MacLeod wasn't sure how he was supposed to get from New Mexico to California by ship but he figured to go along with the man pretense for the moment. "A woman came with me. She was killed by Indians at the river. Only my son and I escaped."

"Killed?" Captain Martín questioned. "And where was this woman killed? I have not recently heard of any people being killed."

"It was a big river east of here some ways. Not sure what it was called."

"Ah, very well. You left this ship and you and this woman wandered about until you came to a river where she was killed. That is what I will put in my official report. No more of your lies now." The comandante scratched at the accumulated dried food on his beard. "This woman was your wife?"

MacLeod hesitated, then said. "No, sir, though we were planning on it, soon as we could."

"I see, not your wife. Who is the mother of this son you speak of? You say she was not your wife. What kind of woman was this? Was she an Indian also?" He laughed.

MacLeod fingered the stock of his rifle. All he wanted to do was get this paper they were all so damned concerned about and go back and get his son. What he was going to do after that he hadn't thought out yet. He took a deep breath. "Comandante Captain Martín," Macleod said. He figured the use of the man's full title might be a good way to start. "The woman's name was Maria de Cordero. If the Indians had not stolen just about everything we had, I would have given you the greetings of Governor Fecunda Melgares of New Mexico. He signed our passports himself."

Captain Martín puffed out his chest and nodded. "Yes, I see what you mean. I only wish you still had this paper. It would have made my position easier, you see. I have these rules I must follow and you have no papers."

MacLeod shuffled his feet, feeling the tiredness in his body from the weeks of little food and three days of riding. He felt as if he could use a week in bed.

A peel of bells cut through the stillness of the courtyard outside the comandante's window. MacLeod had come to recognize the staggered schedule of the bells, thinking this one was the call to the evening meal. At least he hoped that was what it was since the corporal had neglected to stop after they left the mission that morning.

"So," Captain Martín continued, while drumming ink-stained fingers on the table top. "What is it you want me to do, I ask? What am I to do with you? I have no counsel here. There is no one but me. Do you not have papers from your America place you can show me? Something at least that tells me a name?"

MacLeod shook his head. "We don't carry any papers in the United States. I guess it's because our government doesn't feel the need to keep track of its people."

"I am astonished you would say this," Captain Martín said. "All countries must know where their people are. It is impossible to rule without this knowledge."

"We're doing pretty well without it," he retorted. "All I'm asking here is for some kind of paper I can show this fellow so I can go back and get my son. Not asking for anything else. Seems a trifling thing for you to do to put your name on a piece of paper."

Captain Martín gaped in awe at the outburst. His jaw worked a few times before he spoke. "And if I were to give you this paper you speak of, the one I have not yet made my decision on. What would you do with it? Where is it you want to go with this bastard child you say you have? What is it I must put in my report to the governor? He will ask what ship you came on. He will want to know how you plan to leave, since you cannot stay."

MacLeod looked out the window and across the sweep of sand and weeds to the cool lapping waters of the Pacific Ocean. More to himself than the blustering official behind the table he said, "Home, I want to take my son and go home, that's what you can tell him. Soon as a ship comes in I'll leave."

Captain Martín pushed one stack of papers aside and drew another in front of him. He pursed his lips, then reached for the mug of wine before speaking. "Our Most Excellent Governor Luis Antonio Argüello has authorized me to make certain decisions on his behalf, on things like this. Therefore," he said, again wiping up spilt wine with his sleeve. "My decision in this matter is to not make a decision at this time."

MacLeod laughed. He couldn't help himself. He was tired, hungry, his body ached, and the only man authorized to allow him to go back to the mission of San Gabriel and pick up is son couldn't make a decision.

"Corporal Rodríguez," Captain Martín bellowed. "Take your prisoner and put him in the jailhouse until I decide what to do with him."

MacLeod felt a deepening sense of what had happened in the past with Mexican officials and their jails. Rough hands grasped his arms while the corporal reached over, pulled the pistol from MacLeod's waist, and seized the rifle. The comandante had already returned to laboriously signing his name to another piece of paper.

8

A full moon, round and white against a sea of stars, crept across the narrow window in his cell. MacLeod sat with his back against the rough stone wall, his knees drawn up to his chest, and measured its progress as it passed behind each iron bar in the opening. Sleep came in brief intervals, interrupted by terror-filled dreams in which Maria still lived, standing across a deep chasm with her arms out, pleading to be rescued. He would awaken suddenly to find himself drenched in sweat, his heart pounding against the wall of his chest, only to discover he still lay confined in the stone structure overlooking a vista of sand and sea.

It had been a week, as best as he could figure. A week of waiting for the man in charge of the ill-managed military town to make his decision. MacLeod couldn't help wondering if the man remembered having put him in the cell. One of MacLeod's problems was what to do, if and when, they decided to let him out. He had to go back to the mission where he had left Diego in care of the two women. But what then? His promise to Maria had been to continue on to California. What had she wished for after that? They had talked about it all winter at her father's hacienda, outside of the tiny town of Taos in New Mexico. From the stares and whispers of those who had come by the hacienda on a pretext of some sort, it was obvious the women would never let Maria live a normal life among them. She had been taken by an Indian, and used, maybe by many, he heard one say. The others had nodded their combined heads in mutual agreement and hurried off to tell whoever would listen. And Maria had this child, and who might have fathered it? Certainly the tall, strange *Americano* had blue eyes, like the child, but might it not also be possible the child was Indian?

During the long months of winter, MacLeod and Maria had talked about their options. Maria wanted to try for a new life in California. So they made the decision one night as they lay in each other's arms. The pueblo Indian, Sebastian, agreed to guide them. He said he knew of a trail to the river and California was beyond. It seemed so long ago.

MacLeod reached inside his shirt and removed the thin silver chain and cross. He let the cold chain slide across his fingers and into the palm of his hand, then drew it up to his mouth and touched his lips to the cross. It was all that remained of her. No, not exactly. He had Diego, the infant being cared for by two women he knew nothing about, and who had expected him to return for the child in a few days. Would they still be caring for him?

The moon dropped from sight, leaving the cell in darkness. MacLeod folded his arms over his knees and laid his head down. *Tomorrow I will try again to see Captain Martín.*

Hours later voices woke him, morning voices, low and slurred, calling out to each other across the plaza. Then the first bell rang, loud and clear, followed by the others in a slow roll of tones announcing the call to the morning meal. MacLeod pushed himself to his feet and walked the two steps to the barred window. Three presidio troops huddled against the morning chill at the adobe wall of the compound, waiting to be relieved. Whining voices called out, followed by harsh orders from the obese officer in charge of the guards. A trooper picked his musket out of the dirt and lined up alongside a half dozen others who had emerged from the sleeping quarters, half dressed in what resembled uniforms. They came to attention, and the officer performed a cursory inspection before dismissing them. MacLeod shook his head. He had watched the same comedy routine each morning, only broken up when the comandante replaced the regular officer to do his imitation of an inspection.

From somewhere outside his cell, a series of low groans were followed by invitations to meet a real man of Spanish blood who could make her a woman. MacLeod recognized the ritual. The guard at the gate to the plaza removed his hat and bowed, offering to do for her whatever she wished of him. The girl told the gallant guard to find a sheep instead and marched toward MacLeod's cell. Each day she brought him his meals and sat in his cell while he ate.

He had returned to his spot on the floor when the sound of a far off cannon came rolling in on the back of a fresh sea breeze. He jumped up and rushed to the cell window. The scene outside reminded him of a night in the mountains north of New Mexico many months before when a dead tree crashed to earth near their camp. The little Frenchman, Belanger, cried out that they were under attack, and everyone had scrambled about in the dark, trying to remember where they had put their rifles. The panic MacLeod saw in the plaza reminded him of that night. He watched three of the soldiers assigned to the cannons attempting to load the rusted hunk of iron.

MacLeod followed the line of their panicked glances and saw the bow of a ship appear around the point of land guarding the natural harbor. The ship lowered a few sails, its speed slackening as it began a slow turn into the wind and finally dropping the rest of its worn canvas as men scurried over the deck. The ship dropped its anchor and swung with the current until a second anchor splashed into the water.

The door to the comandante's office flew open. Captain Manuel Martín rushed out as a cannon from the presidio roared in reply.

MacLeod saw the slow flight of the ramrod that the gunners, in their haste, had failed to remove. It struck the shore like a spear and buried itself in the sand.

The torrent of orders from the comandante managed to get through to the gunners and they stood silently by their guns, dropping a second powder charge at their feet and shrugging in unison while pointing toward the ship safely at anchor in the bay.

MacLeod had seen the same flag in the harbor in Boston a few times. The tricolor of France waved in the ocean breeze as sailors on board slowly lowered a launch into the water. MacLeod realized the cannon from the French ship was the announcement of its arrival and not an attack on San Diego as perceived by the presidio artillerymen.

The rowers reached the shore, pulled the launch up on the beach, and helped two people onto the sand. Captain Martín, hands clasped together at his back, awaited their arrival at the presidio.

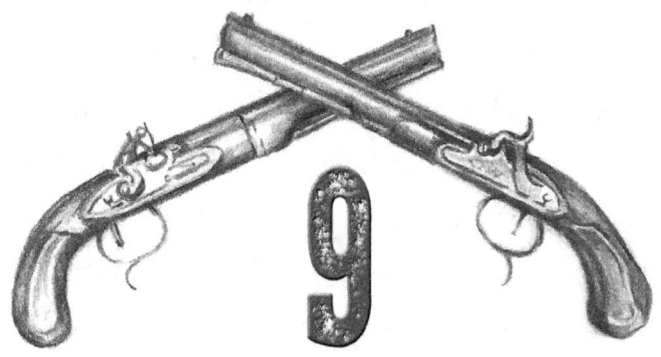

A WAY HOME

Four days later, the roar of cannon fire once again brought MacLeod to the window of his cell. Earlier, he had overheard Captain Martín say that an American ship was sailing south from San Pedro and would be putting in to his port.

Could this be it? he wondered. He searched the sea for a sign of another ship. Then he saw it as it rounded the point, the westerly wind on its starboard side, and sailed neatly into the harbor. MacLeod felt the excitement grow in his chest when he made out the Stars and Stripes at the top of the mainmast. The flag began its decent in acknowledgement of the foreign port, too quickly for MacLeod to count the stars. Before he had left Boston, Maine had just joined the Union and word was Missouri would be next. He wondered if James Monroe was still president. But here was an American ship, possibly out of Boston. Could he know someone on the ship? Was this his answer, a way home? Home, with his mother again. Somehow he would learn to live with his stepfather and the man's children. Could he convince Captain Martín to let him go back for Diego and leave on the ship? It would solve everyone's problems. Moments later the ship's launch splashed into the water and the rowers took their seats. Two men dropped over the side and sat in the launch's stern, the rowers pulled toward the shore.

Hours later MacLeod's cell door swung open, one of the guards stuck his head inside, and grinned a broken-tooth smile. Captain Martín had ordered the guard to bring the prisoner to the comandante's office immediately.

MacLeod ducked his head under the low doorway and entered the office. Two figures sat on a narrow bench to the left of the commandant, while two men stood beside the table with papers in their hands.

Captain Martín held his arms out in welcome, a vast change from his refusal to see MacLeod for the last week or two.

"Ah, the *Americano*. I am happy you are here. This man has come to talk of trade, and this one...." Martín said, pointing to a short, bearded figure who stepped forward with his hand outstretched, "is Captain Fanning of the American ship you see in my port there."

MacLeod shook the calloused hand, grinning at the thought of reverting to English. "William Wallace MacLeod, sir, from south of Boston. Don't suppose you're from thereabouts?"

"Surely, sailed from that very port not six months ago," Captain Fanning said. "Man here said he had an American lad in their jail. Whatcha do to get up their ire so?"

"Not much of anything except come here. Had papers but they won't believe it when I try to tell then the papers were taken. Even had to admit I came by ship to suit their thinking. Still, the man hasn't decided whether to give me a passport so I can pick up my son."

A tall man in a frock coat stepped forward and held out his hand. "Name's Hartnell, William Hartnell."

As he took the man's outstretched hand, MacLeod glanced over at the two who had not been introduced. A thin-lipped man sporting a small, pointed beard and pencil-like mustache sat with his legs crossed, talking to a striking-looking young woman. She turned her head away from the man speaking to her and glanced at MacLeod. The man halted his speech and followed her gaze. MacLeod felt a cold chill as their eyes met for the briefest moment. MacLeod had a funny feeling it would not be the last time they would meet.

"It can be something of a challenge in dealing with these people," Hartnell said. "I've been trying to convince them of the opportunities available to them through the company I'm associated with."

"I had no idea Americans were trading here yet," MacLeod said. "I met a bunch out of St. Louis who brought a mule train of goods to Santa Fe."

"Actually I'm with an English company, John Begg and Company, dealing out of Lima, Peru. My partner is a Scotsman, Hugh McCullough. We've opened an office up the coast, in Monterey. I'm here to get some papers signed and the good Captain Fanning here offered me passage down. It's a good thing we can speak their language. I picked it up in Lima doing business there. Haven't met one yet who speaks English."

Comandante Martín interrupted. "Yes, so, I will need to look over these papers and see if my commission allows me to permit this," he said to Hartnell. "I also have papers to sign for Señora Montero, and this gentleman from the country of France, Señor Dupré. There is so much work to be done in these matters I must apologize for the waiting." The comandante sat down and shuffled through the various papers waiting for his signature. MacLeod took the opportunity to speak with the captain of the American ship.

"When might you be expecting to return to Boston, Captain Fanning?"

The short, stocky man stood with his legs spread as if on the pitching deck of his ship and contemplated the question for a moment. "Well now, we've been down in South America a spell. I heard about the trade here in Mexican California opening up so I came to find out if it were true. I've nothing to trade on this trip but figure I would spend a couple of weeks exploring the possibilities. Why do you ask?"

MacLeod felt a rush of excitement. "Might I buy passage home for me and my son? I can pay our way."

"Mind you, we're a trading ship, not much room for passengers and such. But I am short a second mate. Suppose I could let you have his berth. Where is this son of yours. Can't be much more than a young'un, judging by your age."

MacLeod grasped the man's hand. "He's might little right now, but I can manage him. He's with some people at a mission place they call San Gabriel, until I can arrange papers. All I'd have to do is hurry on back and get him. Meet you back here in a week or so, if you'll be here."

"Well then, I wish you good luck, but you didn't mention your wife. Will she be with you?"

MacLeod shook his head. "Afraid not. We ran into some Indians a couple of weeks back. She was killed."

Captain Fanning bowed his head. "I'm right sorry to hear of that, but you and your son are surely welcome to travel with us back to Boston."

While they talked, the woman rose from the bench, followed by the one called Dupré. They passed MacLeod on their way to the door. She held his gaze for a brief moment as she passed. MacLeod caught his breath. The woman couldn't have been much more than a girl but carried herself with a rare dignity.

The Englishman stood beside the desk, explaining the reason for the papers the comandante had before him, and requested his signature. MacLeod turned to watch the woman and Frenchman as they left the comandante's office.

Captain Martín appeared flustered, shaking his head, then dropping the papers on the desk and reaching for a glass of wine. The wine seemed to help him make his decision. He used a small knife to shape the end of his quill pen and dipped it in a pot of ink. With a flourish he began the laborious task of signing his name.

MacLeod waited for him to finish before speaking. "Captain Martín, with the captain here willing to allow me to book passage, all I need do is go back for my son. Suppose I need papers for that?"

"We will discuss this in time. I have much to do today as you can see by the papers on my desk. You may wait outside until I decide."

MacLeod followed the Englishman, Hartnell, and the American ship captain out into the dusty courtyard. The two who had left earlier were walking together toward the row of cannons facing the harbor.

Hartnell spoke. "I hope the good comandante here is reasonable about your situation. Seems like giving you a temporary passport is a good way for him to deal with the problem of you being here."

"I hope so, too. What are the others waiting for?" MacLeod asked.

"It's not clear what the Frenchman wants. He is said to be buying or trading for otter skins which he hopes to take to China to sell. But from what I've heard, the hunting hasn't been too good lately."

"Is the woman his wife?"

"No, though he appears to have taken quite a fancy to her," Hartnell said. "Her name is Doña Marisol Montero. She's quite a beauty, although there's not much known about her. Her husband is quite a bit older than her, an influential fellow up the coast at the Pueblo de los Ángeles. Gets himself involved a great deal in the political situation here since the Spanish got themselves turned out."

"So what is she doing here?"

"I understand she's taking the French ship down to South America, and then travelling to Spain to have her child. That way the child will be considered a Spaniard."

MacLeod remembered something about the status of those born in Spain compared to those born in Mexico. He had never been able to understand why they made it such an issue. "Seems a far way to go to have a baby."

While they talked, MacLeod had watched a small boat leave the French ship and land a man on the shore. The man mounted a horse, rode up to the presidio, and approached Dupré. They walked off by themselves to talk, leaving the woman alone.

She walked casually toward MacLeod and Hartnell. When she reached them, she offered a gloved hand. MacLeod took it and bowed slightly. "Ma'am."

The briefest shadow of a smile creased the sides of her face. He understood why she would be considered a beauty, in any country.

She placed a gloved hand gently on his arm. "I understand a little of your language. I heard of your loss, and of your concern for your son. How old is he, and his name, please?"

She was taller than most women he had known, even taller than Maria, though just as slim. MacLeod found himself lost in the depth of her black eyes and her voice, low and husky. Her eyes captured his and held them, waiting for an answer. He felt she truly wished to know.

"He's no more than half a year," he said. "Just a little fellow, señora. We've had a troublesome time, his mother dying and all. I was forced to leave him with a woman who offered to take care of him. He was too weak to travel."

"I am sorry about his mother. What is his name?"

"Diego, and thank you for your concern."

"I heard it said you are from America. What will you do now?"

"The captain here, of the American ship, is bound for Boston. He said he'll give us passage home."

Dupré finished his conversation with the French ship's captain and strode toward them. He appeared upset that the woman had stopped to talk with MacLeod. He took her elbow and began to walk off with her. MacLeod caught the smell of a sickly perfume as he passed.

The woman stepped away from the man's grasp and turned back to face MacLeod. "I wish you and your son good fortune, sir, and a safe passage."

MacLeod bowed. "And to you also, señora."

He watched them walk toward the shore, wondering if she knew what the Frenchman at her side wanted.

"Only met her once," Hartnell said. "There are few who would take on such a voyage as she has ahead of her."

MacLeod said his goodbye and walked back to the comandante's office to find out about a passport.

Captain Martín picked up the paper in front of him and held it up for MacLeod to see. "I have signed this for you. I have the authority to only allow you another five days here in Alta California. It is a good thing the good captain has said he would take you, otherwise I would have to put you back in my jail. You can go back to San Gabriel Arcángel and pick up this child you say is yours and return here or…." Martín sat back in his chair and laughed. "You can leave the way you say you came. But since this is a lie, I expect you will return and take this ship. I do not even know whether this child is yours."

MacLeod took the paper and tucked it inside his shirt. *Five days should be sufficient.*

M arisol Montero stood at the ship's rail, the soft sea breeze swirling her hair around to caress her cheek. She lifted her hand to tuck it back behind her ear, wishing she had spent a moment to pin it before leaving the cramped quarters of her cabin. She watched the walls of the presidio slowly make their way toward the ship's stern as the tide ebbed out of the bay, swinging the ship as far as its anchor would allow.

The woman sighed as she thought about the long voyage ahead. A voyage of necessity. A voyage to keep her secret—and husband's secret—safe.

Marisol recalled the first time she had seen Vicente. She was sixteen, living on the streets of Vera Cruz. He had picked her up and taken her to his hotel room, and demanded she clean herself up before he would have her. Somehow, through the tangled hair and thread-worn clothing she wore, he had seen the raw beauty that would cause men to want her. Vicente Montero had seen it, and hoped his desire would overcome his problem. They had made several attempts over the next few weeks, but he was unable to perform the act.

She had not laughed at him, or ridiculed him, and even offered to return the money he paid for her. Then he offered her a chance to leave the streets. He would marry her and take her with him to Alta California. He would give her whatever she wanted in the way of clothing, servants, and a tutor who would teach her the ways of manners of a woman of wealth. A life she had never dreamt possible. In return, Marisol would act as his wife and never reveal his secret. She knew the value Spanish men felt for their sexual prowess. She would be the proof of his.

She had not regretted the four years spent with him, and she never had a desire to break her promise. Even though many men had attempted to lure her into a clandestine *liaison*, the latest being the attention lavished on her by the Frenchman Dupré. But Marisol knew the ways of men. She knew how to make them desire her. She knew how to turn that attention elsewhere. The Frenchman was no different, regardless of his titles and stories of royal bloodlines. And she had seen the way he reacted to the attentions she had given to the *Americano.*

The launch pulled up alongside the ship and two men boarded. Dupré smiled as he approached her. He removed his hat and bowed, apologizing for being unable to continue on with her, that he would be transferring to the American ship.

Marisol acknowledged his bow. Yes, she thought, the ship sails soon, and I will be away from you and your unwanted attentions. But she did not want him to have gained any illusions about their relationship. It was time to step on him.

"What will they do with him, the one from America?" she asked.

Dupré tossed his head. "I suppose they will make an example of him, so others do not follow. It is of no concern of mine."

"Did you not believe the story he told about the child, and the woman?"

"An impossible story. He is obviously a deserter from one of their ships here to buy the skins of the cattle. They are all of a less than bourgeois character."

Dupré removed a scented cloth from a coat pocket and held it to his nose. "You should not suffer the worry of what they will do with him. You have a long journey to perform. I only wish that I might have accompanied you across the seas. There is much I would like to have told you."

Yes, Marisol thought, and it would have been all about you. But her questions had not been answered about this strange man with the yellow hair and blue eyes. She would never know what happened to him. She would sail in the morning. But that was fortunate also. She would not have to face him again. She would rather remember him as he was, and not have to discover she was developing feelings for someone who would test her resolve. Yes, she would sail, and he would, what? Was it possible he might still be there when she returned? Oh, God, she thought, please let him be gone.

G aston Dupré screwed up his lips at the first taste of the sour liquid they served and dared called wine. He wondered how these people could drink such swill and believe it enjoyable. And the food served on the unclean dishes in this mission in this primitive place they called San Diego was no better.

He tore off a piece of the hardened tortilla and chewed on it, hoping to quell the rising bile in his stomach while watching the two priests at the long wooden table silently devour their bowls of gruel.

Their filthy habits were a testament to how the whole business at this place was conducted.

This was the second day spent negotiating with the priests for supplies for the ship. Earlier he had decided to send the ship down the coast to Lima to trade some of the items brought from France for the more primitive goods sought after in Alta California.

Dupré swallowed another mouthful of wine and wiped his mouth. He expected the ship to return in three months, and by then he hoped to have hired some of the Alaskan natives the Russians used for hunting the otter. These natives he planned on sending out to the islands at the mouth of the harbor of San Francisco. Those in the north had told him the islands were hunted out, but he doubted most of what they said since they had no boats of their own to hunt the animals themselves.

For a moment he reviewed what the ship's hold already contained in the way of skins. Only what few he had been able to obtain from the priests in some of the most northern missions who had accepted them from Russians as payment for fresh fruit, meat, and vegetables.

The elder priest at the far end of the plank table rose from his bench, scratched at his groin, and farted before shuffling out of the dining area to return to his quarters for his afternoon siesta.

Dupré swore he would never return to this land of peasants and savages. It was bad enough having to sit through their morning services in the church and listen to battered Latin mumbled through lips stained with sacramental wine. He had even heard a rumor that the consecrated water sent north from San Blas had not been properly packed and some of the containers had leaked. Not having anyone in Alta California of high enough office in the Church to bless new water, they had used olive oil to extend what they had.

While waiting for the other priest to complete his meal and issue the order for the supplies, Dupré's thoughts wandered back to the woman, the tall, dark-eyed woman who carried herself with the dignity of royalty, and who would sail on his ship to Lima. What was she doing in this cultural desert? But again his blood rose as he remembered the look that had passed between her and the half savage, the American who wore bloodstained animal skins. And their last moments together, on the ship, when she dismissed what he had to say and asked him about the fate of the American.

But, of all the perceived insults he felt he had received, none could equal the smirk on the face of the tall American savage when the woman pulled away from Dupré's grasp and spoke to him.

He rose from the table and made his way into the fresh air of the courtyard. His rented horse stood waiting to return him to the American ship. Dupré swore that if he was still in this backward country when Marisol returned, he would have her.

An early morning fog blanketed the harbor and buildings of the presidio. Captain Martín had released MacLeod from the jail but had not signed his passport. Not only that, but Corporal Rodríguez had been allowed to return to San Gabriel, with MacLeod's guns. What would the two women at the mission think when Rodriguez returned alone? It had been two weeks since MacLeod left Diego with them. Would they still be caring for him? Or would they have passed him over to others?

The skiff the American ship used to transport supplies to the ship sat at the water's edge. MacLeod hailed it before the crew had a chance to push off. They made room for him among the heaps of vegetables and fresh meat.

When they reached the ship, MacLeod climbed aboard and moved toward the stern, where he saw Captain Fanning watching the French ship leave the harbor. MacLeod turned to look and saw the woman he had spoken with standing beside a small Indian girl. She tilted her head in MacLeod's direction, and he lifted a hand in recognition. He then resumed his walk to the stern and approached Fanning.

"Do you have a few minutes, Captain?" MacLeod asked.

"Of course," Fanning replied. "If you have a mind, why not step below and join me for breakfast. It isn't often we have fresh meat and such for our meals. I believe Mr. Hartnell will be joining me as well."

Fanning led the way below, MacLeod ducking his head as descended the steep steps and into a small cabin at the rear of the ship. Hartnell was already seated and drinking coffee.

MacLeod grinned as Fanning's man offered him a steaming mug. "Haven't tasted coffee in months. Hot chocolate I can tell you all about, but, lord, this is going to be a treat."

MacLeod cradled the cup in his hands. "Captain, the comandante is allowing me only five days to go back where I left my son and return here. It appears he doesn't want to be questioned later for overstepping his authority."

Before Fanning could respond, Hartnell laughed and said, "Well, it's unfortunate you don't stay. I could offer you employment, and when you come to Monterey you could ask the governor for more permanent papers."

MacLeod sipped his coffee before answering. "I do appreciate your offer, but with what I've been through the last couple of years with these Spanish and Mexican people, I figure the sooner I get out of their damned country the better."

"I can understand," Hartnell replied. "They do business a bit different. It takes some getting used to, and some head shaking, but this land here, I don't believe they know what they have. They better take notice soon before someone takes it way from them." Hartnell stood and picked up his hat. "I think I'll wander the deck a spell."

MacLeod addressed the captain again. "You're taking that Frenchman back with you, I hear."

"As far as San Pedro, then he and Mr. Hartnell will catch another ship to go farther up the coast."

"The man appears to anger easily."

Captain Fanning pushed his coffee mug away and pursed his lips. "The man is a strange one, if you can believe half the stories he tells. Claims to have Bourbon blood in his veins. But, as I understand it, his wife has the lineage. Still, that doesn't stop him from making other claims. Calls himself Gaston Dupré, Le Chevalier de la Légion d'Honneur."

MacLeod chuckled and asked, "What's he doing here?"

Fanning shook his head. "He had a notion to fill up his ship with sea otter skins and take them to China, but it hasn't proved a success.

I did a trip a few years back. Used the profits to buy an interest in this ship, but the market isn't what it used to be; least the supply isn't. Russians saw to that. Anyways, young fellow, what can I do for you?"

"Well, that arrogant little toy soldier who brought me here left and took my guns. I feel kinda naked without them, and thought you might have a pistol to sell."

Captain Fanning went to the door of his cabin and spoke to a man swabbing the deck nearby. Turning back to MacLeod, he said, "I've sent for the mate. We don't carry much in the way of arms, but we do have a few for personal protection when we're ashore, and of course for the occasional dispute at sea. Just enough for my first and second mate and myself, but I do believe we might have an extra."

The man returned a few minutes later and laid a weathered flintlock on the captain's table, along with two small bags, one of which hit table with a dull thud.

"Thank you, Captain," MacLeod said. "I'm hoping to claim my own, and I'll return this one. If you're held up a day or two, I might find a spot up the coast a ways to watch for your ship."

MacLeod shook hands with the man and picked up the pistol, tucking it beneath his sash and pocketing the powder and balls. Neither the comandante nor Rodriguez had thought to search him, so he still had the silver coins nestled in the buckskin bag tied to his belt. He used them to purchase woolen pants and a couple of shirts. He would be damned if he would wear the silly-looking pants the local men wore. But he would need some new moccasins soon, if he could find some skins to make them with. In the meantime, boots would suffice, so he grabbed a pair from the few trade goods left from Fanning's venture in South America.

On deck, MacLeod found Hartnell waiting to speak to him. "If things were to change and you decide to stay, let me know. I've got more than I can handle, and too many places to try to be. And the killing season will be upon us shortly."

"Killing season?" MacLeod said.

"Aye, all the missions do their slaughtering at the same time. It's called *la matanza* and takes place from July through September. If you're still around, you'll recognize it from the unholy smell."

"Thanks again for the offer, but I hope to make it back here to meet the captain in a week or so. Then it's home for me and my son."

"Well, good luck," Hartnell said. "If you ever get up to Monterey, look me up. Company's called McCulloch and Hartnell, but the Mexicans call it *Macala en Arnel*."

Back at the presidio, MacLeod found Captain Martín haranguing a slope-shouldered soldier who stood in front of the desk, looking as if he hadn't slept in a week. The unshaven youngster scurried out of the room, leaving the comandante still muttering his complaints.

Captain Martín handed over the passport and said he had informed Corporal Rodríguez of his decision. He denied giving Rodriguez permission to remove MacLeod's guns from the office.

MacLeod found his horse and gear at the back of the corral and fastened his purchases behind the saddle.

A CHILD FOR THE CHURCH

MacLeod sucked in a deep breath and exhaled heavily, glad to be on the road and away from the oppressive confines of the San Diego Presidio. The smell of the ocean and the sound of the crashing surf brought back memories of home and trips to Boston to see ships entering and leaving the harbor.

A series of late-spring storms had filled the streams and small rivers that carried the water from the surrounding mountains and dumped it into the sea. Combined with the early summer weather, it had clothed the hills in a mantel of lush green grasses and chaparral. Fat cattle grazed in the fields, competing with herds of horses as he approached the San Luis Rey Mission. He thought again about what might have been, if Maria had lived. They could have brought up Diego in this country, acquired land, and begun raising their own cattle. Perhaps, after a time, he would have considered joining their church, or at least making it look as if he had. Then they could have married.

MacLeod shook his head to rid himself of the thoughts. Maria was dead, and Sebastian, the old Navajo Indian who had led them to California, also lay back there, near the river. He swore that they would never be forgotten. He had made it to California with Diego, fulfilling his promise, and Diego would know of their sacrifice. But he had not promised to stay. He no longer feared his bible-totting stepfather, not after what he had been through, losing his trapping partners in New Mexico, then having to search for Maria, then losing her.

The afternoon sun neared the far edge of the Pacific Ocean, casting its golden rays on the tan walls of the mission at San Luis Rey. MacLeod turned his horse over to a youngster, and found food and drink placed before him. Nothing was asked of him in return. The next morning he found his horse saddled and standing by the corral gate.

When he reached the mission of San Gabriel, the Indians working outside the walls stopped to watch him pass until driven back to work by an *alcalde*. The warm air hung heavy over the mission grounds. The sweet scent of the spring blossoms fought a losing battle with the thick pall of cooking fires and the pungent smell of the cattle. Some distance off, men were dumping loads of firewood beside the cooking vats, while four soldiers lounged beneath the shade of a large tree.

MacLeod stepped to the ground and untied the bundle from behind his saddle, then turned the horse over to an old man, who led it away without a word.

He heard the excited chatter of children and, turning, saw Father Fernández, a large crust of bread in his hand, being led toward him. He smiled upon seeing MacLeod.

"Señor Americano, I see you have finally returned."

"I'm afraid it took much longer than expected. I had a hard time convincing the authorities in San Diego that I had no intentions of overthrowing your government or starting an Indian uprising," MacLeod said.

Fernández chuckled. "I must warn you that talk of such things, even in your manner of jest, would be reported and cause you much trouble."

MacLeod shook his head. "Well, Father, I suppose your Corporal Rodríguez would be more than willing to report any effort on my part to cause Indian trouble. He has returned, hasn't he? Don't suppose he told you what happened down there?"

Father Fernández frowned. "I have not spoken to him since I returned."

"There was an American ship in the harbor. I've arranged passage for the boy and me, but my passport gives me little time to return to San Diego and board the ship. Right now I'm awful tired and would like to see my son."

The good Father led MacLeod across the dusty plaza toward the little room where MacLeod had left Diego. The door hung open. Father Fernández entered first, halting abruptly in front of MacLeod. The room sat empty, the beds stripped of their blankets.

Fernández pushed past MacLeod and hailed a neophyte. The child hurried over and nodded his understanding of Fernández's orders, then ran off.

The priest turned to MacLeod, his faced etched with concern. "Someone has had them moved. I have sent for Father Torres; he was here in my absence. He is sure to know where they have been put. It is possible Father Pérez moved them while I was away."

The neophyte came hurrying back, followed by a young priest who held his robe up to his knees in order to keep up with the child.

"Where is the one who was here when I came?" MacLeod asked.

"When I returned, I was told that Father Pérez was recalled to the Mission of San José de Guadalupe by the Father Prefect for counseling and meditation. That is why they have sent Father Torres here, even though he is still very young."

Fernández assured the young priest that he had done nothing wrong and asked the whereabouts of the women and children who were using the room.

Father Torres shook his head. "I am sorry, Father, but they were sent away."

"Sent away? By whose orders was this done?" Fernández asked.

"It was Father Pérez."

"Did he give you a reason?"

"He said that the woman had the mark on her. She was evil and would destroy the good work we are doing here. He said there were things that she had done that I am not to be told."

"What about the child. Where's he?" MacLeod demanded, feeling the first signs of panic smoldering in his gut.

A look of fear crossed the face of Father Torres as he stepped back from MacLeod. "She took the child with her. Her and the other woman."

Fernández held out his hands to calm the agitated young man. "Where did Father Pérez send them?"

"He did not say, only that they must leave."

"But they could not travel without permission," MacLeod said.

Father Torres shrugged, his chin hanging to his chest. "He said it was of no concern. God would punish them as he saw fit."

MacLeod clenched his hands, raising them slightly as if about to punch someone, and Father Torres took another step backward. Then MacLeod, not wanting to further frighten the man, dropped his arms and sighed in exasperation. "Did they have horses, supplies, anything? Did you see which way they went?"

Father Torres relaxed and a shy smile creased the edges of his mouth. "Father Pérez told me to turn my back on them so their temptations would not follow me, but I watched as they left. I heard the old one say she knew of people at San Antonio de Pala. They would go there."

"So the women and children were going to this Pala place?" MacLeod asked.

"No, only the old woman and the child the young woman carried."

Father Fernández held up a calming hand. "Father Torres, think about it. There were two little children staying in this room. Where is the boy? Did the woman give him to another woman here at the mission?"

The young priest shook his head. "No, Father Pérez took the other one with him. He said the child was born in sin and only a life dedicated to the Church would save him. He said that is where the child now belonged, so he left and took a woman with him to care for the child."

MacLeod reached out to prevent Father Torres from leaving. "And no one tried to stop him?"

Father Fernández placed a hand on MacLeod's arm. "There was no one here who could prevent Father Pérez from taking the child."

"Why? What right does he think he has? And where did he come up with the notion my son was born in sin? He knows nothing about me."

"I am afraid I am responsible," Father Fernández said. "He asked about you and the child. My mind was troubled with the story you told of this woman, the one you say is the mother of the child. I wished to discuss my decision to allow you to remain. You cannot imagine our difficulties here. We are only two priests for each of the Lord's missions. I should not have spoken of it to Father Pérez."

"It's done now. Where is he going, and how long has he been gone?"

"He was to report to the mission in San José. It is many days away. He will follow El Camino Real, the same road you travelled to get here. But you will not be allowed to follow him without the proper passport. They will certainly arrest you."

"Well, they can try, but I'm about out of patience. I'd be obliged if you can find me a fresh horse. I'll need to travel fast."

"He has been gone many days now. It will be difficult for you to elude the soldiers long enough to catch up with him."

"You said he's been called back to this San José. Is that another one of your missions?"

"Yes, but Corporal Rodríguez and his men...."

MacLeod pointed toward the back gate of the mission courtyard. "Speaking of the corporal, here he comes now."

Rodríguez, carrying MacLeod's Kentucky rifle, kneed his horse over to where the American stood. MacLeod noted the Bates of London pistol that had belonged to his trapping partner tucked under Rodríguez's belt.

"Have you returned with permission? I would see your papers now," the corporal said.

MacLeod pulled the packet from beneath his shirt and handed them to the little corporal. "I see you brought my guns back."

Rodríguez took a moment to study the papers, ignoring MacLeod. When he finished, he dropped the papers in the dirt at MacLeod's feet. "You must hurry if you expect to return to San Diego in time."

Father Fernández stepped forward. "The man's child has been taken away. He wishes to stay until he can find the boy. I am certain he will follow his orders when the child has been found."

"I have no knowledge of this. My comandante questioned the validity of this man's story, and of the woman he claims was the mother of this child. He has little time left on his passport. I will return in the morning to see that he leaves." Rodríguez spun his horse around and trotted back the way he came. Not once did he address the stolen rifle and pistol.

MacLeod watched the corporal as he passed through the gate, then turned to Father Fernández. "I expect there will be trouble between us, and probably pretty soon unless he can rethink his position. I'm not asking for much, just a few days to find the boy. That's all. I buried the woman I loved in some rocks out in that desert. I won't leave your country without my son."

"They will come after you. They have nothing else to do and Corporal Rodríguez is looking to gain stature in our new country. He will make the most of your refusal to follow the laws of the land. I do not counsel you to cross him."

MacLeod's smile displayed no humor. "I expect they will, Father, but I have no other choice."

"I will pray for you, and that you find the child."

"Thank you, Father," MacLeod said, noting that the priest had dodged the issue of the child being MacLeod's son. "Maybe you could save a few of your prayers for Corporal Rodríguez there. If they try to stop me, I'll feel obliged to act in a way that will not be in the best interests of either of us."

Father Fernández bowed his head. "You are a violent man. I do not wish your troubles to lead you to these things you say."

"I was not always this way. I was taught the good things out of the Bible. But people here and back there in New Mexico have changed me. I'll have to depend on the Lord to decide whether to punish me or not. I can't turn the other cheek, Father. If they would simply let me go in search of my son, I would leave your country. So, if you get a chance, you might say so to that Rodríguez fellow. It might save me from doing something I don't want to do, and maybe save his own life in the bargain."

Father Fernández spoke softly. "There is the possibility of another way."

MacLeod waited.

"If you were to go to a place not far from here. It is called El Pueblo de la Reina de los Ángeles. You might find sympathy to your cause from the *alcalde mayore*. Perhaps he might give you the permission you seek."

The huge bells hanging in the openings in the high façade of the church began a new round of peals. MacLeod searched the old man's face for sign of deceit. He saw none. "How do I find this place?"

"You will follow the road over by the river. It will take you there."

THE ASISTENCIA OF PALA

O nce MacLeod took the time to think about it, he realized
Father Pérez had too much of a head start to be caught. He sat
in the dirt with his back against the adobe bricks of the blacksmith's
shop. A three-quarter crescent moon slowly edged its way across a
cloudless sky, pulling the new day up from beneath the darkness
beyond the mountains. He hadn't slept. He had too much to consider.
Father Fernández thought he might obtain an extension on his
passport from the *alcalde mayore* at the nearby pueblo, but MacLeod

wanted to explain this new situation to Captain Martín or Captain Fanning, or leave a message for him.

Standing patiently for him to make his decision, the big black mule leaned against a midnight-black gelding Father Fernández had given him to ride. The mule had been put into a high-walled pole corral to await its fate after putting two Indian vaqueros out of commission. Apparently they had made a wager about who could ride the mule the longest. Both lost.

MacLeod had found the mule with its head through the poles and nose to nose with the gelding. He opened the gate and let it loose to find its own fate, but the mule would have nothing to do with a permanent parting.

MacLeod pushed himself to his feet and slipped his saddle onto the gelding's back. He then loaded the mule with the supplies the good father had provided, along with what he had purchased from the ship's stores.

MacLeod led the stock to the corral and looped the mule's lead rope over a railing. The last thing he needed was having the two following him. He moved into the darkness beside the building where the troops were quartered. He crept along the wall until he found the door. It stood ajar, allowing the fresh breeze to cleanse the interior of a portion of the smells of unwashed bodies and partially digested spicy foods. He eased the door fully open and waited. With his hand hovering over the butt of the flintlock, MacLeod entered the room and crouched down while his eyes adjusted to the gloom. Loud snores competed with short gasping breaths and restless bodies turning in their beds.

The beds were lined up along both sides of the room, five on each side, as far as he could make out. He wasn't sure if the mission garrison was fully staffed, or whether Corporal Rodríguez brought others back from San Diego with the pretext of containing any other incursions by foreigners. Anything over one outnumbered MacLeod, but he had out maneuvered whole garrisons of troops in New Mexico and figured he could do so again.

Pegs had been driven into the walls above the beds to hang clothing and pieces of gear, with wooden footlockers at the ends of the beds. MacLeod crept down the narrow corridor, looking for Rodríguez's bed, although he doubted the man would sleep among the common soldiers. Which meant he would probably be at the end of the room, or in another room altogether.

As he crept past the fourth row of beds, a grunt from behind caused him to drop back into a crouch and pivot slowly, his hand grasping the butt of the pistol. The man grunted again and sat up before swinging his legs out of the bed and shuffling out the door.

MacLeod made his way to the end of the room before dropping down as the man returned to his bed. Minutes passed while MacLeod waited for the man's deep breathing indicated he slept.

Other bodies stirred but none appeared to awaken. Finally MacLeod turned and moved toward the last row of beds. Then he noticed the narrow doorway leading into another room.

He glanced over his shoulder to make sure no one had come awake, then slipped into the back room. A narrow bed sat beneath a shuttered window with a small table and one chair beneath it. On the bed, the form of a sleeping figure lay without a blanket over it, facing MacLeod. MacLeod paused, looking for what it was he sought.

He saw the rifle leaning against the whitewashed wall at the head of the bed, then the pistol, clutched in the hand of the figure on the bed. Was the person awake, waiting to identify who had entered the room before shooting?

MacLeod eased his own pistol out from his belt and thumbed back the hammer. He fought to control his breath, his heart racing. If he had to use the pistol, he wondered what his chances were of making it out through the troopers in the other room.

Another minute passed. The room began to lighten as dawn approached, and he still had much to do if he expected to evade Rodríguez. Figuring he would have been shot by then if Rodríguez was awake, MacLeod tiptoed across the room, where he picked up the rifle and the hide bag containing his bullet mold and tools. He stood beside the bed trying to determine how to go about getting the pistol out of the sleeping man's hand. He was damned if he was going to leave his prized Bates of London behind. He hovered over the sleeping Rodríguez, unsure how far he could go without waking him. Rodríguez stirred and shook his head, as if shaking off a mosquito. That gave MacLeod an idea.

He reached across and ran a fingertip along the edge of the sleeping man's ear. Rodríguez squirmed again and MacLeod repeated the gesture. The second time, Rodríguez released the pistol and slapped the side of his face to drive away the irritation. With two fingers, MacLeod lifted the pistol off the bed and stepped back to see what happened when the man's hand returned to the bed. Rodríguez rolled over without waking. MacLeod backed out of the door and snuck past the other beds and into the early morning light. He sprinted across the plaza to where the stock waited and slipped the old flintlock beneath his gear. The rifle and Bates of London pistol he kept at hand.

The road to the Pueblo de los Ángeles followed the Rio San Gabriel to the coast. MacLeod had no intention of going to the pueblo and putting his freedom in the hands of some *alcalde mayore* who could turn him over to the authorities and dissolve himself of having to make a difficult decision. But he could at least make it look as if that was where he intended to go.

Two miles from the mission, MacLeod cut off the road and cut through a thick band of willows, then backtracked until he found the road he had come up the day before. He hoped those following would race down the ten miles or so to the pueblo and have to return slowly to try to discover where he had turned off. By then he hoped to have disappeared.

By late afternoon, MacLeod had put thirty miles behind him. He guided the gelding across a stream and up a tree-covered slope until he found a spot where he could watch his back trail for any sign of pursuit.

Late the following afternoon, MacLeod rode the gelding up toward the single bell tower of the mission church at San Luis Rey de Francia. He found a narrow bench beneath a shade tree and dismounted, looping the reins over the back of the bench, and went in search of someone to answer his questions. Father Fernández said the old woman with Francesca was heard to say she would go a place called Pala. Fernández informed MacLeod it was a little mission attached to San Luis Rey.

An hour later the black gelding worked its way up the trail alongside a flowing stream. Ahead, the valley appeared to spread out into fields of early summer grains waving gently in the ocean breeze and surrounded by rocky, barren mountains. Indian men and women labored in the fields, cultivating crops to feed the little place they called Pala as well as the much larger mission below.

MacLeod didn't know what to expect, the priest at San Luis Rey had claimed to know nothing of two women and a child who might have travelled down the coast from San Gabriel. Figuring he at least owed her the time it would take him to check this *asistencia*, as the priest had referred to it, Macleod rode up to the door of the church and corralled the first person he could find. He had no more patience for shrugging shoulders.

He learned from the priest they had come there, some seven or eight days before, an old woman leading a horse carrying another woman and a child. She had sought food and information on where they could house themselves, turning down his offer to stay at the mission.

MacLeod figured they would not stray too far from the little mission, so he thanked the man and pointed the gelding back to the river and a narrow path that led past more fields of grain and kitchen crops.

He saw the shack, about two miles above the mission, stark against the bleakness of the rock and scrub, and tucked under the shade of a large cottonwood. A shaky affair of branches and twigs built thirty or so feet from the stream. It seemed too small to house two people and a child, but MacLeod had seen three or more adults live in huts as small as this.

A woman came out and picked up a crying child from a basket by the front of the shelter. MacLeod recognized the old woman, Rosalie. She let out a cry when she saw him and backed away before turning and entering the shelter. At first he didn't recognize Francesca as she came out into the sunlight. He had only caught a brief glimpse of her in the room at San Gabriel as she fed Diego. Before he could speak, the old woman rushed out of the hut and picked up a long stick with one sharpened end and shuffled toward him, screaming out orders for the other woman to run.

Francesca backed up a step, her arms wrapped around her body, her hand in a tight fist covering her mouth. She shook her head. "He is not with me. I do not have him. They took him from me."

MacLeod realized she thought he had come for the child. He nodded. "I know this. I saw Father Fernández and the other one. They told me the one called Pérez took my son."

Tears flowed down her cheeks, and the long thin hands that had held Diego so tenderly she clasped at her chest. "He is such a good child. He and my Catalina played together as if they were a family. I tried to tell the priest I would look after him until you returned, but he said no, he would take the child to a place where they would care for him and bring him up in the teachings of the Church because you are no good for him. Always the Church. Why is this?"

"I suppose it's what they think keeps them in power. This is not the only place this happens."

"I am so sorry for what has happened. I was afraid of what you would do," Francesca said. "Father Pérez said you would be angry and would take my child in place of yours. He said that is why he was sending us away. To protect us. If he wanted to protect us, why did he send us away with no place to go?"

"That is not what he told Father Fernández." MacLeod wasn't sure what words to use without offending her. "He said the soldiers could not do their work when you were near."

"And the young one," she said bitterly. "He was the worst."

"Corporal Rodríguez."

"Yes, that one. He told Rosalie that it was my wish. I pleaded with him to leave us. He laughed. It was only because Rosalie held a knife to him that he left. He was very angry."

"I'm sorry for your having to leave San Gabriel. I came here to thank you for taking care of the boy. I wished to ask you how he was, had he recovered his strength."

The shy smile he had seen at the mission lit up her face. "Yes, he gained his strength back very quickly. He is a beautiful child. I have never seen one with the eyes of blue, like yours. And your wife, it is sad what has happened to her on your journey."

Relief coursed through his body with the news, and knowing nothing he could ever do would be enough to thank this woman for what she had done. He wondered what Father Fernández might have already told her. He figured she would understand if he told her the truth.

"The boy's mother and I never had the chance to marry," he said. "We hoped to do so once we reached California. I wish you could have met her. You are much like her." He looked at the shelter they were living in. "But why are you here, and not at the little mission?"

Rosalie placed the little girl on the ground and found some sticks for her to play with, then continued digging up the soil. MacLeod wondered what she was up to, figuring it was a little late to be planting crops.

"I am so sorry. You possibly have not eaten," Francesca said. "Please sit here while I bring you food." She went to a small fire and returned with a wooden bowl.

MacLeod leaned over and took the food from her.

"I wish we had more to offer," she said. "Rosalie has been gathering things that grow along the river."

MacLeod ate the thin soup knowing they could not survive long on such meager rations, then realized she had evaded his question. "Wouldn't they let you live at the mission?"

"Yes, but I cannot stand to be locked away at night with the others. I have a fear of such close places."

"Why would they lock you up?"

"All the women who do not have husbands are locked away in the *monjerio* at night. They lock the doors and give the keys to the *majordomo* and another to hold until morning prayers. They say it is for our protection."

MacLeod nodded, then thanked her for the food and said his goodbyes. He reined the gelding around and headed back to the little mission.

He found the one in charge and made arrangements to purchase vegetables, fresh meat, and a milking cow. A young boy agreed to bring the cow the next morning. Francesca sat and wept when MacLeod returned, bearing the much-needed supplies.

"Thought a few things might be useful, seeing as you didn't seem to have much."

Rosalie came out of the shelter with the child and handed her to Francesca, then went about preparing a fire.

"She is from my village," Francesca said. "I would not be here without her."

"Seems a mighty big help to you. Father Fernández saw fit to depend on her at the other mission."

"Yes," she said. "She came up from Mexico as a child. She was placed on the steps of the place for unwanted children, Real Casa de Expositos, in Mexico City. Her name, Lorenzana, is given to all the children from this place. It is in honor of Francisco Antonio Lorenzana who founded the home. I do not know why but she has placed herself at my side from my first day."

"Señora, the priest said your husband was killed in an accident. Do you not have a home you could return to?"

Francesca turned her back as she spoke. "My father did not approve of my husband. He believed he was not of the proper class.

His parents were born in Mexico, and my father desired me to marry someone of more Spanish blood. My father wishes to be a part of the government here and felt this would have diminished his hopes. When I refused to follow his wishes and not marry the one he chose, he sent me from the house."

MacLeod did not to comment. The same type of situation had caused the troubles in New Mexico that had led to him and Maria leaving for California.

Francesca placed the child on the ground and turned to MacLeod as he tightened the gelding's cinch. "I cannot say what I feel. You have done so much . . ."

Then her eyes went wide as MacLeod hollered, "No!" and pushed past her to run toward the big black mule. The child had crawled over to the animal and was attempting to pull herself to her feet by clinging to the mule's leg.

The mule lowered its head and inspected the child, who stood with her arms wrapped around its hind leg. MacLeod saw visions of the bodies of those Indians who had attempted to approach the mule, and he himself had been the victim of more than one attempt at maiming by the animal. The mule shifted slightly, again turning to check on what was clinging to its leg. The child babbled away and MacLeod would later admit that, if an animal could look confused, this one did.

As Francesca rushed toward her child, MacLeod held out an arm. "Wait," he said. But his warning came too late. She spoke to the animal in hushed tones, then knelt down and gently removed the child's arms from around the mule's leg. She lifted the child up, cradling her in her arms, and ran her hand along the mule's side. The mule lowered its head to have its ear rubbed, causing MacLeod to stand in awe.

"Of what was your concern?" she said. "The animal appears lacking in hostility."

MacLeod bit his lip, not willing to frighten her with the stories about the mule. He had developed a love-hate relationship with the big mule, having been in need of its strength and durability in a number of situations. He mounted the gelding and wheeled the horse around. "I've got to go to San Diego to straighten out my papers before I can go in search of my son. Perhaps I'll stop again, if I'm able."

The shy smile creased the corners of her eyes. "I wish that very much, and we thank you for your help. I wish you well in your search."

Rosalie rose from her dirt patch and stretched her back, then called out that someone approached.

"It's probably the boy bringing a milking cow I traded for. Figured it could be a help to you."

"No, I do not think it is only him." She pointed down the path leading to the mission.

"There are others," Francesca said.

The youngster led the cow to the side of the path to let four soldiers pass. MacLeod sat on the gelding, wondering if he could talk his way out of another arrest. The heavy figure in front reined his horse to a stop, then inspected MacLeod and the scene. He said nothing but indicated to one of the others to search the area.

The one who appeared in charge waited until the one sent out to look around reported back, then urged his horse toward MacLeod and held out his hand.

MacLeod handed him the paper signed by Captain Martín. The man appeared to be an older version of Corporal Rodríguez, but much larger. His dark complexion indicated to MacLeod that somewhere in the man's family history someone had strayed and met up with a compliant Indian. His long black hair hung down his back in a braid. Heavy mutton-chop whiskers framed a thick-lipped face and a nose flattened in some earlier encounter. He spoke to the troops before handing the papers back to MacLeod. The men spread themselves out, their hands hovering over the hilts of their swords. When the one in charge seemed satisfied he rode back over to MacLeod but stopped some distance off, eyeing the rifle resting on the front of MacLeod's saddle.

"It is illegal for you to have these weapons that you have there. I am arresting you for this. You will hand them over to me."

In a pig's ass MacLeod muttered, then said, "Captain Martín didn't have a problem with my weapons. I don't see why you should."

Francesca stepped between them and spoke. "This man came here for information about his son. He has done no wrong that you should arrest him."

"I am Sergeant Pasqual Pacheco, of the Mazatlán squadron, Señora. This man is not allowed to carry such weapons. It is my duty to arrest people who do not follow the laws of our land. And you are not at the mission, so you must also have papers. I would see them to."

MacLeod knew he needed to direct the man's attention away from the woman and back to himself. "Sergeant, I am returning to see Captain Martín and ask him to re-issue my passport. I'm hoping he'll allow me the right to go to the Pueblo de los Ángeles. If you are travelling to San Diego perhaps we could ride together."

Sergeant Pacheco continued his inspection of Francesca for a time while ignoring MacLeod, then said, "I think I will allow you to ride on to San Diego while I remain here. I think perhaps I may be of assistance to the señora in some way before I continue, and I can also then see her papers. I will not arrest you this time. My men will lead you back to El Camino Real so you may not be lost."

One look at Francesca prompted MacLeod to realize the sergeant would not be a welcome visitor. "I thank you for your offer, Sergeant," MacLeod said. I believe I can find my way. He kneed the gelding up alongside Pacheco's horse. "A word with you before I go perhaps."

MacLeod led off down the road toward the little mission, turning to be sure the sergeant followed. When he figured they were far enough away not to be heard, he spun the horse around and stopped a few feet from Pacheco. He wanted to be sure the man understood what he was about to say.

"I want to thank you for allowing me to return to San Diego to see Captain Martín. I haven't the time to explain this situation here, with the señora, but I'm sure your intentions are, as we say where I come from, honorable. Do you understand this?"

Sergeant Pacheco stared at Macleod, then grinned, revealing a row of yellow teeth. "What is it you are saying to me here, that she is for you only? You are warning me, are you? You will probably not be allowed to remain in this country and then she may need my protection."

MacLeod nodded, kneeing the gelding a step closer, placing the muzzle of his rifle inches from the sergeant's thick belly. "That's true, Sergeant. The woman is someone special to me. So before you decide to bother her, you got to ask if it's worth dying for. You understand?"

Sergeant Pacheco backed up his horse a few steps, his eyes travelling up from the muzzle of the rifle to MacLeod. "You are threatening an officer of the Republic of Mexico?"

MacLeod noted the lack of force in his threat. "No, Sergeant, I would never think of doing anything like that. However, I believe there is a good chance Captain Martín will grant me new papers, so I believe on my return I will stop by and see how the señora has fared since I left. I would not like to hear that anyone has caused her pain. I am afraid I would be forced to seek out those who did so." MacLeod tipped his hat and spun the gelding around to say his goodbyes to the women.

San Diego Presidio and the surrounding buildings reminded MacLeod of places that had been abandoned and left to return to nature. MacLeod nodded to the half dozen soldiers milling around outside the comandante's office and stepped into the gloomy interior.

"Ah, good, I see you have returned in time to go on that ship there. You have brought this child?"

"Well no, sir, seems one of the priests up there at that mission where I left him thought my son would be better off in his hands and not mine. Appears he took him to some place called San José. I can't leave without my son, Captain. I've come back to ask you to allow me to go and find him."

Captain Martín shook his head. "I have no authority to do this. You are not of our country. You are only permitted to remain in Alta California for a few days or a week or something like that. You are, how do you say, over your period of time. If Our Excellency, the appointed governor, should be told I have violated my authority I would be dismissed and sent to Mexico. I do not want to return to Mexico. If you want to remain here. Perhaps you can take a ship up to Monterey and speak with the governor and say you wish to become a citizen of the Republic of Mexico."

"Well, Captain, not planning on doing that since I don't plan on staying once I find my boy, so you can arrest me now and save yourself the effort of chasing me down, because I'm not leaving," MacLeod said. "And there's something else might come to your attention pretty soon. I'm afraid I had some words with your Sergeant Pacheco up there near San Luis Rey. I'm sure he'll he lodging a complaint."

"Pacheco, who is this Pacheco? I have no one in my command of that name. He is most probably from los Ángeles. So do not go there if you wish to have no more trouble with him. But, you cannot go there without my permission. I think you should have left our country already."

Captain Martín began shuffling papers on his desk and building small piles amidst the cups and plates littered with half eaten meals. MacLeod remained silence, knowing if he said what he felt it would only put himself further up the line in the captain's black list. The one thing his mother had said to him so often was he was he own worst enemy at times.

The bells from the mission began their toll, announcing prayers, or a birth, or that someone had died. MacLeod had never been able to figure out how anyone could tell the difference.

Finally, Captain Martín found what he was looking for. He held it up for MacLeod to see. "This paper here, this is for that ship out there to leave. It is my permission that they may leave. You are to go on it also."

MacLeod left the office with the comandante's words ringing in his ears. He had seen the ship in the harbor when he rode in. He hitched a ride out to the ship on a boat loaded with meat and vegetables from the mission. He found Fanning in his cabin.

"We were turned back by the wind," Fanning said. "It pushed us out to sea, and we found ourselves fighting a losing cause, I'm afraid. However, I have permission to leave on the morning tide, so we will see how our luck holds this time. Bring your son aboard anytime."

After MacLeod explained what had happened, Fanning suggested he sail with him and approach the *alcalde mayore* at the Pueblo de los Angeles who might be somewhat more understanding.

MacLeod thought it over, but something crawled through the back of his mind like an itch he couldn't scratch. He had to go back and find out how she was, and whether Sergeant Pacheco had heeded his warning.

"There's a little matter I need to address before I go, Captain. I thank you for your offer. I guess I'll have to find a way to convince Captain Martín here to change his mind."

"Come with me." Captain Fanning pushed himself to his feet and went up on deck. "I hear these men have not been paid in some time. Perhaps they could be convinced a different way."

"You saying I might consider doing something to get on the good side of the man?" MacLeod said. "Afraid that idea never took hold before. Now that you mention it, I recall him complaining of not having any tobacco sent up from Mexico in months. Don't suppose you have any to spare?"

You know," Fanning said with a grin. "I might have a plug or two I can part with."

Carrying a sack of tobacco plugs, MacLeod dropped into the ship's launch. "If things work out, I might see you up there where you're headed. Perhaps you could put in a good word with whoever's in charge."

"I'll see what I can do young man. In the meantime try to get along with these people, as difficult as it might seem at times."

Captain Martín wrung his hands, complaining about stretching his authority in signing a new passport, while eyeing the tobacco MacLeod had placed on the desk. Finally, he succumbed to the offer and scrawled his signature across the paper giving MacLeod permission to travel to the Pueblo de los Ángeles. MacLeod thanked him, hoping Captain Fanning's influence would get him the passport he needed to travel farther north. He had no idea how far, or even where, this San José mission was. He expected someone would be able to tell him.

Captain Martín cleared his throat and pulled a new batch of papers forward for signing. "This Sergeant Pacheco you speak of," he said, without raising his head. "I think I remember him, yes. I would not want to allow him too close. I sent him to los Ángeles because he was creating many, many problems here. He is a dangerous man."

MacLeod's eyes narrowed. "Thank you. I'm much obliged for everything."

Outside the stifling office, MacLeod leaned against the gelding and contemplated the captain's last remark. With Corporal Rodríguez at San Gabriel, and Sergeant Pacheco appearing to be at los Ángeles, he would need to stay out of their clutches in order to start his search. He swung into the saddle and kneed the gelding toward the gate.

With darkness approaching MacLeod, stopped at a small adobe house nestled beneath half a dozen tall sycamore trees. A young boy with a leafy branch kept a family of chickens from scratching their way through the family garden. MacLeod shared their meager meal of *atole* and attempted to pay, but he was beginning to find out that all they wanted from him was news of local happenings. During their conversation, MacLeod discovered that even they needed a passport to visit relatives a few miles down the road.

He passed the large mission of San Luis Rey early the next morning. Two soldiers sat on their horses talking with a group of Indian girls. Both took a moment to watch MacLeod approach but soon lost interest when the Indian girls took the opportunity to escape into the mission courtyard.

A mile below the women's shelter, MacLeod passed a pole and adobe house that appeared deserted, remembering it from two days before. Whoever chose the spot did so wisely. A small stream gurgled over rocks behind the house. MacLeod guided the gelding into the shade and dismounted, letting the horse wander about and pick at the clusters of grass.

MacLeod stood and surveyed the house and tiny pole corral. He had an idea. He pushed aside a rough plank door hanging on leather hinges and stuck his head inside. A family of rats scurried through a hole in the wall and disappeared beneath a mound of rubble. He figured a day's work would make it as habitable as any home he had seen in this part of the country.

He found the priest attending the little *asistencia* amiable to his offer of a few coins for the use of the house.

A few hours later Rosalie entered the little house. It had taken a good amount of persuasion to convince her and Francesca to move from the lean-to. Rosalie came out and gestured to Francesca, who handed her daughter to MacLeod and followed Rosalie inside. MacLeod felt a sudden warmth as the tiny child reached up and pulled on a length of his hair.

Francesca emerged from the house and walked toward him, attempting to stifle the smile lighting up her face. Two tears streaked her cheeks. "I am happy they did not arrest you, and now you can go and look for your son. But I do not know why you do this for us. We have done nothing to deserve this. Is there something from me you want for this?"

MacLeod felt the heat of a scarlet blush beneath his beard. "No, ma'am," he said. He hoped his intentions weren't being misread. Yet, looking into her eyes, he thought he saw a deep hurt, something from her past that made her unable to accept his gifts without having strings attached. "I couldn't think of any other way to thank you for what you did for me and my son."

She smiled with embarrassment, tilting her head and saying, "If what I did for your son saved his life, I accept this that you have given us. I hope your search is successful. If you ever travel this road again, this house is yours to stay at."

"Maybe someday, but I'm hoping to return to my country if it's possible." MacLeod mounted the gelding and spoke briefly with the old woman, informing her she could pick up supplies he had bargained for. As he passed, Francesca reached out and touched his arm, bowing her head in thanks.

As MacLeod rode past the corral, the black mule and Francesca's mare lifted their heads to watch before dipping their muzzles into the grass Rosalie had gathered.

The next day MacLeod found himself whistling a silly little ditty his French-Canadian trapping partners sang around the campfire. He chuckled when he realized what he had been doing. It was the first time he had felt optimistic since he had entered the country.

He rode through fields of mustard that grew as tall as a man on horseback and pastures filled with grazing cattle before finally crossing a shallow river and entering the Pueblo de los Angeles. It appeared to be a much-improved version of San Diego, comprising about fifty or sixty houses, flat roofed and topped with a black pitch-like substance. He rode past the outlying houses and spoke with a man herding a half-dozen sheep. The shepherd told him where to find the *alcalde mayore*.

A dozen people stood in front of a squat, whitewashed building at the end of a narrow lane. Two soldiers shooed the crowd away from the door to let a tall, thin-faced man enter.

MacLeod reined the gelding to a halt half way down the lane. He wondered how long it would be before he ran into Sergeant Pacheco. Hopefully not until he had a chance to speak to the man who issued passports.

The people waiting to be called into the office stood aside as he walked up to the soldiers and pointed at the door. One stepped in front of him to block his entry. MacLeod had no desire to wait, remembering how long it took officials in San Diego to dispense with business.

"Should only take a minute fellows," he said as he pushed past the soldier and ducked down to pass through the low doorway.

The man who he had seen enter before him sat behind a low table piled high with papers and rolled documents. The man continued to read while holding up his hand to ward off any interruption.

MacLeod figured his best approach would be to wait to be acknowledged.

The man placed the paper to the side of the table and studied MacLeod for a moment. "You are this one I have been told to expect?" he said, without raising his head.

"I guess that might be me," MacLeod said.

"You have a paper to show to me?"

MacLeod pulled the paper Captain Martín had given him and placed it in front of the man. "I expect Captain Fanning has spoken to you?"

"I am to understand from Sergeant Pacheco that you were attempting to come here," the man said. "This man Captain Fanning you speak of has not arrived. He may be in San Pedro but he is not here, nor have I spoken to him recently. Sergeant Pacheco has told me of your disturbing action with this woman at San Antonio de Pala. He has told me that he was forced to defend the woman's honor and that you escaped his wrath and rode away. Is this true?"

MacLeod knew his chances of remaining in Alta California long enough to search for his son depended on his response to this accusation. All morning he had rehearsed his argument for staying to look for Diego. He hadn't anticipated this further complication.

"Well, sir…."

The man stood. "Excuse me. I am José María Castañeda, the *alcalde mayore* of El Pueblo de Nuestra Señora la Reina de los Ángeles." He sat back down. "Now, you will explain to me your story."

"Yes, Señor Castañeda," MacLeod said. "This Sergeant Pacheco has misinterpreted what the lady and I were doing. I was only trying to help her. I'm afraid I was upset about my son's disappearance and had words with your Sergeant. I apologize for my harshness."

"Good, I will pass along your apology. There are times this Pacheco tells me things that are not so true. Now," Casteñada said,

"Captain Martín has failed to indicate what it is you wish from me. I see by this paper that your time in Alta California has expired."

As calmly as he could, MacLeod explained the death of Maria and having to leave the boy at the mission of San Gabriel. Casténada clasped his hands together, his elbows on the table, and settled his chin on his fists while MacLeod told of the priest taking the child. At the mention of the priest's name, Casténada nodded. MacLeod concluded by saying, "I was told by Father Fernández that this Pérez was recalled to the north. He took my son with him. I want to get my son back."

Casteñada leaned back in his chair and studied MacLeod. "I have listened to this story of yours. There is a question I have. This woman who you say was the mother of your child was killed by these river Indians, what two, three weeks ago, and you are already involved with this other woman Sergeant Pacheco speaks of?"

"Not involved in any way, sir. The woman he speaks of saved my son's life. That's the reason I was helping her." MacLeod figured the less said about the matter the better. He couldn't see why it had any connection with allowing him some time to find Diego.

Casteñada picked up the paper again and continued his study of it. "I will need to think about this matter before I make my decision. I do not believe you have any idea how large a country this is. Myself, I have never been to the north, to San José de Guadalupe. If this priest is travelling to this place, who is to say he would take the child with him all the way. He could leave it anywhere. There are many missions between here and where he is going."

MacLeod was about to ask what there was to think about but held his tongue. "When should I come back for your answer? I'd hate to be accused of overstaying my passport while I waited."

Casteñada pushed MacLeod's papers back across the desk. "Perhaps while you wait you can think about whether you wish to take on such a task in so big a country as Alta California. And how long would you need to stay? I would need to put a date on any papers I sign. Return in a day or more, but wait outside the next time with the others who wish my attention also."

THE HOME OF DOÑ VICENTE MONTERO

The sun lay a few hours above the horizon, its brilliant rays causing MacLeod to shield his eyes after leaving the dank interior of the *alcalde's* office. He wondered how long it would take the man to decide, knowing each day put Diego that much farther out of reach. He paused as the cooking odors filling the air made him realize how hungry he was, and knowing he would need to find someone who might share their meal with him. It was never a problem at the missions. They were always willing to feed a traveller. But in the pueblo it was different, at least he figured it would be, since none of the little adobe dwellings looked too prosperous.

He led the horse down the wide street, preferring to stretch his legs after the long ride. Small plots of ground between the houses showed early summer vegetable gardens. He followed the road out a mile, passing a half dozen men carrying water from the river and being prodded along by another on horseback. In the fields, others shoveled dirt into wooden forms, using digging tools carved from tree branches, and poured in jugs of water. Two Indians stirred the mixture, using crude wooden pitchforks to add straw. MacLeod stood and watched, amazed at the slow progress as other Indians placed wooden forms on a cleared section of ground and filled the forms with the mixture. He walked on past to a spot were the wooden forms were being emptied and the oblong adobe bricks placed in long rows to dry.

He returned to the center of the pueblo, passing a *carreta* piled high with firewood and pulled by a yoke of oxen. An old man, his broad-brimmed hat pulled low over his eyes, shuffled along beside the squealing wheels, flicking a switch over the heads of the team. MacLeod noted no increase in the tempo of the animals, figuring the old man had done it so often both he and the oxen had worked out a mutual agreement. MacLeod doubted the old man could walk any faster.

At the edge of town, he watched two men approach on horses. Both appeared well dressed. He was still trying to come to a decision when he heard his name called out.

"I hadn't figured on finding you here in los Ángeles. Thought you'd be well on your way by this time," one of the men said.

MacLeod grinned, recognizing William Hartnell. "Thought the same as you, though I recall Captain Fanning saying he hoped to meet up with you here in town before you caught a ride up the coast. You haven't heard from him, I suppose?"

"As a matter of fact I have. I received word this morning he anchored at San Pedro yesterday afternoon. Expect he'll be in town in time to dine. My apologies," Hartnell said. He turned to the man beside him who rode a magnificent cream-colored horse that had a silver-white mane and tail. "This gentleman is Doñ Vicente Montero. He has been so kind as to offer the good captain and me lodging while we are here in los Ángeles."

MacLeod bowed his head in acknowledgement. "Doñ Montero." The man's dress spoke of a certain degree of wealth. His graying hair framed a thin face and hawkish nose. MacLeod felt the weak chin would be better served by letting his whiskers grow. Still, the man put out a feeling of superiority.

Hartnell said, "This is William MacLeod, the young American I spoke of. The one whose son has been abducted by a priest who would serve better by worrying about the treatment of some of the Indians at the missions. He is having a problem obtaining the needed papers so he can search for the boy."

"I must apologize for this. Is this not necessary in your country?"

"No, sir. Like the country Mr. Hartnell is from, we don't find it necessary to do so. The lady I met in San Diego, Señora Montero, is she your wife?"

"Yes, Doña Montero is on her way to Spain. We wished to have our son born there, in true Spanish fashion."

"So it was explained to me. She appears a fine woman, sir."

Montero tilted his head. "Yes, a very fine woman. Mr. Hartnell and Captain Fanning of the American ship will be dining with me this evening. If you have not made other arrangements, I also invite you."

MacLeod tried to remember when he last ate a full meal. "Thank you, sir. I'm much obliged and would be honored."

As he reined his horse, Montero posed a question. "This priest you speak of, the one who has taken your son. Do you know his name?"

"His name is Pérez. Apparently there were other issues with him, and he was being recalled."

Montero chuckled. "Yes, so I have heard. We will eat when it is cooler, but come whenever, and we can share a glass of wine and talk more about this problem you have with our authorities."

Hartnell pointed down the road in the direction they were heading. "You can't miss the house. It's the large one at the end of the road." He hesitated a moment before adding with a narrowing of his eyes. "Doñ Montero has also invited Mr. Dupré, the other gentlemen you met in San Diego."

MacLeod bit back the remark that formed the moment he heard the name. The arrogant Frenchman had thought his words spoken to the captain of their ship, down in San Diego, were not understood by any in the group. MacLeod had not spent two years living with French trappers from St. Louis without a thorough understanding of their language. Dupré's disparaging remarks about Americans and Mexicans had not gone unheard. He nodded his understanding to Hartnell and thanked Montero again for the invitation.

By late afternoon the warmth began to fade as the sun dropped toward the waters of the Pacific Ocean. Thanks to his having purchased a razor from the ship's stores in San Diego, MacLeod felt somewhat refreshed after bathing again in the river and shaving with a proper razor.

Montero's house stood off the road, nestled beneath a grove of trees. Beyond the trees, a large area enclosed by an adobe wall had been planted with a variety of flowers and vegetables. MacLeod could see three women working between the rows. As soon as MacLeod dismounted, a young Indian boy led the gelding away and began unsaddling the horse.

Doñ Vicente Montero greeted MacLeod as soon as the Indian servant opened the door. The room was larger than MacLeod expected, with four windows looking out onto a shaded patio built around all four sides of the house. Solid wooden furniture and a hewn plank floor made the house unique to what he had seen so far in this country. The walls appeared to have been whitewashed recently.

MacLeod thought Montero was impressed that he had taken time to clean up before making his appearance.

"I am happy you have accepted my invitation. My house here in Alta California is not what I am used to, but it is all I could manage to have constructed by the local people. A few of the Indians from the mission have been taught the rudimentary craft of carpentry, but they cannot build what they have never seen. However, it is the home that Doña Montero and I share here in los Ángeles."

"I assumed you and the lady had lived here always. I don't know why."

"No," Montero said. "We were married in Vera Cruz, but political problems with those in current power forced us to seek a home elsewhere. I am sure you are not interested in this," he said, taking MacLeod by the elbow and leading him into the room. "Mr. Hartnell has said that you have recently buried the mother of your child. This is true?"

MacLeod nodded. "Unfortunately, yes. Her name was Maria de Cordero. Her family was also from Vera Cruz."

"Certainly not Doñ Antonio de Cordero? I was to understand he had moved his family to *Nueva Mexico*."

"As a matter of fact it is."

A look of deep concern swept over Montero. "I knew the family well. He had also lost a son, I believe?"

"Yes, he had. And I have to find a way to let him know about Maria."

Montero turned away as a young Indian woman answered the knock at the door. "Ah, here is Captain Fanning now. I believe you met in San Diego."

"Yes, we met."

"William MacLeod, I did not expect to see you so soon," Captain Fanning said, breaking away from Hartnell and offering his hand. "I've just been told about your latest problem with your papers. Seems to follow you everywhere," he said with a wide grin.

"It appears that way. I see you finally got the wind to go in the right direction for a change."

"About time. I hope my luck holds and will let me leave before the infernal wind turns against me again. Until it does we'll see if anything can be done about your problem. Young Hartnell and I have just been discussing it, and he might have the perfect solution."

MacLeod felt a ray of hope. "What might that be?"

"I'll let him tell you about it. I see the Frenchman has arrived. I hope you mind your manners with him, son. He is a dangerous man with an explosive temper."

MacLeod wondered how much Montero knew about Dupré's obvious infatuation with his wife. "I'll do my best, Captain, but I would ask another great favor before you sail. I believe I might have mentioned that my mother lives in Walpole, on the Boston Post Road. She hasn't heard from me since I left. Do you suppose you could have someone deliver a letter to her for me?"

"I'll do better than that. You write your letter and I'll deliver it myself. I'm sure she would like to hear from someone who has had the opportunity to speak to you. And it so happens I have kin who live nearby."

MacLeod walked across the room to where Hartnell and Dupré appeared to be engaged in an animated conversation.

On seeing MacLeod approach, Dupré stepped forward. "*Je suis Le Chevalier Gaston Dupré,*" he said, offering his hand.

"William Wallace MacLeod," MacLeod answered in Spanish, not about to admit he spoke the man's language. He barely had the opportunity to touch the man's hand before it was withdrawn. He remembered the look that had passed between them in San Diego and refused to break off eye contact. He wasn't about to back down to Dupré's bullying challenge, in spite of the warning about his reputation.

Hartnell stepped up. "Well now. I've been meaning to ask you how you plan on going about searching for your son if you can solve your travel problems. I don't know if you realize how big a country this is."

"I've been told that already, but it was a long way from New England to Santa Fe, and then to Alta California."

"There's nothing more formidable than a man on a mission. I certainly wish you luck. Now Monsieur Dupré here has a far different problem we've been discussing. He had hopes of filling his ship with otter skins to sell in China. A mighty lucrative business. The problem is the Russians from Sitka, have pretty much cleaned out the ocean of otters. Oh, they'll come back if left alone but that will take a spell. He's been inquiring if I know anything about the Russian fort up above the Farallons. I told him I hadn't had any contact with them, then laughed. I heard this story about the Russians sailing into San Francisco Bay. Their ship, *Predpriatie,* Captain Otto van Kotzebue, came in to try and purchase supplies and flying the Russian flag, of course. Well the proper salute for a foreign ship entering the port of another country is a cannon salute. So, whoever was in charge up there at the San Francisco Presidio had to send someone out to ask the Russians for enough powder to render the appropriate salute."

Fanning joined the conversation. "Mark my word, the day will come when some country will send a ship here and take this country over. I don't believe the people here realize what they have. Right this very minute there's a British frigate anchored out past me in the bay. Seems they came in on the sly, hoping to fill their water barrels, and an altercation took place between an officer and one of the men. If you know anything about His Majesty's navy, you know that could mean a hanging. I guess the fellow recognized what he had done and went over the side. They were out there looking for him when I left."

Dupré said, "I also have been telling the leaders of France about the great possibilities this country offers. It would necessarily need a new form of government to succeed, and I have offered them my services in this matter."

MacLeod couldn't resist putting in a word. "Seems if France wanted any part of this country, Napoleon wouldn't have sold most of it to us already. At one time you had everything from St. Louis to Santa Fe, and up to the border with the British."

Dupré's manner froze. "France will be better served once the people realize how much better off they were with the monarchy. We will again serve France, as my people, the Bourbons, have done for centuries. It is too bad you Americans cannot see what you have lost with your republican type of government."

MacLeod was glad of the schooling his mother had insisted on. "Somehow I don't think this is going to happen. Look at the mess old Ferdinand has caused in Spain. I recall something Thomas Paine said about monarchies. The first king in a monarchy was the best; all others were simply products of his loins, and there wasn't any guarantee of the outcome. I think France will prosper as a republic."

Hartnell walked off to speak with their host, leaving MacLeod alone with Dupré.

"What would you know," Dupré muttered through clenched teeth. "A pup with no education. Look at you."

"Well now, Mister Chevalier, least I can take care of myself, probably better than some," MacLeod countered. "And there's no one paying my way," he added, recalling Fanning's story about who financed the French ship's voyage.

Dupré's cheeks flushed. "Si vous étiez autre chose qu'un agriculteur commun j'appellerais vous pour cela. Il serait un plaisir de te tuer."

MacLeod knew he had pushed the man too hard. He smiled, not wanting Dupré to realize he understood the threat. He had no desire to end up in a duel with this man. Yet the man had just said it would be a pleasure to kill him.

"Ah, there you are," Montero said. He took MacLeod by the elbow and turned him away. "I am curious what you think of our country now that you have been here a few weeks."

"Well, sir, I don't think it would be fair to judge it so soon. The only people I've met have been either officials who can't make a decision, or priests who believe my soul needs mending."

"Yes, I understand. We who live in the pueblos are somewhat immune from the priests, and usually the soldiers also."

"You said you were forced to leave Mexico for political problems," MacLeod said. "Were you not in favor of independence?"

Montero chuckled. "No. I believed we were far better off remaining in the hands of Spain, and in fact most of the *Californios* were for Spain, including the priests, but that was only a portion of the problem. I do not know how to explain this to someone who had no knowledge of certain, how shall I express this, groups of people. There were two groups that were very influential in the politics of Mexico. One was called *Los Escoceses* and the other *Los Yorkinos*. I belonged to the *Los Escoceses*, and they were not in favor at the time."

MacLeod frowned. "This group, Scottish something?"

"Yes, I think in America it is called Scottish Rite, but you would not understand."

"My father was a Freemason. He also belonged to the Scottish Rite."

Montero's jaw dropped. "You are certain of this?"

"Yes, sir, no doubt. He and General Pike attended a lodge in Boston when Pike visited," MacLeod said.

Captain Fanning came up and addressed him. "I also belong to the Fraternity, as do many of our leaders. Why, eleven of the signers of our Constitution were Freemasons."

Montero ran his hand over his hair. "Perhaps this bit of information can be used to influence the *alcade*, although I would have to discover what his beliefs are. There is a strong movement in Mexico that is anti-masonic. I will approach him tomorrow. Would it be possible for me to explain that you would be in favor of becoming a citizen of Mexico? You must join our church first, of course."

MacLeod knew he needed to walk carefully and not offend this generous offer of Montero's. "Thank you, sir, but once I find my son I wish to go home, to New England. We intended on making California our home, but now there is nothing here for me."

"That is unfortunate, but I understand. You have experienced difficulties with the officials you have met so far. They are the cause of much of the frustrations we face here. Even though I supported Spain, I could see that those they sent out to serve as our leaders were without ability. There are those of us who feel Spain may still reoccupy Mexico someday and, by sending us stronger leadership, lead this country back to greatness."

Gaston Dupré broke away from his conversation with Hartnell and approached Montero. "I am expected back on my ship this evening. It is long ride, so I must ask you to excuse me from dining. I had not realized the lateness of the hour," he said. He tilted his head to Montero and walked away without acknowledging MacLeod.

Vicente Montero watched the Frenchman leave and without turning spoke to MacLeod. "I am afraid I overheard the conversation you had with him. You have a young man's desire to say whatever it is you feel. You lack restraint. Do not be offended. I had a similar reaction to my peers when I was your age. I do not know what the man said to you in his own language, but I presume from the manner in which it was spoken that it contained a threat of some sort. The tone had much menace in its manner."

"I hope that I have not been the cause of his leaving, Señor Montero. The man has a pretense of superiority, and I just can't abide by it," MacLeod said. He wasn't about to repeat Dupré's threat.

"He is a dangerous man. If you would take the advice of someone who has witnessed the results of uncontrolled anger, you would not allow yourself to be drawn into a disagreement."

"As I have been told, it's a big country. I doubt we will see each other again."

At least he hoped they wouldn't meet again. He had no desire to fight the man. He wondered again if Montero knew of the attentions the Frenchman has paid to Doña Montero.

After the table was cleared and brandy served, MacLeod cornered Hartnell. "You mentioned something earlier about you and Captain Fanning having a possible solution to my problem."

"Yes, especially if this Father Pérez has taken your son any distance. There are many places he could leave a child and who is to say it would not be at one of the many missions."

"Seems I heard the same thing earlier today, but I don't have much choice. I have to start somewhere, and if his saying the boy was in need of salvation, where else would he leave him, unless he expected to take him as far as this San José de Guadalupe?"

"You are not of this country, nor are you of their Church, and that will have a definite bearing on how much help they are willing to give you," Hartnell said.

They stood outside Montero's home talking until Captain Fanning said his goodbyes to Montero and joined them.

Fanning said, "I plan on weighing anchor on tomorrow's tide if the winds should bless me. So if that letter you wish me to deliver is to go with me, you had better see to it. I believe the tide will turn at a little after six tomorrow morning. It's twenty miles to the harbor, so mind you don't dawdle, son. The tides wait for no man." He tipped his hat and mounted his horse. "And hear what Edward here has to say. I believe it will be in your interest."

"Thank you, Captain," MacLeod said.

"Let's walk a spell," Hartnell said. "And listen carefully before you make your decision. You might be fortunate and discover he has left your son at the first place you stop. However, if you find it necessary to go further, you might find a more welcome reception if you have something to offer."

"What do I have to offer?"

Hartnell smiled. "Come to work for me, and you'll have a reason for your stay. Become an agent for McCullough, Hartnell and Company. You would be doing the priests a great service and offering them a fair price for their hides and tallow."

MacLeod wasn't sure how much help he would be since he knew nothing of this hide trade. "How can I help, and why me?"

Hartnell took a moment to answer. Finally he said, "First you need a reason to stay. If we can show the *alcalde* you'll not be wandering all over their country without their knowledge, he's bound to be more apt to grant you papers. And, frankly, I need someone to sign up the missions to contracts."

It had merit, MacLeod had to admit. "You still haven't said why you want me. Surely there are plenty of men who know the country and this business who could do it better?"

"Look around. How many men do you see working at any type of labor? Furthermore this whole business of trade is in its infancy. They're just beginning to understand it now that it's legal."

MacLeod nodded. "You're right, I haven't seen many working, now that you mention it."

Hartnell reached for a cigar and bit off the end. "This country is unique. The *gente de razon,* as they refer to most of the non-Indians, are mostly retired or invalided soldiers, or those sent up from Mexico in an attempt to settle this vast country. Unfortunately Mexico couldn't always get volunteers so they emptied their jails and sent up what they call *chollos,* who we call riffraff."

Once Hartnell's cigar was lit, he led MacLeod over to the fenced gardens and pointed to it. "These gardens provide crops for the people here in the pueblo. They're cared for by Indians. You were at San Gabriel, what did you see?"

"Pretty much a mess of Indians working at different jobs. Actually, I don't recall seeing any white people, other than the priests."

"Right, and those Indians grow the crops, herd the cattle, do rudimentary blacksmithing, saddle and shoe making, tanning. All the things that workers in other countries do to make a living. How much do you think they pay the Indians for their labor?"

The bellowing of nearby cattle cut the stillness of the night air. MacLeod said, "I see your point. There's no way to compete with free labor."

"That's right, and they have soldiers at the missions to make sure the Indians perform their duty. But there is one other factor, and that's where you come in. The men I might find capable of doing the job have no real desire to work. Oh, they might put in a week or so, but once they have a *real* or two in their pockets, they want to find ways to rid themselves of it as soon as they can. Drink is a problem, so is gambling. With Indians to do the work, there's no need for them to do it. I assume you have some schooling, at least enough to read some and do some figures?"

"I think I can manage that."

"Good. I can go over what I'm offering with you tomorrow if you decide to accept."

The offer seemed too good to pass up, especially as it was explained. The *alcalde* in the los Ángeles pueblo would have a good reason to issue the passport. "Do I get paid, too?" MacLeod said, grinning at the idea of getting paid to search for Diego.

Hartnell took MacLeod's arm. "You have no idea how many hides are marketed each year. I would guess the number is around forty-to-fifty-thousand, and growing each year. I'll give you ten percent of all the hides coming from the missions who sign contracts. At one dollar a hide, that's a tidy sum you could count on, and that's not counting the tallow."

All MacLeod could picture was forty or fifty thousand cattle slaughtered each year, and nothing had been mentioned about the rest of the steer. "If you think I can handle the job I'll give it a try. Can't be any harder than skinning beaver and tending camp for two Frenchman and an Englishman bent on making my life miserable."

"There will be other factors involved, of course. It won't be all sun and honey."

"Figures," MacLeod said. "But nothing has ever come easy. I suppose there's a season you'd like me to sign up for?"

"*Matanza*, as they call it, runs pretty much from July through September. You'll see the activity around the missions start to increase in the next couple of weeks."

Hartnell laughed. "I warn you, come September you won't be able to draw a breath without choking on the smell of putrefying flesh. You'll be wanting for winter to come as quickly as it can. Of course, you'll also need to take a hand in seeing the hides and bags of tallow make it to the port. The ships travel the coast and sometimes you have to wait to load. There'll be things needing done to the hides once they reach the shore. Then they'll be off-loaded in San Diego to finish the process. San Diego has the best bay and weather for this."

"I'm much obliged for your offer. I hope I don't let you down."

Hartnell tossed the cigar away and offered his hand. "That's what I was hoping you would say. Now, if you're going to see that letter is on the ship, you best write it quick and ride after Fanning.

Doñ Montero has offered me lodging until my own ship arrives, so look me up as soon as you get back. We'll go over the contracts with you and see about getting you permission to stay."

MacLeod caught up with Fanning and rode with him to the harbor at San Pedro. He obtained paper, pen, and ink from the captain's desk and sat for some time thinking about what to say. Once he began to write, he couldn't bring himself to tell her about Maria. He simply said she was a grandmother, and he would send more information later. He did explain that he was in Mexican California, and about his frustrations with the authorities over his need to remain. Her being Scottish and raised Presbyterian, he thought better than to mention the need to become a Papist in order to stay. He finished by admitting that the country was magnificent, the possibilities immense, and the people too lazy to take advantage of it.

MacLeod rode most of the way back to the los Ángeles pueblo before finding a spot beside the road to catch a few hours' sleep.

The next morning, accompanied by Vicente Montero, he walked past a recently built adobe wall surrounding a few acres of sprouting vegetables. He asked how a four-foot wall of mud bricks would keep deer and other animals from destroying the plants before they could be harvested. Doñ Montero explained that following the slaughter, the heads and horns of the dead cattle would be mounted along the top of the wall, forming an impenetrable barrier. He also said MacLeod would see other efforts to keep foraging animals out of gardens, wherever he travelled.

Montero spoke to the soldier standing at the door of the *alcalde's* office and handed over the reins of his horse. He waited until the man led the horse away before speaking to MacLeod. "It would serve better, I believe, if you would not enter with me. I would like to speak to him first."

MacLeod settled himself on the ground and leaned back against the rough adobe wall, his hat tilted down to protect his eyes from the glare of the sun. Having ridden most of the night to return from the ship in San Pedro, the warmth quickly caused his eyes to close and his head to drop toward his chest.

He woke at the sound of approaching voices, one harsh with authority, and threatening, the other whining in response. MacLeod eased the brim of his hat up an inch. Sergeant Pacheco saw him at the same time. The soldier kneed his horse over to the office building. He dismounted in front of MacLeod and walked a couple of steps until he stood blocking the sun. He held his hand out and wiggled the tips of his fingers in what MacLeod had come to recognize as a demand for papers.

MacLeod used his thumb to point to the office.

Pacheco waited a moment before nudging MacLeod with his boot, indicating for him to rise. When MacLeod still sat, Pacheco kicked him in the side. "Passport."

MacLeod slowly pushed himself to his feet and spoke in English. "You do that again you son of a bitch and I'm going to break that foot off and make you shallow it whole."

Although Pacheco did not understand the words, he appeared to interpret the threat. His hand dropped toward the hilt of his sword.

MacLeod's own hand rested on the butt of his pistol.

Pacheco turned aside as Montero emerged from the office.

"Ah, Sergeant Pacheco. I believe you have met this man who is new to our country," Doñ Montero said. "I have been discussing his stay here with Doñ Casteñada." He turned to MacLeod and took him by the elbow. "Come, he wishes to discuss your request."

Before entering the *alcalde's* office, Montero whispered a warning in MacLeod's ear. "He will instruct you as to what your limits are, and he may even request you to attend him when you are in los Ángeles. Agree with everything he asks. He will soon forget everything, but he feels it is his duty to warn you, and he worries that others, of higher authority, will question his decision. It is always the way it is."

They stood at the door to the office while Montero gazed at something behind MacLeod's back. "There is one other thing I should say to you. Although I have known you for such a short time, I have come to know you do not seem to take advice easily. But, I will warn you anyway, and then it is up to you. My hands will be clean. The authorities have great power here. This Sergeant Pacheco knows how to use his power. He is an expert in the use and abuse of his authority."

"I understand. I'm afraid I lost my temper. The sooner I'm on my way the better."

"Yes, that would be good. Now, I have given Doñ Casteñada my pledge you will not break the rules of our country. I hope you realize how much this pledge means to me?"

MacLeod bowed his head in acknowledgement and followed Montero into the small, stuffy office. Sergeant Pacheco followed.

The *alcalde mayore* rose and directed Montero to a chair in front of his desk, letting MacLeod stand. "Doñ Montero has asked me for a very special favor," Casteñada said. "He has asked that I give my permission for you to remain here in our country and that you be permitted to work for the business of *Macala and Arnel.* After much thought, I have decided to allow you to remain here. I warn you now, in front of Doñ Montero, one of California's most illustrious citizens, that you do not abuse this privilege I have given you, and you follow our laws and obey our authorities. Do you agree to this I have said?"

MacLeod nodded, feeling it necessary to humble himself, and give the man the notion he was intimidated by the threat. "I understand, Doñ Casteñada. I appreciate your allowing me to stay."

"Good," Casteñada said. He picked up the paper before him and held it out to MacLeod. "This will allow you to travel in the work you are to do for Señor Hartnell. If anyone of authority, like Sergeant Pacheco here, asks to inspect it, you must produce it immediately. Do you understand this?"

MacLeod took the paper and nodded.

Casteñada indicated that MacLeod leave and began speaking to Montero, then called out as MacLeod reached the door. "That paper I have given you is only good as far as El Presidio Real de Santa Bárbara. However, there is a note on the paper that you should show to the comandante at the presidio there. It will be up to him to allow you to travel further."

MacLeod sighed. "Beg your pardon, but where is this mission they call San José?"

"San José de Guadalupe? Oh, that is much further. Perhaps he will allow you to go there. That is up to him."

THE IRISH DESERTER

"This lets me go as far as Santa Bárbara, that's it. They said the priest was going to the mission called San José," MacLeod said.

"As I see it, William, you have two choices. You can fight their system or you can do as I do. Live with it. He's given you permission to make a start. Perhaps you can convince whoever's in charge up there to let you continue on."

"I reckon you're right. I'll see where it leads and figure it out later. Why don't we go over these contracts and such?"

Hartnell smiled and led MacLeod to a low bench beneath a cottonwood tree by the river. For the next two hours he explained the hide and tallow trade. "The contracts are for three years, but not all the missions will sign them, preferring to work with someone else, or whoever shows up first. The prices we're offering are fixed. We guarantee a dollar a hide and two dollars per *aroba* for tallow. They're about twenty-five-pound bags. You'll also have to see they get to the shore to meet the ships. I think I mentioned that before."

"You did," MacLeod said. "Now, since you're going to be at your office up in Monterey, how do I pay them? Don't suppose I'll have to carry bags of silver around?"

"Well, you would think so wouldn't you? But the missions prefer trading for goods off the ships rather than coin. There's nowhere they can use the coin, and having silver in hand makes it easier for the government to find a way to tax them. The one thing you'll discover here, William, is that a man's word and handshake are honored. Any *gente de razon* who enters a contract will honor it. Not to do so would ostracize him in the community and nobody would do business with him."

So, no coin," Hartnell continued. "Someone from the mission will come on board the trade ship and take in goods what their hides and tallow are worth. You'd be surprised how anxious they are to board the ship with credit in hand. My lord, the women can't wait to pick up a yard or two of silk, or linen, or even fine wool cloth.

Ribbons are a must and, of course, threads for all the fancywork you see."

Hartnell drew a rough map of the four missions within the area MacLeod had permission to travel, and warned him again about staying out of the reach of Sergeant Pacheco. MacLeod figured he would keep Hartnell in the dark about his run-in with Corporal Rodríguez.

Doñ Montero felt privileged to help him purchase two pack mules. Over MacLeod's claim that his own saddle would manage, Montero bargained for a beautiful, hand-tooled, Mexican-style saddle that MacLeod reluctantly admitted fit him better than the one he had. The only thing MacLeod refused to accept were a pair of the needlepointed spurs many of the Californios used. He had no use for the brutal treatment of a good animal

Two days later, trailed by the two loaded pack animals carrying a sample of goods for trade, MacLeod followed the river road toward the San Gabriel Mission. He figuring the best place to start was with Father Fernández. If he couldn't convince Fernández to sign a contract, he didn't know how he was going to sell any of the other missions.

With the sun overhead, MacLeod reined the gelding off the road and into the trees by the water's edge, figuring to let some of the heat from the sun drain off before continuing.

He leaned the rifle against a tree trunk and dipped his hands into the cool water, set on washing away the layers of accumulated trail dust from his beard and hair.

A twig snapped nearby.

He froze, waiting to see what approached.

A figure burst from the bushes, short and whip-thin, shoeless with a tattered shirt and ragged trousers. His pale skin accented the long hair and beard the color of a raw carrot. The figure crouched, grasping the hilt of a wicked-looking knife, ready to spring.

MacLeod had left his pistol on the saddle and the rifle was not within easy reach. Without wanting to encourage the man to charge, MacLeod reached for the leather-wrapped handle of his skinning knife.

"I would not do that. I've experience with this here blade," the man said, licking his lips.

"I'm sure you have," MacLeod answered in English. "It's easy to see you know how to use it. Course, it might be better to just tell me what you want."

"Now that I've met a man speaks the good King's English I'll just say I've a mind to be taking that rifle you got there, and that horse, I suppose. And whatever it is to eat you might be carrying."

"You can be having all the food I got. I'm afraid the horse and rifle are not part of the bargain," MacLeod said. He couldn't remember ever seeing anyone quite like the man, although there was something about the accent that stirred MacLeod's memory.

The man's tongue darted out and licked the moisture from his lips. "You forget I be holding the knife," he said.

"Listen, first you tell me who you are, and then maybe I'll let you have what's in the bag on my saddle." MacLeod watched the man's eyes travel to his saddle, figuring he had guessed right. He rose slowly. "I'll just amble over and get that bag for you. Save you the trouble."

"Now don't you be reaching for that pistol I see hanging from your saddle. I can toss this knife 'fore you grasp it."

Then it came to him. He had heard that accent on the streets of Boston. He untied the leather bag, tossed it in the dirt at the man's feet, and walked back to the water's edge.

The red-haired man tore open the bag, pulled out a tortilla, and crammed it into his mouth while keeping an eye on MacLeod.

"Don't suppose you're the one jumped ship a time back? I heard tell they were looking for someone assaulted an officer. Did some fearful damage to him I hear. Would that be you?"

MacLeod waited for an answer, but the man packed another tortilla into his mouth and tried eating a hunk of cheese at the same time. MacLeod reached over and picked up his rifle. "When you're done with that mouthful, why don't you lay that knife on the ground and tell me who you are."

A terrified look washed over the man's face but the food took up all of his attention. Finally, he swallowed the last of the food, placing the knife on the ground within easy reach. "You wouldn't be thinking of taking me back, would you? If you are, we might as well fight it out right now."

"What happens to you if I do?"

"They'll run me up to a yardarm. Not like your regular hanging where a fellow's neck goes snap. Oh, no. They haul you up while you kick away and slowly twist around until you strangle, and all the

officers and young gentlemen standing there in their finest to watch.
"

"Hang you? For getting in a fight?"

"Oh, they'll hang me all right, without so much as a God bless the Pope. It was an officer I hit. Wish I'd done him in and save me shipmates from him."

"What did he do?" MacLeod asked.

"Tried to bugger me, he did. I won't be buggered by any man. Young lord that he was, he's been getting away with it on others. Poor young midshipmen right off the farm don't know no better, especially when it's an officer. Their word being the law and all. Don't suppose you've anything else on that saddle of yours to eat?"

"Afraid you've had it all," MacLeod said.

The man laid his hand on the ground, close to the knife. "You've not answered me question. You planning on taking me back for the reward?"

"Reward? I hadn't heard of that, but lucky for you, your ship's sailed. I hear it left San Pedro two mornings ago."

The man grinned. "Well now, I be thanking the Lord for that. So, what do we do now?"

"Don't know about you, but I'm heading for the mission up the road. You're on your own."

"As you can see," the man said, pointing to his feet, which were blistered and bleeding. "I lost me shoes when I went over the side. If you could find your way to take me along to this   mission place, I'd be mighty thankful."

MacLeod bent down and picked up the pistol. He couldn't leave the man, not in the condition his feet were in. "First you'll be telling me who you are, then maybe we can come to an agreement."

A wide grin revealed a row of good teeth. "The name is Concannon, Shaun Concannon, from Galway."

"Irish, are you?"

"Aye."

MacLeod shook his head. "A Papist, I suppose? Seems I can't get away from them."

"If you be meaning the Church, you have it right, although I will have to say it's been awhile since I did my speaking to a priest. Be good to clear my soul."

"Well, if you've a mind to clear your soul to some priest, they're not far away and you can do all the talking to them you want." MacLeod led his horse over and helped the man on.

"Now you be taking it easy there," Concannon said. He grasped the front of the saddle with both hands, a look of sheer terror cloaking his face.

MacLeod laughed. "You figuring to strangle that saddle? And you were going to steal my horse. You've never been on one before, have you?"

"I'll be learning right quick," Concannon said. "It can't be any more difficult than walking a yardarm in a storm. You suppose it'll be approaching time to eat when we get there?"

MacLeod picked up the lead rope of the pack string and started down the road, wondering why he had gotten himself involved.

The Irishman grasped the saddle tighter as the horse took a step and followed. He called out from behind. "These priests, what do you suppose it is they will do with me?"

"No idea, but you'll learn soon enough."

With the towering façade of the bell tower in sight, MacLeod hadn't really thought about it. He had enough problems of his own to worry about, the first being how long it would take him to reach this San José mission and Father Pérez. "Well, you being one of them already with their church, I hear they might just let you become a Mexican citizen if you ask."

Father Fernández met with them at the bottom of the stairs leading to the second floor of the mission church. Concannon immediately knelt and asked the priest for his blessing. MacLeod could only shake his head while hiding his grin. The Irishman had a way with him. It didn't take long for the priest to send for someone to look after Concannon's feet and see that he was fed a proper meal. The priest assured him he was welcome until he could travel to San Diego to seek permanent residence, and he expected to see him at evening prayers. MacLeod wondered how much of Father Fernandez's words the Irishman understood. That was not his problem. He wouldn't be seeing the man again.

THE CEMETARY AT SAN MIGUEL ARCÁNGEL

By the time the bells called the neophytes to evening prayer, MacLeod and Fernández had concluded their business. Father Fernández signed a three-year contract committing the majority of the mission hides and tallow to Hartnell's company. With a contract from this, the queen of the Alta California missions, MacLeod felt the others would at least hear what he had to offer. He promised to be back in time to help oversee the work to be done before the hides were ready to load on the ship.

He followed the river north, with the high pine-covered peaks of the San Gabriel Mountains on his right. He glanced back occasionally to catch a glimpse of the snowy dome of the highest peak in the range. The sun cast long shadows as it continued on its daily journey toward the depths of the Pacific Ocean.

MacLeod stopped in a grove of ash and cottonwood alongside slow-moving waters. He picketed the stock, threw a blanket on the grass, then lit a fire using branches cast up at the high-water mark from the winter's flood. Not for the warmth but to keep him company. He ate what was left of a dozen corn tortillas and a hunk of beef from the mission kitchen. Nights were the worst, when he had nothing to do but think, but that day he felt that the miles traveled were the first in his real search for Diego.

He rose at dawn and watered the stock, anxious to be on his way. By late morning he had passed through a narrow pass and dropped down into a long valley.

The mission buildings and their distinctive red-tile roofs came into view as he left the river and picked up the road. He had been told that this particular mission suffered a great amount of damage from the last earthquake. At the rear of the low buildings, comprising the shops and soldiers' quarters, smoke rose lazily into a cloudless sky from fires burning beneath the vats rendering the fat into tallow.

MacLeod dismounted and left his horse by a trough of water. He passed a group of Indian women herded along by a mounted Indian swinging his *rieta* at those bringing up the rear.

He cupped his hands into the pool of water beneath a stone trough and doused his face and hair. When he looked up, he spotted them, two dark-skinned Indians with their heads and hands protruding from thick, axe-hewn yokes. He walked over to where they sat in the dirt, their backs coated with drying blood. He wondered what major offenses they had committed to have had the lash used to such an extreme.

The priest authorized to sign contracts agreed to supply two thousand hides for this season and the next two. The man lacked the enthusiasm shown by Father Fernández at San Gabriel, and the disorderly state of the mission grounds was testament to the attitude that seemed to prevail.

Of Father Pérez he and his fellow priest would only say they remembered the man passing by, but could not remember any Indian woman travelling with him, or of a child. MacLeod wondered how accurate their memories were after noting the sad condition of the habits they wore or the heavy sweet smell of wine surrounding both priests. They thought Father Pérez had come by two weeks before, but even that bit of information appeared to be vague.

MacLeod tightened the cinch on the black and reached for his water bag. He strode over to and knelt beside the first Indian locked in the stock, pouring water slowly into the man's mouth. He did the same for the other before mounting his horse and leading the stock onto the narrow road.

The information he received was much the same at the next two missions he passed. Father Pérez had stopped for the night but they were unaware of an Indian woman travelling with him, or of a child.

A few days later MacLeod rode into the small settlement of Santa Bárbara. He recognized the presidio office by the tattered hand-sewn flag flapping on a pole alongside a narrow building. Two guards leaned against the adobe wall and watched him approach, neither making a move to intercept him. He dismounted, slowly stretching the aching muscles in his back and shoulders, then entered the building. The man behind the desk wore a sweat-stained uniform, the collar open to accommodate the rolls of fat surrounding his neck. He looked up and waited.

"If you're the comandante here I expect you're the man I've been told to see," MacLeod said. He placed the letter from Castañeda on the desk.

The man picked up the letter and checked the seal before slitting it open with a thin blade. He read it slowly, then placed it carefully on the desk. "You are this man, this MacLeod?"

"Yes, sir, William MacLeod. I'm working for William Hartnell, of the firm McCullough, Hartnell and Company, buying hides from the missions. I'm also looking for my son."

The comandante picked up the letter again. "I see, and you are asking of me what again?"

"I'm seeking permission to travel up to the mission of San José. I have reason to believe my son might have been taken there by a priest.

"And how did this happen?"

MacLeod explained it to the man, wondering how many more times he would have to repeat it.

"Priests, they are a troublesome lot," the man said. "I have them here to contend with. A greedy bunch who refuse to feed and clothe my troops like they are supposed to. But that is another issue, is it not. If this priest took your son, I will not even ask why he should do such a thing. They do matters that I cannot understand every day. I see here Doñ Castañeda has asked that I grant you a passport to travel. I can do this as a favor to him."

MacLeod bowed his head. For the last few days he had wondered what he would do if this man refused to allow him to go farther. "I thank you, sir. I can tell you that as soon as I've found my son, and finished the work I was hired to do, I'll return to los Ángeles."

The comandante nodded in acknowledgment. "Yes, I wish you good luck in your search."

MacLeod thanked the comandante again and left the office, figuring to put in a few miles before darkness covered the trail.

Four days later MacLeod, stood outside the courtyard of the San Luis Obispo mission. One of the padres in the beautiful valley remembered Father Pérez, and said he had a child with him. Pérez had said he would stop to rest for a day or two at San Miguel Arcángel.

MacLeod pushed the animals as much as he dared, riding through fields of drying grass and scattered oak trees, and eating cold tortillas prepared for him in the mission *pozolero* before he left. Mission San Miguel Arcángel sat alongside the Rio Salinas River, its gardens surrounded by fifteen-foot cacti planted side by side and forming a barrier to keep foraging animals at bay.

The old priest, who was summoned to the courtyard, listened with bowed head as MacLeod told the story of his search for Father Pérez and the child. The priest nodded a time or two, then told MacLeod that orders from the Father Prefect were waiting Pérez's arrival, with instructions that he continue on immediately. The priest led MacLeod through the courtyard to a high wooden gate that opened onto the mission cemetery. Along a narrow path between the graves the priest stopped at a small mound of fresh dirt and made the sign of the cross. There they had buried a child brought to them by Pérez. Of the neophyte woman said to be travelling with Pérez, he knew nothing.

MacLeod fell to his knees, numb with grief. Maria lay behind a wall of rocks far out in the eastern desert of Alta California and now Diego, their son, lay in a shallow grave at a place that MacLeod probably would never again be allowed to visit.

Days later a small band of soldiers on their way back to Santa Barbara found him still sitting by the grave.

Gaston Dupré studied the gray ash accumulating at the end of his cigar, his mood in sharp contrast to the warm, scented breeze flowing through the window of Marisol Montero's room and mingling with her lingering scent. He sat on the side of the low bed and stroked the covering, imagining her naked body lying beneath his hand. What did she see in the blustering fool she had married? If in France, he would pay her court and delicately propose a liaison of mutual benefit. But that was not a possibility in this primitive land. He would have to kill Vicente Montero before he could possess her.

No, he thought, it would not do. At least not until his business was complete. But that was the problem, or at least one of a number of problems, he faced.

Dupré slipped out of the door into the cool shade of the courtyard and reread the letter delivered to him that morning. It had come months before and had only just caught up with him. He had recognized his wife's writing immediately. The same questions as before. Those who had outfitted and financed the expedition were asking for an update on the results so far. Did he expect to return soon, and how successful had he been?

Her family expected their investment to reap profits, and why not? Did the ship not carry the best products of France? How was he to know the people in this land had no need for what he had to trade? And few had the means to pay. They did not use coin as civilized countries did. They counted their wealth in the dry, sun-baked skins of dead cattle. But a ship filled with the skins of the sea otter and taken to China, that would have given him the money to rid himself of her and her family, as well as give him the life he deserved as a Chevalier. Dupré smiled. How could Marisol turn him down if he possessed such amounts of money?

Three Indian women swept the ground to remove the fallen leaves beneath the tree, while another carried jugs of water to a trough for the horses. Doñ Vicente Montero had invited him to ride but Dupré asked to be excused.

The letter had also mentioned rumors that threatened his name and honor. The father of the young man he had killed in a duel, the last one before he left, spread the word the boy was only seventeen, and was defending the honor of his sixteen-year-old sister. How could he have known that the boy was not yet a man? It had happened so quickly, and the boy would certainly have killed him.

"Ah, there you are, Señor Dupré," Vicente Montero said. "I see you are taking some air. I have just returned from speaking with the *alcalde*, Doñ Castañeda. We have been discussing some of the problems we must endure with these fools in Monterey. Since we have suffered independence, there is no money coming up from Mexico to pay the soldiers. The priests do not want to share their profits or feed the soldiers and their families as they are obliged to do."

Dupré had no wish to enter into a political discussion, but there was no way he could avoid it. "What can be done?"

"I do not know. Already there have been problems with some of the soldiers in the north. They are close to a revolt unless money can be found to pay them. It was only a few years ago that the idiots in Mexico sent cigars up instead of silver. They worried that silver in the hands of the soldiers would not be used wisely."

"Cigars?" Dupré said.

"Yes. The thought was the cigar would calm the soldier and he would not think as much about the money he was owed."

"Did you not expect trouble with your independence?"

Montero sent one of the young Indian women into the house for cups of chocolate. "Independence. Do you know that by the time the news arrived here in Alta California that Iturbide had declared himself Emperor and the fools celebrated for a week, that Iturbide had already been executed?"

Dupré shook his head. From what he had seen the country was ripe for takeover. "But were you not for independence, Monsieur Montero?"

"Certainly not," Montero said. "Spain is the true ruler. We could have worked out our problems with the proper leadership. But those sent from Spain knew nothing about running a country. They came in search of personal wealth and with family names meant to impress us. Even the priests were against independence. They still refuse to take the oath of allegiance."

"And you, have you taken this oath?"

Montero paused in thought, then said, "I have not. I was also not in favor of those in government in Mexico. That is why I live here in this small home and not in Vera Cruz, but that is an issue for another time. Tell me, do you remember the young American who was here the last time you visited? I believe I introduced you."

How could this fool not think I would remember this, Dupré thought. "I seem to remember, although he did not impress me."

"If you had the opportunity to spend some time with him, you would have seen something in him it is easy to miss at first. I spoke with Captain Fanning of the American ship that was here at the time. You remember him, of course."

Dupré relit his cigar and nodded. "Yes, although I have not spoken with him since."

Montero rubbed the side of his face. "Where was I? Yes, the American. His story of how he came to our country is one you would have enjoyed hearing, I am sure."

"I am sorry that will not be possible now that he has left. But, I do not believe he will be missed," Dupré said. The look that had passed between them the last time they met angered him still. "Perhaps if he remained I should speak with him."

Montero handed his empty chocolate cup to a passing Indian woman and sat on the bench beneath the tree. "It is still possible. He has not left."

Dupré felt uneasy with this information. "You say he has not left. Are you certain of this?"

"Señor Hartnell offered him a job with his company, and the young man saw this as an opportunity to search for this child he said was taken."

Dupré pushed aside his anger. What did it matter that he was still here?

"I have not had a moment to ask you what you intend on doing if you cannot find these animal skins you seek," Montero continued. "If those in Mexico had sent up a warship to deal with the Russians, we could have profited from these sea otter ourselves. Now it is too late. They have ravaged the seas and left very few of them. It is too bad you have not seen the opportunity that lies with our hide and tallow trade. It is our future."

This would not be necessary if he was successful in his plan, but he wished to keep that to himself. "If this trade you speak of is your future here in Alta California, then perhaps it is not too late to become involved."

"Oh, but it is, at least for those missions who have signed contracts for a term of three years." Montero rose and seemed for a moment lost in thought. "You know I have been told my wife met this young man when her ship was in San Diego. I hope she had a moment to speak with him. I believe she would have liked him."

Dupré remembered the looks that passed between Señora Montero and the American. If simple glances could pass so much meaning, he could only wish he had been on the receiving end. "I believe they were introduced. I do not believe they spoke. However," Dupré said, "you should be aware of this person. I believe there are certain things about him that may change your attitude."

Montero frowned. "You know of something I have not heard?"

"Only vague rumors, of course, and my honor will not allow me to repeat them."

"Yes, certainly. I would not want you to say anything that cannot be proven, but I hope you are wrong in this. I liked the young man. Anyway," Montero said, rising. "I wish you good fortune in whatever it is you wish to do while you remain here in Alta California. For me, I only wish my wife and our child would return soon. It is lonely without her presence."

Dupré had no desire to comment on that. He, too, wished Marisol Montero would return soon.

JUNE 1823

Sergeant Pacheco slouched against the adobe wall of the stuffy office, his weathered face creased in a mocking sneer. He nodded in agreement as the comandante of the Santa Barbara Presidio wore out his anger on MacLeod.

"You have violated your parole here in Alta California, as well as your word to me and to Doñ Montero."

MacLeod had not slept since the troops passing San Miguel Arcángel found him in the cemetery behind the mission. Exhaustion combined with depression to make the comandante's words meaningless. He didn't give a damn what official rules he had violated. Possibly, if he had found Diego, or information that he was still alive, he might have cowed to the man and offered an apology, but it didn't matter. They could do with him as they thought fit. Maria and Diego lay buried in the hot, dry soil of Alta California. He wanted to go home.

The presidio comandante continued. "But, I have been informed by some that this would create a problem. I am asked not to use my authority and banish you from our country, at least not until *la matanza* is over, since we have need for the sale of our products and it will begin in a month."

"But," MacLeod heard, or thought he heard. He fought to recall what the comandante had said. "But," then something or other. He didn't know whether he should interrupt the man and ask him to repeat what he had said. And if he was saying MacLeod could stay, MacLeod wondered why he would want to stay.

"Sergeant Pacheco here has advised me to send you away immediately."

I'll bet he has. And shoot me the first chance he gets. MacLeod also seemed to remember Corporal Rodríguez offering to take him out and see him on his way.

"So," the comandante continued without realizing MacLeod was lost somewhere back at the beginning of his speech. "They have asked me to allow you to remain and finish the work you have started for Señor Hartnell. When you have finished this important work, I will again review your situation."

They can't find anyone who wants to work to see the hides and tallow get to the shore and loaded on the ships properly, MacLeod figured. Why else were they so willing to let him off? Damn! He had given his word to Hartnell, and the man's business depended on it. Although, if he were truthful, he knew he had thought little of how the whole process worked. If he had to stay until the business was complete, he didn't want leather-jacketed soldiers shadowing his every move, and Hartnell had said there might not be a ship returning to Boston for another year. So he had a choice, work or sit in one of their jails.

All right, MacLeod thought. Get through the upcoming season and collect the money owed him. With it and whatever silver he had left, he could buy a farm back in New England. Most of the money made from the sale of the furs he had trapped with his partners lay buried in a rocky cache far out in the desert, only a few feet from where he laid Maria's body. He could never return for it, even if he thought he could find the spot. What if her bones had been dragged from beneath the rocks and lay strewn about? No, he thought, the silver bars and coins would remain in their hidden cache.

"Very well, what do you say about this?" the comandante concluded.

It took a moment before he realized the man had stopped talking. MacLeod took a deep breath and gazed at the cobwebs accumulating in the corners of the windows. "I'm sorry for this inconvenience I've caused, Comandante," MacLeod said. "Would you say again what I'll be permitted to do?"

It appeared obvious the man expected more in the way of an apology, but that was all MacLeod was prepared to give him.

"Yes, I will repeat it once again so there is no mistake this time. You will be allowed to travel only where it is I permit."

MacLeod turned to look over his shoulder at Pacheco. "Perhaps you could have him remove these shackles. Then we could talk about your offer."

The comandante nodded to Pacheco, who took his time finding the key. He twisted MacLeod's arm to locate the keyhole, tearing away the scabs that had formed on MacLeod's wrists from the chaffing of the rusted iron cuffs.

MacLeod inspected his wrists, unblinking as he stared at Pacheco, then turned slowly back to the comandante. "If you want me to finish what I've begun, you can't restrict me in my travels. I need to be able to go from that San Miguel place where you found me down as far as San Diego."

The comandante's mouth hung open. "I cannot allow this. How can we know where you will be?"

"Well, sir, I don't reckon more than a few of these folks who ask for my papers can read anyhow. If you say in those papers why you're taking this onto yourself, I'm sure they'll understand."

MacLeod could hear the man's breath slowly escaping as he began the task of writing out a new passport. "You understand, *Señor Americano,* this authority of mine I give you here does not permit you past the time of *matanza.* Then you will present yourself here again in front of my desk, and I will consider again what to do with you."

MacLeod had no intention of putting himself back under this man's authority, but he'd worry about that later. "Most certainly, Comandante. Now would you tell your Sergeant here to give me back my rifle and pistol? I figure I best be starting on my way."

After several inquiries, MacLeod was directed to the house of a man he was told might assist him. The old Indian who answered the door led MacLeod into a large room. Woven tapestries hung on the newly whitewashed walls. Salvador Hidalgo rose from the seat where he had been reading and offered a nominal bow. He was a heavy-set man, light skinned, and about MacLeod's height, his face framed with a thick mustache. He bore himself with a manner of self-conscious authority.

MacLeod returned the bow. "Doñ Hidalgo, I was told you might be able to help. I'm working for Mr. Hartnell, who has a business out of Monterey buying hides and such. I'm in need of two or three men who know the trade. I'll need them for the season, but I need men willing to work without me watching over them."

Hidalgo returned to his seat and crossed his legs without asking MacLeod to sit. "And how is this that you have come to me?"

"The comandante has suggested I speak to you."

"I see. And what are the limits of these contracts you have?"

"I can work the missions from San Miguel Arcángel all the way south to San Diego de Alcalá."

Salvador Hidalgo frowned. "And he is allowing you this. It is over half of Alta California."

MacLeod touched the folded paper in his pocket. "I'll stop in and see Señor Castañeda, in los Ángeles. Wouldn't be fair to him to be travelling through his territory without talking to him about it."

"Ah, yes, Doñ Castañeda. And was this where you met with Señor Hartnell?"

MacLeod shuffled his feet, anxious to be out in the open air. He hadn't bathed or shaved since finding Diego's grave and felt the need to clean up. But at that moment he needed Hidalgo's help. "No, sir, met him first in San Diego, him and a Frenchman, name of Dupré, then again at Doñ Montero's home in Los Angeles."

Hidalgo visibly paled. "Montero?"

"Yes, sir, he was a big help in convincing Señor Casteñada to let me stay. Can't figure out what I would have done without his help. Do you know him?" MacLeod turned his head as a door opened and a heavy-set woman entered the room and stood, waiting to be acknowledged.

Hidalgo shook his head and waved her off. She retreated quickly.

"To answer your question, yes, I know Doñ Montero. We have had a number of discussions about the welfare and future of Alta California, and the one agreement we have come to is that we will never agree on the form of government we need. I hope you do not depend on this man for information. He is a fool."

MacLeod took note of the obvious dislike that Hidalgo held for Montero. "I understand Doñ Montero was displeased with your gaining independence from Spain?"

Hidalgo rose and walked to the window overlooking his orchard, his hands clasped behind his back. "Yes, I believe in a republican form of government. You speak of this Frenchman you met. Do you know he has received one of the highest awards the French government has to offer their citizens?"

MacLeod was surprised Hidalgo knew and held such high regard for Dupré. "He made it a point in his introduction," MacLeod said.

"Señor Dupré and I have many things in common. I believe, like he, that Alta California, should look to a country like France for leadership, and possibly join with her as a territory of that great country. Señor Dupré believes that a strong republican government will not last in France after the debacle that was Napoleon, and they will return to a monarchy. I do not agree with him on this, but if France should look with interest to us here in Alta California, I have offered to be put forward in any movement to see them succeed if they should ask."

Frankly, MacLeod was tired of listening to the political views of everyone who felt the need to express them. Their own independence was a mere two years old, and some were already looking to promote themselves by selling out their new country. "Well, Doñ Hidalgo, I figure there's others who might feel some other country besides France might have an interest in Alta California. The Russians I hear have a fort up there above your last mission, and above them there's the English Hudson's Bay Company. I figure they'll be sending people down here before long looking for beaver in your rivers. Of course, it may be that none of them are allowed to stay. Captain Fanning told me our President Monroe has told all of them to stay away from you. I wonder why?"

Hidalgo turned back and waved his hand. "I do not know of this, but the Russians are peasants, that's what they are up there. Filthy peasants who should never have been allowed to remain."

MacLeod wanted to be on his way. "Yes, sir, but I don't want to take too much of your time. Would you know where I can get a couple of men to help me? I'll be glad to pay them."

Hidalgo ran his hand over his chin and nodded. "Yes, I have a couple you can use." He called a young Indian woman over and told her what he wanted. She scurried out the door, returning five minutes later, followed by three Indians. They stood outside the door to the house, their wide hats held in their hands.

MacLeod couldn't help noting the fear on the faces of the two squat-bodied younger Indians. The other one was taller and thick across the chest, with very dark skin. He stood to one side, a look of hatred in his smoldering black eyes.

Hidalgo waved a dismissive hand at the big Indian. "This man has worked as a vaquero. He knows the business you are engaged in, and I no longer need his service. I feel it is my duty, however, to tell you that you should be careful with him. He has run off a number of times, and I have been forced to punish him for his behavior. I call him José. The other two are Chumash. They are from the mission up the road. They are neophytes, at least that's what the priests tell me, but they have worked with cattle before."

"Guess I'll have to take a chance on them, since I need help. What about horses for them?"

Hidalgo nodded and spoke to the tall one, telling him to pick out three horses. "You will need to go back to the comandante's office for papers for them. Only vaqueros are allowed to ride horses."

The one Hidalgo called José returned riding a leggy cinnamon gelding and leading a pair of mares. MacLeod thanked Hidalgo, glad to finally be away from the man and his superior attitude. The comandante appeared eager to rid himself of the problem and issued the papers for all of them.

With the sun at midday, MacLeod wanted to get started right away. He pointed at José and asked his name, surprised at how well the man spoke Spanish. "I am Sisquoc, not José."

MacLeod nodded. "Sisquoc, you call me William."

"Guillermo, *si*," Sisquoc said. He pointed at the others. "Miwak, Malibu."

"All right, now that we know who we are, I think we can get the hell out of here and you can begin telling me how this hide trade works. MacLeod swung into the saddle and watched the three Indians vault into theirs, grinning amongst themselves.

At the edge of the pueblo, Sergeant Pacheco met them with four of his soldiers. He had them dismount and unfold their new papers, taking his time until he reached MacLeod. He casually inspected the paper before letting it float to the dirt at his feet.

MacLeod bent to retrieve the paper, then straightened up. "It's been a real pleasure getting to know you, Sergeant."

Pacheco's heavily lined face broke into a grin. "Do not let me catch you alone. This is a very big country, and they would never find you, even if there was someone who would look, like that señorita who is in need of a man. Perhaps you, too, like this woman, but think I will have her for myself."

MacLeod nodded and took a half step forward, his hand on the butt of his pistol, forcing the bigger man to step back. "Touch that señorita and I will hang your *testículos* from that excuse the comandante has for a flagpole over there. Now we both understand each other."

After they departed, Sisquoc rode up alongside MacLeod. "He is a bad man. He will kill you if he gets the chance."

MacLeod turned to Sisquoc. "Expect he'd try."

FRANCESCA'S HORROR

Francesca Hidalgo reached down for the corner of the cloth she used as an apron. She wiped the tears from her eyes before continuing to scrub the pile of vegetables that sat before her.

It had been three weeks since the party of disgruntled neophyte Indians from San Diego de Alcalá had went on a rampage and swept through small outlying ranchos, killing a few settlers and carrying off two small children, including the young son of the governor's sister. That day Francesca had left Catalina with Rosalie and walked to the mission for supplies. She had returned to the little shelter to find it ravaged, and Rosalie and Catalina missing. She had searched the nearby woods and along the stream, fearful of what she might find. Finally, exhausted, her clothing in tatters from charging through the bushes, she ran to the mission, collapsing at the feet of the young priest. She begged him to order the soldiers to go after the Indians and bring her child back.

The priest had summoned the two soldiers assigned to the mission annex, directing them to find out what they could. She was later told they followed the tracks for a distance but turned back in fear of being ambushed. They reported the incident to their corporal at San Luis Rey. Not having the authority to act on his own, the corporal led his own small party of soldiers to San Diego to report to Captain Martín.

A week later, a party of soldiers from San Diego passed by Pala, following what tracks they could still find. They told Francesca the Indians would probably head inland, toward the *tulares,* and maybe even farther north, to the big river they called the Rio San Joaquin, or one of its many tributaries.

Each day her fear grew, knowing that the soldiers rarely found those responsible, or they believed the Indians were too numerous to attack.

At first Francesca had stayed at San Luis Rey, but the two soldiers left behind to guard against further atrocities found their attention drawn instead to her. The old priest had her locked up at night in the *monjerio* with the other single Indian women. But that had not dulled the desire of the soldiers who had nothing else to do but shadow her every movement, hoping to catch her alone.

Two mornings ago she had risen at four with the other women and, following the traditional morning prayers, she slipped through the gate and ran back to Pala. There she worked in the kitchen, helping to prepare the meals served each day to the neophytes.

Francesca looked up from her work, a painful smile creasing her face. She thought of the tall *Americano*. He, too, had suffered the loss of a child. But he was able to search for the one taken. How she envied him. Perhaps he had been successful and was at the moment returning to his own land with his son in his arms. Francesca blushed beneath the streaks of dirt on her cheeks, thinking of his child at her breast, and him standing there looking at her. Had he seen her nakedness? Did he think of her the way she thought of him? At night, when she sought to dispel the thoughts of her Catalina and where her daughter might be, she thought of him, and dreamed about what he might do if he knew. Such foolishness, such dreaming that could only lead to more despair. And would she again confess these thoughts to the young priest, who had admonished her for these lustful ideas. But she still had the thoughts, and she knew they would only lead to more unhappiness. She was a damaged woman, driven from her home and family, and without her child. She had nothing to live for.

"No," she whispered, she would not give up hoping. As long as there was a chance Catalina was alive, she would go on, the way he was going on. But how?

FALL 1823

MacLeod watched the last of the ship's heavily laden longboats approach the ship. The last load of cured and sun-dried hides meant the *matanza* was over. With the killing over, all that remained was the thick sickly smell of rotting flesh.

He would return to San Gabriel and pick up the contracts he had given to Father Fernández for safe keeping, then ride to San Pedro or San Diego and wait for a ship sailing up the coast to Monterey.

MacLeod felt the weariness of the many hours in the saddle. Activity at the missions was returning to the daily routine that would last until the next summer. Already he could see the change in the season, the hills a golden brown, the mornings cooler. He figured he had been in Alta California for about six months. If the winds favored them, a ship could make it around the Horn and up the coast to Boston in nine months. MacLeod pictured himself walking down the road past the crossroads. He could see the trees surrounding the house, and the barn with its silo, and the fence around the garden.

MacLeod climbed into the saddle and turned the gelding onto the well-used track up the river to the mission, knowing in his heart he wanted to see Francesca one last time. She would want to know about Diego; she deserved to know.

The tolling bells at San Gabriel greeted him as he dismounted beside the stairs leading up the side of the mission.

At the top of the stairs, Father Fernández held his hands apart in greeting. "I did not know you would return so soon. You are welcome, of course. But first I must know if you found the child?"

"Yes, I found him, but I was too late. He died on the journey. I don't suppose he had enough time to regain his strength. The last time I was here I was in a heap of a hurry. Did I tell you I found the woman, Francesca, the one your Father Pérez drove away?"

The old priest bowed his head. "I pray she is well. I am sorry for what happened to her. Father Pérez saw things that were not so. His vision of how we should all live could not be met by most."

"Well, you should be thankful he's no longer here. I'm afraid I might do something mighty sinful if I ever came across him again."

It appeared as if Father Fernández was not accustomed to such bold words. He tucked his hands into the sleeves of his smock and bowed his head.

MacLeod said, "Father, I stopped by to pick up that bundle of contracts I left with you, and to thank you for your hospitality."

"And you? Will you remain with us, here in Alta California?"

"No, it hasn't been a happy place. I'm fixing on catching a ship home soon as I square away my business."

He heard the commotion before the cause. Loud voices, giggling, laughing children, then the red-haired Irishman, his hair hanging down his back in a pigtail, and a face full of hair to match. He came trotting toward MacLeod, trailed by a passel of Indian children.

"And a good day to you, Father," Concannon said. He turned to MacLeod, grinning. "And I did not expect the pleasure of seeing you again. What are you be doing here?"

MacLeod couldn't help breaking into a smile. "Well now that you ask, I'm passing through, bound for San Diego. I see you've made a few friends."

"Oh, that is for certain, though I expect some were wishing I was gone. The good Father here would agree, I'm certain. I'll have to admit not speaking their language has been a bit of a worry."

"I would think it's better than hanging."

Concannon's face lit up. "I'm certain of that, though at times hanging would be better than hearing those bloody bells ringing every moment of the day. There's no sleep to be had. It's as bad as being at sea."

"I guess you're going to have to live with it. You could ask to join up with their country, give yourself one of those long names they use. I expect you could get hired on one of their ships that go back and forth to Mexico."

"Well now, I suppose I could, though now that you're here I'm thinking I would rather go with you. I hear there are Irishmen in your Boston town, if you be returning soon."

"Suppose there's a few, though I doubt any ship's captain will be willing to take you back without paying passage, and it may be some time before I find a ship."

"You would be right there, but you said it yourself. I'm a top hand on any ship. There's bound to be help wanted. I'll work my way back."

MacLeod had hoped to be away as soon as Fernández returned with the contracts, and he had no desire to shepherd someone all the way to San Diego who couldn't sit a horse. "Afraid I can't take you. I'll be riding fast."

Concannon clasped his hands together as if in prayer. "Oh Jesus, Mary, and Joseph, have you no mercy? Take me with you, or go ahead and shoot me where I stand and put me out of my misery. You have no idea what it's like having all the praying, and being locked up at night with them damned Indians so I won't be bothering the women folk."

"Like I said—"

"I'll ride, I'll learn, you can teach me. I'll do anything. Tie me on your godforsaken beast, or drag me, but get me out of here.

They've had me in their confession booth so many times I feel the good Lord must be tired of hearing me voice."

A closer look revealed bruises on Concannon's face and cuts on his knuckles. "Are those the only reasons? Looks to me you had a few disagreements."

"Oh that wasn't any matter to speak of," Concannon said. He made a fist and studied it. "These soldier fellows were in need of a lesson or two in manners. They do not a farthing's work themselves but stand around with their arses hanging out and telling you what to do."

MacLeod watched the burly figure of Father Fernández hurrying over empty handed, a look of concern on his face. "I will need more time to search for these papers you gave me," Fernández said, wringing his hands. "They are not where I believe I placed them. I will speak with the woman who cares for my room."

"You can't find them?" MacLeod said.

"The woman will know. She has placed them somewhere, but she has been given permission to visit her village. She will not return for some days."

MacLeod had this problem with no contracts to turn over to Hartnell, and the Irishman groveling about taking him along, and all he wanted to do was tie up some loose ends and sail away, leaving this country and its foolish way of doing things.

"Father, I can't be waiting for her return. Would you be so good as to send them up to Mr. Hartnell, in Monterey, when you find them?"

The bells began to toll. After agreeing to do so as soon as the woman returned, Father Fernández stood watching as the *majordomo* and a few Indian *alcaldes* began herding the Indians toward the church for mandatory prayers. The look on Concannon's face made MacLeod laugh.

"I'll take you as far as San Diego. Mind you, they might arrest you, with no papers. But somehow you're going to have to learn to stay on a horse. You sure as hell can't run all the way."

"Oh, you are a true gentleman, a right wonderful fellow. I'll learn to ride. I swear on my Mother's grave."

The look on Father Fernández's face told it all when MacLeod translated. He grabbed the arm of a passing Indian and directed him to bring an animal for Concannon. Fernández cautioned MacLeod about a band of Indians that had been raiding near San Diego and San Luis Rey, and had not been caught.

MacLeod led his little cavalcade west, following the river before picking up the road south, glad to be away from the mission fields and rotting carcasses. Concannon had not stopped complaining about the obvious lack of intelligence in the mule since it failed to stop, or turn, as directed. At times, MacLeod considered shooting him to shut him up.

Concannon fell off the animal twice. The first time, the mule, feeling no direction from the rider on its back, began to feed along the way and walked below a low hanging branch. The branch plucked Concannon off the mule's back, depositing him in a heap of the gelding's steaming dung.

His voice rose in anger, "Go hifreann leat. Go stroice an diabhal thú."

MacLeod reined the gelding around and leaned on the front of the saddle. "I suspect you weren't apologizing to that poor animal. Need to keep your eyes peeled for them branches."

"I saw the damned branch," Concannon said. He stood beside the mule and attempted to shake the clinging wet dung from his pants. "The cursed animal refused to honor my command."

"Afraid it only understands them in Mexican. You need to be learning their talk." He reined the gelding back around and continued down the road. "Better figure a way to be getting back on that poor animal. We got a long way to go today."

The second incident happened while crossing the Rio Santa Anna. MacLeod heard the curse first, then the splash. He turned around and urged the gelding back into the water in time to grasp the collar of Concannon's shirt and lift up the gasping man.

"I can't swim and you ride through these raging rivers with no concern for others," Concannon managed to say while attempting to breathe.

"We call these here rivers gentle little streams," MacLeod said, making an effort to keep from laughing. "And the raging river is only two feet deep. Now grab the tail of my horse and follow along."

From San Gabriel south they had seen no one of authority who might ask to see papers. MacLeod figured the Indian scare and troops sent out in search of the raiding party had left only the oldest soldiers behind, and they seldom left the security of the missions.

A short distance beyond San Luis Rey, MacLeod turned up the narrow track to Pala.

"Are we to be going up there?" Concannon said. "I figure the other place is down that way, that being where the water is."

MacLeod ignored him. He felt his excitement grow at the thought of seeing her one last time, even though the news he carried would not be what she hoped to hear.

Two hours later MacLeod halted, a cold fear gripping him as he stared at the scene before him. The small adobe structure lay in ruins, the poles of the corral scattered about.

Concannon rode the mule up alongside. "Is this what you came to see?"

MacLeod nodded.

"What do you make of it?"

"Indians. That party everyone went after must have ridden through here on their raid."

"Did someone you know live here?"

"Yes, someone special."

"Do you suppose they took that one also?"

MacLeod ignored the question. He stepped out of the saddle and searched the area around the house and corral, not knowing exactly what he expected to find.

Concannon said, "I expect they may know something about her at those buildings we passed."

"Expect they will. Let's go and find out."

When they reached the structures, it took a moment for him to recognize her, the woman carrying an armful of branches.

Francesca's clothing hung sack-like on her thin figure, her hair a bird's nest of tangles. She backed away as he approached. Then recognition flooded her face and she broke into a smile.

"I saw the house," MacLeod said. He stepped out of the saddle and walked toward her. "I heard about the raid but no one spoke of you. What happened?"

She seemed to struggle with the words, and MacLeod feared what he thought she might say.

"They have her."

"Your little girl?"

She nodded. "They took her. They took the woman, Rosalie, also. I was not here. I am to blame," she said. Then her arms released their load, and she sank to the ground and wept.

He knelt beside her, folding her into his arms.

They sat together for some time until her body ceased its trembling and she could talk.

"I went for food, to the mission, like I did always. They came when I was gone. Every day I stand by the road and watch for the soldiers to return." A new round of tears flowed down her cheeks.

"I'm told the soldiers are looking for them. Probably found them by now. Should be back any day."

Francesca pushed herself away. "Do you think this is true?"

"Surely, since the other child they took is a relative of the governor's. He won't let them stop till they find them. From what I can tell, there's a big party out there searching."

Concannon took the opportunity to slide off his mule's back and drink from the creek.

MacLeod helped Francesca to her feet, embarrassed at having clasped her so close but also aware how thin she appeared.

Francesca brushed off her dress and tided her hair, color rising in her cheeks, her eyes losing some of the dullness he saw earlier.

"Then I will wait and pray, and hold it in my heart to hope," she said. With a gasp she clasped her hands together as if in prayer and asked. "And your child, the little one. I have not asked. What about him?"

MacLeod lowered his head. "Yes, but it was too late. I guess he just wasn't strong enough yet. He died on the way to wherever the priest was taking him."

"I am so sorry for this. With my Catalina, as you say, there is still hope. What will you do now?"

"There's no reason to remain here. In San Diego I hope to catch a ship for Monterey. Then I'm going home."

"Your home, this America?"

MacLeod grinned. He couldn't help it. These people knew so little about what lay on the other side of this continent. "Yes, to America, actually to the city of Boston."

"City? Is this like Santa Barbara?"

He laughed. "No, Boston is a big city. Last I heard maybe forty thousand people or more, and a harbor full of ships from all over the world."

Francesca clasped her cheeks in her hands. "I cannot think of so big a place. But that will be good that you can go to your home, is it not?"

The idea of home kept him from grieving more. Green fields of clover, milk cows peacefully grazing, summer showers, and people building a country on hard labor and hope. And the sounds of voices speaking his own language. "Do you not have anyone to go to, a family possibly?" he asked.

Her eyes teared up again. She bit her lip and shook her head as if afraid to speak the words.

MacLeod knew he couldn't remain any longer. He couldn't help her. Her pain he recognized; he had suffered it also, and he knew it would eat at her mind and body until she knew one way or the other. He couldn't bear the thought of what it would do to her if her child was lost.

He took her hands in his. "I hope they bring her back to you. My Diego would not have lived to be taken by the priest if you had not cared for him." He dropped her hands and turned away, not knowing what else to say. He picked up the gelding's reins and mounted, not daring to look back.

Concannon rode up alongside, clinging to the front of the saddle. "That's a fine looking colleen that one. Would be nice to bed."

MacLeod spun the gelding, forcing the mule to sit back on its haunches and dumping Concannon in the dirt. "Irish, if you want to get to San Diego alive, I will not hear your voice again."

"Oh, now, you be saying I am not to question you?"

"Another word Irish and I'll shoot your sorry ass and leave you by the side of the road for any vulture still hungry and tired of feeding on rotten beef. No one will miss you. You're not even supposed to be here. How in tarnation I ever let myself be talked into bringing you along I'll never know."

Concannon pulled himself onto the mule's back. "Can't understand why you have gotten yourself so upset about me saying what is on my mind."

MacLeod pulled the pistol from his belt and pointed it at Concannon. "Not another word do I want to hear from you. Understand?"

M acLeod watched the last of the ship's heavily laden longboats approach the ship. The last load of cured and sun-dried hides meant the *matanza* was over. With the killing over, all that remained was the thick sickly smell of rotting flesh.

He would return to San Gabriel and pick up the contracts he had given to Father Fernández for safe keeping, then ride to San Pedro or San Diego and wait for a ship sailing up the coast to Monterey.

MacLeod felt the weariness of the many hours in the saddle. Activity at the missions was returning to the daily routine that would last until the next summer. Already he could see the change in the season, the hills a golden brown, the mornings cooler. He figured he had been in Alta California for about six months. If the winds favored them, a ship could make it around the Horn and up the coast to Boston in nine months. MacLeod pictured himself walking down the road past the crossroads. He could see the trees surrounding the house, and the barn with its silo, and the fence around the garden.

MacLeod climbed into the saddle and turned the gelding onto the well-used track up the river to the mission, knowing in his heart he wanted to see Francesca one last time. She would want to know about Diego; she deserved to know.

The tolling bells at San Gabriel greeted him as he dismounted beside the stairs leading up the side of the mission.

At the top of the stairs, Father Fernández held his hands apart in greeting. "I did not know you would return so soon. You are welcome, of course. But first I must know if you found the child?"

"Yes, I found him, but I was too late. He died on the journey. I don't suppose he had enough time to regain his strength. The last time I was here I was in a heap of a hurry. Did I tell you I found the woman, Francesca, the one your Father Pérez drove away?"

The old priest bowed his head. "I pray she is well. I am sorry for what happened to her. Father Pérez saw things that were not so. His vision of how we should all live could not be met by most."

"Well, you should be thankful he's no longer here. I'm afraid I might do something mighty sinful if I ever came across him again."

It appeared as if Father Fernández was not accustomed to such bold words. He tucked his hands into the sleeves of his smock and bowed his head.

MacLeod said, "Father, I stopped by to pick up that bundle of contracts I left with you, and to thank you for your hospitality."

"And you? Will you remain with us, here in Alta California?"

"No, it hasn't been a happy place. I'm fixing on catching a ship home soon as I square away my business."

He heard the commotion before the cause. Loud voices, giggling, laughing children, then the red-haired Irishman, his hair hanging down his back in a pigtail, and a face full of hair to match. He came trotting toward MacLeod, trailed by a passel of Indian children.

"And a good day to you, Father," Concannon said. He turned to MacLeod, grinning. "And I did not expect the pleasure of seeing you again. What are you be doing here?"

MacLeod couldn't help breaking into a smile. "Well now that you ask, I'm passing through, bound for San Diego. I see you've made a few friends."

"Oh, that is for certain, though I expect some were wishing I was gone. The good Father here would agree, I'm certain. I'll have to admit not speaking their language has been a bit of a worry."

"I would think it's better than hanging."

Concannon's face lit up. "I'm certain of that, though at times hanging would be better than hearing those bloody bells ringing every moment of the day. There's no sleep to be had. It's as bad as being at sea."

"I guess you're going to have to live with it. You could ask to join up with their country, give yourself one of those long names they use. I expect you could get hired on one of their ships that go back and forth to Mexico."

"Well now, I suppose I could, though now that you're here I'm thinking I would rather go with you. I hear there are Irishmen in your Boston town, if you be returning soon."

"Suppose there's a few, though I doubt any ship's captain will be willing to take you back without paying passage, and it may be some time before I find a ship."

"You would be right there, but you said it yourself. I'm a top hand on any ship. There's bound to be help wanted. I'll work my way back."

MacLeod had hoped to be away as soon as Fernández returned with the contracts, and he had no desire to shepherd someone all the way to San Diego who couldn't sit a horse. "Afraid I can't take you. I'll be riding fast."

Concannon clasped his hands together as if in prayer. "Oh Jesus, Mary, and Joseph, have you no mercy? Take me with you, or go ahead and shoot me where I stand and put me out of my misery. You have no idea what it's like having all the praying, and being locked up at night with them damned Indians so I won't be bothering the women folk."

"Like I said—"

"I'll ride, I'll learn, you can teach me. I'll do anything. Tie me on your godforsaken beast, or drag me, but get me out of here.

They've had me in their confession booth so many times I feel the good Lord must be tired of hearing me voice."

A closer look revealed bruises on Concannon's face and cuts on his knuckles. "Are those the only reasons? Looks to me you had a few disagreements."

"Oh that wasn't any matter to speak of," Concannon said. He made a fist and studied it. "These soldier fellows were in need of a lesson or two in manners. They do not a farthing's work themselves but stand around with their arses hanging out and telling you what to do."

MacLeod watched the burly figure of Father Fernández hurrying over empty handed, a look of concern on his face. "I will need more time to search for these papers you gave me," Fernández said, wringing his hands. "They are not where I believe I placed them. I will speak with the woman who cares for my room."

"You can't find them?" MacLeod said.

"The woman will know. She has placed them somewhere, but she has been given permission to visit her village. She will not return for some days."

MacLeod had this problem with no contracts to turn over to Hartnell, and the Irishman groveling about taking him along, and all he wanted to do was tie up some loose ends and sail away, leaving this country and its foolish way of doing things.

"Father, I can't be waiting for her return. Would you be so good as to send them up to Mr. Hartnell, in Monterey, when you find them?"

The bells began to toll. After agreeing to do so as soon as the woman returned, Father Fernández stood watching as the *majordomo* and a few Indian *alcaldes* began herding the Indians toward the church for mandatory prayers. The look on Concannon's face made MacLeod laugh.

"I'll take you as far as San Diego. Mind you, they might arrest you, with no papers. But somehow you're going to have to learn to stay on a horse. You sure as hell can't run all the way."

"Oh, you are a true gentleman, a right wonderful fellow. I'll learn to ride. I swear on my Mother's grave."

The look on Father Fernández's face told it all when MacLeod translated. He grabbed the arm of a passing Indian and directed him to bring an animal for Concannon. Fernández cautioned MacLeod about a band of Indians that had been raiding near San Diego and San Luis Rey, and had not been caught.

MacLeod led his little cavalcade west, following the river before picking up the road south, glad to be away from the mission fields and rotting carcasses. Concannon had not stopped complaining about the obvious lack of intelligence in the mule since it failed to stop, or turn, as directed. At times, MacLeod considered shooting him to shut him up.

Concannon fell off the animal twice. The first time, the mule, feeling no direction from the rider on its back, began to feed along the way and walked below a low hanging branch. The branch plucked Concannon off the mule's back, depositing him in a heap of the gelding's steaming dung.

His voice rose in anger, "Go hifreann leat. Go stroice an diabhal thú."

MacLeod reined the gelding around and leaned on the front of the saddle. "I suspect you weren't apologizing to that poor animal. Need to keep your eyes peeled for them branches."

"I saw the damned branch," Concannon said. He stood beside the mule and attempted to shake the clinging wet dung from his pants. "The cursed animal refused to honor my command."

"Afraid it only understands them in Mexican. You need to be learning their talk." He reined the gelding back around and continued down the road. "Better figure a way to be getting back on that poor animal. We got a long way to go today."

The second incident happened while crossing the Rio Santa Anna. MacLeod heard the curse first, then the splash. He turned around and urged the gelding back into the water in time to grasp the collar of Concannon's shirt and lift up the gasping man.

"I can't swim and you ride through these raging rivers with no concern for others," Concannon managed to say while attempting to breathe.

"We call these here rivers gentle little streams," MacLeod said, making an effort to keep from laughing. "And the raging river is only two feet deep. Now grab the tail of my horse and follow along."

From San Gabriel south they had seen no one of authority who might ask to see papers. MacLeod figured the Indian scare and troops sent out in search of the raiding party had left only the oldest soldiers behind, and they seldom left the security of the missions.

A short distance beyond San Luis Rey, MacLeod turned up the narrow track to Pala.

"Are we to be going up there?" Concannon said. "I figure the other place is down that way, that being where the water is."

MacLeod ignored him. He felt his excitement grow at the thought of seeing her one last time, even though the news he carried would not be what she hoped to hear.

Two hours later MacLeod halted, a cold fear gripping him as he stared at the scene before him. The small adobe structure lay in ruins, the poles of the corral scattered about.

Concannon rode the mule up alongside. "Is this what you came to see?"

MacLeod nodded.

"What do you make of it?"

"Indians. That party everyone went after must have ridden through here on their raid."

"Did someone you know live here?"

"Yes, someone special."

"Do you suppose they took that one also?"

MacLeod ignored the question. He stepped out of the saddle and searched the area around the house and corral, not knowing exactly what he expected to find.

Concannon said, "I expect they may know something about her at those buildings we passed."

"Expect they will. Let's go and find out."

When they reached the structures, it took a moment for him to recognize her, the woman carrying an armful of branches.

Francesca's clothing hung sack-like on her thin figure, her hair a bird's nest of tangles. She backed away as he approached. Then recognition flooded her face and she broke into a smile.

"I saw the house," MacLeod said. He stepped out of the saddle and walked toward her. "I heard about the raid but no one spoke of you. What happened?"

She seemed to struggle with the words, and MacLeod feared what he thought she might say.

"They have her."

"Your little girl?"

She nodded. "They took her. They took the woman, Rosalie, also. I was not here. I am to blame," she said. Then her arms released their load, and she sank to the ground and wept.

He knelt beside her, folding her into his arms.

They sat together for some time until her body ceased its trembling and she could talk.

"I went for food, to the mission, like I did always. They came when I was gone. Every day I stand by the road and watch for the soldiers to return." A new round of tears flowed down her cheeks.

"I'm told the soldiers are looking for them. Probably found them by now. Should be back any day."

Francesca pushed herself away. "Do you think this is true?"

"Surely, since the other child they took is a relative of the governor's. He won't let them stop till they find them. From what I can tell, there's a big party out there searching."

Concannon took the opportunity to slide off his mule's back and drink from the creek.

MacLeod helped Francesca to her feet, embarrassed at having clasped her so close but also aware how thin she appeared.

Francesca brushed off her dress and tided her hair, color rising in her cheeks, her eyes losing some of the dullness he saw earlier.

"Then I will wait and pray, and hold it in my heart to hope," she said. With a gasp she clasped her hands together as if in prayer and asked. "And your child, the little one. I have not asked. What about him?"

MacLeod lowered his head. "Yes, but it was too late. I guess he just wasn't strong enough yet. He died on the way to wherever the priest was taking him."

"I am so sorry for this. With my Catalina, as you say, there is still hope. What will you do now?"

"There's no reason to remain here. In San Diego I hope to catch a ship for Monterey. Then I'm going home."

"Your home, this America?"

MacLeod grinned. He couldn't help it. These people knew so little about what lay on the other side of this continent. "Yes, to America, actually to the city of Boston."

"City? Is this like Santa Barbara?"

He laughed. "No, Boston is a big city. Last I heard maybe forty thousand people or more, and a harbor full of ships from all over the world."

Francesca clasped her cheeks in her hands. "I cannot think of so big a place. But that will be good that you can go to your home, is it not?"

The idea of home kept him from grieving more. Green fields of clover, milk cows peacefully grazing, summer showers, and people building a country on hard labor and hope. And the sounds of voices speaking his own language. "Do you not have anyone to go to, a family possibly?" he asked.

Her eyes teared up again. She bit her lip and shook her head as if afraid to speak the words.

MacLeod knew he couldn't remain any longer. He couldn't help her. Her pain he recognized; he had suffered it also, and he knew it would eat at her mind and body until she knew one way or the other. He couldn't bear the thought of what it would do to her if her child was lost.

He took her hands in his. "I hope they bring her back to you. My Diego would not have lived to be taken by the priest if you had not cared for him." He dropped her hands and turned away, not knowing what else to say. He picked up the gelding's reins and mounted, not daring to look back.

Concannon rode up alongside, clinging to the front of the saddle. "That's a fine looking colleen that one. Would be nice to bed."

MacLeod spun the gelding, forcing the mule to sit back on its haunches and dumping Concannon in the dirt. "Irish, if you want to get to San Diego alive, I will not hear your voice again."

"Oh, now, you be saying I am not to question you?"

"Another word Irish and I'll shoot your sorry ass and leave you by the side of the road for any vulture still hungry and tired of feeding on rotten beef. No one will miss you. You're not even supposed to be here. How in tarnation I ever let myself be talked into bringing you along I'll never know."

Concannon pulled himself onto the mule's back. "Can't understand why you have gotten yourself so upset about me saying what is on my mind."

MacLeod pulled the pistol from his belt and pointed it at Concannon. "Not another word do I want to hear from you. Understand?"

27

"**N**o, and that's all I'm saying. You're not coming, so don't be asking me again."

Concannon shuffled his feet, his hands tucked under his armpits. "I would be a help, you know. Your cooking will kill those pour little creatures, if you are to find them."

The argument had begun as soon as MacLeod returned from the comandante's office and told Concannon to start breaking camp.

"Hell you can't stay on that flat-backed mule for more than a mile. I can't be picking you up out of every river and stream we ford."

"I'll be learning quick, you'll see."

"No."

"I want to come. I promise I won't be a burden."

MacLeod turned and held up his hands in frustration. "Why? The woman is nothing to you. Can't you see this is something I have to do? Probably get killed in the bargain."

"Perhaps you are not the only one," Concannon said. "I'm asking this of you MacLeod. I'm pleading with you. Take me with you."

Something in the look on Concannon's face forced MacLeod to ask again. "Why? I'm going to be riding hard and fast. I haven't time to amble."

"Maybe you are not the only one to lose someone. Maybe I also have a need to search, to help clear my soul."

MacLeod laid aside the saddle repair he was working on and nodded. "All right, you bought yourself a few minutes, no more. Tell me."

Concannon hunched his shoulders and walked a few feet away, his back to MacLeod. "I come from Galway, in Connacht," he said.

"This is in Ireland?"

"Aye. I was a lad, barely breached. Ma and Da went for a pint or two in town, as they did more than most. My little sister was left with me."

A moment passed, but MacLeod felt the man needed time to tell the story. "What happened?" he finally asked.

"I went down by the river for a spell, to fish. I left her in her blanket in the grass. I weren't gone more than a short spell. When I came back she was gone."

"Did you find her?"

Concannon shook his head. "They looked, the village people did. Da and Ma blamed me, of course. I should never have left her. As soon as I could convince those in charge I was of age, I signed onto a ship bound for the coast of France and Spain."

"That's not the ship you came here on?"

"No. After we returned I had it in mind to go back to my village, so I had a pint or two in a pub in Plymouth to help me nerves. Woke to find myself on board that British frigate."

"I thought they outlawed pressing men?"

"Oh, that they did, a few years back, but who is to say you didn't volunteer when you wake to find yourself at sea, and some young gentlemen with a rope telling you your duties."

"So, you're saying I'm not the only one searching for someone to make up for a loss?"

"Aye, it would be like that, I suppose. I have nothing else, MacLeod. I have no one, and nowhere to go. I need to make my life worthy of something."

MacLeod bent to pick up the repair job he was working on.

"Well, Irish, you'd better learn to sit that mule without falling in the dirt, else I'll leave you behind."

Both rose to their feet at the sound of a cannon. "Well, looks like we may be in luck for a change. I figure we could use a few things where we're going."

After hitching a ride out to the ship and finding the captain, MacLeod and Concannon stood beside a pile of goods and supplies. Clothing and boots for both of them, sugar, flour, canvas tarps, and heavy jackets. MacLeod found a box half filled with trade knives and picked out a dozen. "You suppose you might have a pistol or a musket and fixings?"

The man laughed and combed his heard with his hand. "Well now, I might be able to find a piece of sorts, and the fixings as you put it. Mind my asking whereabouts you're about to go?"

"Not rightly sure, Captain, but there's some Indians took someone I'm partial to, and we're going to try and find her."

The captain sent a man below, and he returned with a fowling piece and shot. The captain inspected the piece before handing it to MacLeod. "I took it off a man who thought himself a pirate of sorts. I understand in a crowd it can be very effective, and you won't need worry about accuracy. Might come in handy where you're going."

"I thank you, Captain," MacLeod said. He handed the piece to Concannon. "Learn to use it, Irish. Just be careful about shooting yourself with it, or me."

MacLeod asked the captain for paper and pen and wrote a note to Hartnell, authorizing him to pay for the goods and promising to contact him as soon as he returned, if he did return. If he didn't, he asked Hartnell to see any money MacLeod had accumulated went to

Francesca, who could be found at the Pala mission. He apologized for not knowing if she had another name.

"That wouldn't be coffee I'm smelling would it, Captain."

"Oh, that. Well now, it might be. Am I thinking you might be wanting a pound or two?"

MacLeod grinned. "My mouth is watering already."

A bag with two pounds of coffee beans was included in the pile, which they transferred to the boat. By late afternoon, they rode on the wide track that ran across the rolling coastal plain, dipping down to cross rain-swollen streams before climbing up the shallow banks. They continued northward, to the woman MacLeod knew no longer waited for news and found a spot to make camp for the night. When dawn broke over the eastern hills, they were well on their way again.

The scream came from a thick band of willows bordering a narrow stream some distance below the road. MacLeod halted and listened. It came again, high pitched, then abruptly ceased.

He dropped the pack animal's lead rope and touched the gelding's sides. The horse needed little urging, exploding into a full gallop within half a dozen strides. MacLeod lowered his head as the heavy horse crashed through the willows and emerged on the edge of a small meadow. Two men struggled with a small figure pinned to the ground. One rose at the sound of the horse approaching, his thick hands clenched into fists. MacLeod thought he recognized the tattered uniform of the presidio guard. On the ground, the second figure tried to rise but his pants draped around his ankles caused him to topple over.

A near-naked young girl lay curled at his feet, her thighs smeared with blood.

MacLeod left the saddle before his horse had come to a stop. In three strides he was in front of the big guard, who threw up his hands too late. The barrel of MacLeod's pistol laid open his skull, driving him to the ground.

Concannon joined MacLeod, who stood over the fallen figure. MacLeod still held his rifle in one hand, and he handed it to Concannon. "Here, hang on to this and use your fowling piece on him if he tries to get up."

"I've never shot a gun before."

"Always a first. I'll only need a moment with this other one."

The second guard, thinner than the first and with a face permanently marked by acne, had succeeded in pulling his pants up, but was still in the process of fastening them when MacLeod's fist crashed into his jaw. He went over backward and lay still. MacLeod gathered up an old musket and a rusted sword, and tossed them into the stream. He walked back to where the big guard had managed to get to his knees, blood seeping through his fingers from the deep cut in his skull. MacLeod kicked him in the stomach, causing him to drop his hands and uncover his face. MacLeod's fist caught him flush on the jaw, driving him back onto the ground.

"Bastards," MacLeod said. He knelt beside the girl and as gently as possible helped her up into a sitting position.

"People appear to get hurt when they upset you," Concannon said.

"Irish, climb down off that animal of yours and find their horses and strip off their gear. These fellows didn't come here afoot. We'll take the horses down the road a piece and turn them loose."

"The girl, is she an Indian?"

"Yep. Probably one of the neophytes. Can't figure out why she's so far from the mission, 'less they brought her out here to do their thing."

"And what about them? Are you just going to leave them here?"

"Well now, since they were so anxious to remove their pants, I think we'll do it for them, and their boots. It's a mighty long walk back barefooted."

Concannon let the mule graze in the rich grasses growing along the banks of the stream and went in search of the horses, while MacLeod pulled off the boots of the presidio guards. He stripped off their ragged uniforms, leaving them in nothing but filthy pantaloons, then tied their hands behind their backs with strips of cloth MacLeod cut from their shirts. Both guards struggled to regain their feet, cursing and threatening MacLeod.

He ignored them and looked around for the girl and spotted her creeping toward the band of willows. MacLeod walked over and picked her up. She screamed and lashed out at him until he pinned her arms at her sides. "My god," he said, noting the thinness of her half-naked body. She can't be more than thirteen or fourteen."

"What will we be doing with her?"

"We'll take her to the next mission and talk to them, see if they can keep her. She's no doubt a runaway."

MacLeod rode with the girl in front of his saddle. He had tied her hands together in case she felt the desire to jump and run. He need not have worried. She slept for most of the afternoon.

MacLeod got an idea and passed the big mission without stopping. They came on the remains of the tiny cabin after nightfall. The flickering light from a candle shined through the open window. He hailed the cabin, lifting the girl off his saddle and carrying her toward the house.

Francesca met him at the door, holding the candle up to light his face. "I could not believe it when I heard your voice. You are not supposed to be here. Why have you come?"

Then she saw the thin figure in his arms and reached out for the girl as MacLeod knew she would.

"Who is she?"

"Found her down the road a piece. Some soldiers were having their way with her."

"Come," Francesca said, carrying the girl into the darkness of the room and placing her on a blanket on the floor.

"I wasn't sure I'd find you here, took a chance."

"Yes," she said, lighting another candle. "I have nowhere else to go. You have heard of my Catalina?"

"Yes, ma'am. I spoke with the sergeant after he returned. I'm sorry."

"Why would they do this to her? Why would they kill her?" she cried.

He wrapped her in his arms while she wept, running his hand over her tangled hair. It took a moment before he realized what she had said. "Who told you this, about killing them?"

Through the sobs wracking her body, she told him the soldier said she was dead.

"Which soldier?"

"One that came here. He said the Indians killed them all."

"No, Francesca. I spoke with the sergeant who led the searchers. Listen to me." MacLeod held her at arm's length. "I can't understand why they said that. I know a lot about Indians and I can tell you this. They steal women and children to help strengthen their tribes. Why would they take them all the way up into the *tulares* just to kill them?"

She raised her head and wiped the tears from her cheeks. "You know this?"

Hell, if he was going into this unknown country he had better believe she was still alive. "I believe she is, and if she's alive I'll find her. That's why I came back. I'm going looking for her. The Irishman, too."

She rose from the dirt floor and ironed her dress with her hands. "Then I will wait for your return. If you will gather some sticks for the fire, I will look after the girl. I have little to eat but you must have it."

MacLeod ginned. "You wouldn't believe how good a cook the Irishman is, and we have supplies. I'll have him fix us all something while I look around. Seems the place could use some fixing up."

The next morning, MacLeod and Concannon inspected the damage to the house. The Indian attack had left much of it in need of repair. Holes in the adobe walls and in the roof needed patching, and there was no cooking fireplace inside the house, its previous occupants having used an outside oven for all their meals. MacLeod wanted her to have one inside, to cook in bad weather and for warmth. The problem was, he had no idea how to build it.

"We'll be needing tools of a kind," Concannon said.

"What kind of tools?"

"I'll be knowing them."

MacLeod didn't question him, figuring to take him at his word. "Let's see what's available then. I'm thinking we can also purchase some tiles and a few supplies while we're at it."

Concannon proved to be as adept at building as he was cooking. He said the carpenter's mate went over the side of the ship one night coming around the Horn and Concannon took his place. With his experience climbing the rigging of ships, he scampered over the roof, ripping out what hadn't burnt and installing a foundation of branches for the red tiles.

MacLeod had bargained for the labor of a half dozen skilled mission workmen, who installed a cooking oven in the house. They worked with Concannon to build a crude chimney and patch the walls.

MacLeod had little to contribute and left to see what game was available. He returned that night with two deer tied across the back of the gelding. The next day he skinned both and hung them in a tree to age while he went to work fleshing out the skins and building a form to stretch and dry them.

"You will not be returning the girl to the mission," Francesca said one night as they all sat outside beside a fire. "She will stay here with me."

MacLeod had noticed the bond that had developed in the short time they had spent together. The girl had pushed Concannon away from the cooking pots one night and taken over the duties.

"She appears to be somewhat at peace here with you. I would be aware those damned priests might take offense to her running away and come looking for her. They do feel they're entitled to her once she says she's one of them."

Francesca remained silent while watching the girl work nearby. "She is *Kumeyaay*. Her parents were given to each other by the padres before she was born. Her name is Juana."

"She say why she ran off?"

"Only that one of the padres is very hard. He punishes all who do not believe as he does. She is only a child. When you are finished with the skins I will make her a dress with one of them."

MacLeod slapped himself on the head. "Can't believe I forgot," he said, going over to the pile of gear stacked under the tarp alongside the house. He rummaged through the bundles until he found what he wanted and carried them back to the fire.

She took the bundle from his hands and held it on her lap.

"What is this? It cannot be for me."

"No mistake. Thought you could use it, after last time I saw you."

Tears streamed down her cheeks but she refused to wipe them, hugging the material to her breast. "There is enough here for Juana also. I will walk to San Luis Rey and ask for a needle and some thread."

"No need. I brought along a paper with needles and pins, and the thread the captain said women like." He placed the small package on her lap, conscious of the shaking his hand had developed.

"I cannot take this, it is too much, and not even at the mission do they have such cloth."

"Well, then, I reckon you'll be dressed better than those at the mission 'cause I can't take it back. Ship's already left."

They completed the roof repairs, even if the rust-red tiles looked out of place on the adobe-and-stick dwelling. Without being asked, the Indian workers hung a new door and began stacking wood beneath the overhang for the cooking fires. Neither MacLeod nor Maria spoke again about the gifts, although, at night, with tallow candles burning, both she and Juana cut out patterns from the bolt of cloth, carefully measuring it to reduce waste.

Knowing they had little chance of warm weather in the days ahead, MacLeod figured he would take the opportunity to bath in the stream and wash the accumulated dirt from his hair. He told Concannon to be ready to leave in the morning now that the house would stand up to the winter rains.

He had seen the pool before. It lay beneath the spreading branches of a cottonwood, carved out of the banks by the water cascading down a five-foot waterfall. There the water swirled lazily over a sandy bottom, coming knee high.

She stood in the middle of the pool, naked, her back to him, and her hands combing out the tangles in hair that hung below her waist. He froze, afraid to back into the brush and warn her of his presence, yet immobilized by the image before him. She cupped her hands and reached into the placid water, bowing her head to splash the water on her face and over her body. She was slimmer than he imagined, yet her narrow waist flared over rounded hips and down to long, muscular legs. His heart pounded at the sight of her body; he had never seen Maria like this, even that one time when they had consummated their love in the jail cell. Afterward, Maria had begged him to be patient with her coldness, something Father Alvarez had warned him might occur after she had been sold and raped by the Apache, Romero.

Francesca bent once more to cup the water, her hair falling forward and trailing in the gentle current. Then, as if feeling eyes upon her she turned her head and looked over her shoulder.

As much as he knew he should, MacLeod could not look away, even with her awareness of his presence.

With a grace that stole his breath away, he watched her wring the water from her hair, parting it over her shoulders, and turning to face him from across the short distance that separated them. She folded her hands over the blackness between her legs and tilted her head to the side, then knelt in the water and looked away as if embarrassed at her own lustful display.

MacLeod snuck away and bolted through the bushes, feeling a terrible sense of betrayal at not having withdrawn as soon as he had seen her. What would he say when she returned to the house? How could he face her?

He heard her approach as he and Concannon gathered up their gear and supplies. He had hoped to be away before she returned.

Francesca said, "Please, look at me."

He held his hands apart. "I am sorry, Señorita."

She bit her lip and shook her head. "Guillermo, it was not only you. I am also to blame. I did not turn away as I should have."

It was the first time she had said his name. Whenever they spoke before, she had called him Señor MacLeod, or whatever it sounded like to her.

"I had no right to stand there like a fool and look at you," he said. "If I had left right away you would not have even known I was there."

"But you did not leave, and I did not have to show myself as I did. I wanted you to see me. I wanted you to think of me when you are searching the lands for my child. Will you? And you will please call me by my name, Francesca. I think now we can do this."

MacLeod let his breath, wondering what right he had to answer her with the words forming in his head. "Francesca, I will think of you. I will think of how you looked with my Diego, and of how you looked today, in the stream, and now. It would be impossible for me not to remember how you looked, but if I'm to find your child, I best be going now, else I may not go at all."

A sad smile creased the corners of her mouth. She touched her lips with her fingers in the gesture he loved. "I think, too, you had better go. I think I will have much to tell the priest when I visit the church. I hope it is the older one who hears me. He will tell me my sins are great, but he does not know the feelings I have."

Two mornings before he found the big black mule standing by the pole corral.

"I believed the Indian took it when they took Catalina. I have not seen it since," Francesca said. She walked up to it and put her arms around its mammoth hammer-shaped head.

MacLeod let his breath out slowly. "I would not have believed it if the Lord himself told me that damned animal would let you do that. I think we'll take it along with us though, we can use its strength."

"You meaning this huge devil of an animal. You wouldn't be thinking of putting me on it, I hope," Concannon said.

"No, that would be like sending you back to the British. Both would kill you, but that beast followed me all over New Mexico and out here to Mexico. There's not a better pack animal west of the Mississippi."

When the animals were packed MacLeod picked up the lead rope and climbed into the saddle.

Francesca walked over and laid her hand on the gelding's neck. "I must ask you this. If you do not find her, will you return and tell me this yourself?" she asked.

The question was one he had put to himself. He didn't know whether he could face her if he failed, but she would need to know, one way or the other. "I'll come back, if that's what you want."

Francesca lowered her head for a moment before looking up at him. "Yes, if she cannot be found I would like to hear this from you. Then I would know it is true."

"Well then, I guess I'll be back sometime."

Francesca put her arm around the young Indian girl. "Juana and I will wait. We have much in common."

"You still have credit up at the mission, so you be sure and not go without. And that pistol I showed you how to use. Might keep you safe from some might want to hurt you or the girl."

MacLeod led the mule out. It had taken a liking to the gelding and followed easily. MacLeod thought about his chances of finding the child in this big land. He figured they were slim, but he had to try.

A Burnt Village by the River

"Where will we be stopping, do you know?" Concannon asked the next afternoon.

MacLeod balanced the rifle across the front of his saddle and turned to see Concannon and how he and the mule were getting along. Before they left, MacLeod had fashioned a scabbard of sorts for the fowling piece, knowing the Irishman would require both hands to hang on to the reins and saddle.

"I had an idea we could use a mite more information on the Indians beyond those mountains you see over there," MacLeod said. "Figure the good father might know some." He also wanted to find out if Father Fernández had found the missing contracts.

When they reached the mission, Father Fernández said the Indians were called *tulerenos*. "But that is not who they are. It is what we refer to them as because of this place where they live. They have many names and many villages. We sought permission to build missions there, but the pious fund from our college in Mexico did not have the money to permit this, and the authorities did not want to waste their time doing it."

"What do you know about these people?" MacLeod asked. "The Indians who raided the little ranchos near San Diego have gone there with their captives."

"Yes, this I heard from the soldiers. They passed this way on their return."

"I need to find out how to get through the passes. I could find my own way, but that's bound to take time. Kind of hoping you might have someone who's been there." MacLeod knew it was a gamble. If he had someone who could show them the way, the priest would need to take the chance the Indian would return.

The priest sent a man off, and he returned leading a short, dark-skinned Indian who could have passed for twenty or fifty years old. He wore a thin woolen shirt that hung below his waist and a breechclout of animal skin. His feet were bare.

Father Fernández communicated with the Indian in a mixture of Spanish and hand gestures, then turned to MacLeod. "This is Pucho, he came to us a few years ago because his wife was here and would not leave. He can show you the pass through the mountains."

"Can he ride a horse?"

"He is a *vaquero*. I will give him a paper, but you will meet no one to stop you."

"Meaning to ask you, Father, were you able to locate those contracts?"

Father Fernández folded his hand into the sleeves of his threadbare robe and shook his head. "The woman has said she could not find them where they were put. I beg your forgiveness for such carelessness."

Carelessness? MacLeod wondered. Or someone took them. *I would put my money on that. They are probably ashes by now.*

He and Concannon spent the night with their blankets spread out on the dirt floor in a tiny storeroom. When they woke, they found their horses already saddled and the pack animals loaded.

As they trotted out of the courtyard, Corporal Rodríguez and two of his mission guards sat on their horses, blocking the path. He held up his hand for them to stop.

Concannon kneed his mule up beside MacLeod. "He's a royal pain in the arse. Always sitting on his horse and watching the colleens. He never liked those little dark ladies playing the fool around me."

MacLeod handed his papers to Rodríguez, who made a show of inspecting them before giving them back to a guard, who returned them to MacLeod.

"Why do you think you will find these people when we could not?" Rodríguez said.

"Well now, Corporal, I understood you did find them, least you found some Indians."

Rodríguez stiffened and straightened himself in the saddle. "Who told you this?"

"Sergeant down in San Diego. Said you shot off all your powder and turned tail. At least that's what I make of it."

A moment passed before Rodríguez responded. "What is this turned tail?"

MacLeod knew he should leave it alone but couldn't resist. "Means you skedaddled, turned around and ran back to the safety of your mission."

Concannon said, "He appears a sight upset. What did you say to the little fellow?"

"Said they're a might shy when it comes to confrontations other than the speaking kind. Oh, they get themselves riled up easy enough, but little comes of it but a lot of shouting and fist waving. One thing about their so-called wars against the Indians. It's a lot of show and blowing off their powder and not much else. Hell, I killed more Indians in fifteen minutes than they have in all their chasing and shooting. Besides, he's already riled up. He absconded with my guns a while back, but I rescued them one night when he was sleeping. Far as I'm concerned, they're a poor excuse for soldiers."

Clouds began building in the sky behind them as the Indian led them up the long valley and into the pass MacLeod had carried young Diego through when he entered Alta California. By nightfall, they huddled under waterproof jackets and oilskins, while the rain thrashed their backs, turning the ground into a soggy quagmire.

By morning, the skies had cleared, with white puffy clouds moving silently against a background of brilliant blue. The high desert of creosote and scraggly brush looked clean and refreshed. Where the river MacLeod had followed into the pass turned to the south, the Indian led them in the other direction, across a seemingly endless land of broken arroyos and desert brush. Far ahead a low line of brown hills gradually rose to form what looked like an impenetrable barrier. They rode toward it, Concannon speaking only to complain about the series of swollen blisters on his arse to which MacLeod refused comment.

Darkness crept down the walls of a narrow canyon, the Indian led them out and over a shallow saddle, where he pointed across the open expanse of desert toward the foot of a pass. Without a word, he turned his little roan around and rode back the way they had come.

For two days, MacLeod and Concannon followed the foothills of the dry range of shrub-covered mountains. No more oak trees to dot the land. Instead, scattered sage and creosote and bunch grass, and thin streams carrying the runoff from the storm toward the central valley. Alongside these seasonal streams grew the occasional cottonwood and sycamore but also an abundance of thick willow. The sky filled with fowl rising and dropping into the water. Twice Concannon's fowling piece had filled their bellies with duck, and MacLeod had brought down a curious young antelope who had waited too long to investigate their strange appearance.

"You see that," MacLeod said, pointing to the charred rocks and remains of a campfire on the banks of a stream that led down to a shallow lake. "Looks like more than one fire was built here, and unless these Indians have a passel of horses, I'd say the troops stopped here a day or two, judging by the horse droppings."

Concannon slipped off the mule and stretched. "Is this anywhere near where it is we might be going?"

MacLeod studied the soft earth and a thick line of willows a half-mile into the marsh. "I believe we may know soon enough, 'less I'm mistaken. They've been watching us for the last couple of hours."

Concannon spun around to look at where MacLeod pointed, "Who?"

"Down there in those bushes. Saw what looked like a small boat of some sort. Think maybe we should camp here a spell and see what happens."

They unsaddled the gelding and mule, and stripped the packs from the black mule, then picketed the animals close by.

The sky remained clear as night approached, stars appearing as the sky darkened. From the marshes came the nighttime sounds of birds calling for their mates and the constant croaking of frogs announcing their presence. Other sounds that MacLeod didn't recognize rose above the tules, but the sounds didn't bother him. He focused his eyes on the edge of the heavy growth that promised protection for those who watched. He knew they were there. He had seen the flitting of shadows before the light faded. But would they wait for morning to show themselves?

Concannon rolled over and sat up. "You thinking they might still be watching?"

"Oh, they're down there. I figure about half a dozen, maybe more."

"What are they waiting for?"

"Only an Indian would know. Could be the horses and mules. Could be your scalp."

Concannon edged his fowling piece closer. "Do they really do that, scalping I mean?"

"Not out here, from what I've been told, but what young buck wouldn't like to take that hair of yours back to impress some little squaw he's been hankering over. They ain't never saw the likes of you before. Might help me save mine."

"Well, it would be a costly purchase. I figure on not selling this hair here cheaply." Concannon pulled his blanket up over his shoulders and head, and laid his hand on his gun.

MacLeod grinned. "Wouldn't worry none, just joshing you. They'd rather eat you than scalp you."

A three-quarter moon sank into the earth and dawn woke with a gentle caress of soft light. A bank of fog settled over the marsh, masking the tules. New sounds rose from the hidden waters, and a flock of chattering geese dropped out of the sky and into the fog, and still MacLeod studied the vague line of growth from where he knew they would come.

"Thinking we got company," he said.

Concannon sat up. "Whereabouts?"

"Below us, coming out of the fog now, three or four. Can't be sure yet." He pushed himself to his feet and stretched to shake off the stiffness from a sleepless night.

Four figures began to take shape. Two held their bent bows ready, another carried a musket, its stock wrapped with hide. All wore breechclouts of animal skin and shirts that hung below their waists. They were darker skinned than most; their long black hair hung loose.

Concannon stood, holding his fowling piece across his chest. "That one in front is the biggest I've seen. Looks right mean like. Black as some of those from the Sandwich Islands."

"He only looks mean."

"Now, how you be knowing that?"

MacLeod lowered his rifle and waved. "Believe I know the man."

The big Indian waved in return and spoke to the men with him. They loosened the tension on their bowstrings, all forming a half circle around MacLeod and Concannon.

"Sisquoc, wasn't sure it was you at first. I see you made it back with no trouble. This here's Irish."

A wide grin spread across Sisquoc's face. "You are far from where I saw you. You said you were going to your home. This is not your home."

"Things have a way of changing. I see by the tracks here the soldiers came by. Is this where they stopped?"

Sisquoc nodded. "*Si,* they came and tried to make trouble. They said they were looking for some children and women that were stolen. I told them they were not here."

MacLeod's heart sank.

"The soldiers camped here and some went into the marshes," Sisquoc said. "Then they fired their guns at us, but they were too far away. Then they went home, I guess."

"Sounds about right. I was hoping these people I'm looking for were here. One in particular."

Sisquoc shook his head and pointed to the north. "Not my people. The ones you are looking for are up there. They are with the *Coconoon.* They had some bad sickness and need new people."

"Did you see them?"

"We spoke."

"And they had the captives?"

"They had a few. They said the soldiers were following, and we should be watchful."

The others had circled Concannon and were attempting to touch his hair and beard.

MacLeod laughed. "They just want to see if it's real."

"Well, that may be all well and good for you, but no one's pulling your hair out. Suppose now we can turn back, what with them captives not being here like you figured?"

"How far is this place where these others live?"

Sisquoc pointed up the valley. "It is hard to say. Five days maybe, if the rain does not come again. If it does, you will not be able to cross the river. The villages are on the other side."

Before they left, MacLeod had the big Indian draw a rough map to the village of the *Coconoon*. He invited Sisquoc to come along, but the Indian said he would not be welcomed.

The sky stayed clear, puffy white clouds drifting east against a blue sky, and remained that way as they worked their way up the long valley. Six days later, MacLeod put the gelding into the water and swam across the river without trouble. Concannon followed, holding on to his saddle with a death grip, and chattering in a language unfamiliar to MacLeod.

There they found the still-smoldering remains of a village. MacLeod stepped to the ground and picked up the shaft of a broken arrow. He tossed it aside, reaching down to turn over a body. "Musket shot, no doubt. Not the work of Indians. Looks like soldiers were here."

MacLeod walked the perimeter of the abandoned village. He pointed to tracks alongside a stream that led back toward the east. "There's a passel of tracks following that stream, but they're not the soldiers. You can see the tracks the soldiers' horses made crossing back over the river and going up into those hills to the west. Probably yesterday sometime."

Concannon slid off his mule and sank to the ground beside MacLeod. "You figure it's time we went home?"

"Good question," MacLeod said. He studied the tracks along the stream bank. "Looks like they left in a hurry, people walking and some riding. Didn't even take time to bury their dead."

"Now what you be thinking? I seen that look on your face before." Concannon said.

"Well shoot, we came his far. Another few days can't do us any harm. Long as it stays dry a spell, we should be able to follow those tracks a ways, see where they might lead."

Concannon scrambled to his feet, muttering to himself about no one asking his opinion in the matter. MacLeod chuckled and mounted the gelding. "There be Indians up there never saw an Irishman before. Can't leave them so uneducated, can we?"

"Jesus, Mary, and Joseph," Concannon continued as he climbed back on the mule. "You be using me looks to entertain these savages. You have no feelings. If I had the sense of this mule, I'd turn back and leave you to your own errors, but that poor colleen will be pining away, waiting for your return. Suppose I should go along and look after you."

"Mighty thankful for that. I do need taken care of at times," MacLeod said.

The two days later, the tracks turned north, following a creek coming through a narrow valley between a series of low hills. A thin column of smoke rose from a cluster of huts scattered along both sides of the stream. The black mule shook his head and brayed.

The ears of Concannon's mule flattened.

"I think we've found who we've been following," MacLeod said.

"You think they know we're here?" Concannon asked.

"Well, the ones behind us sure know."

Concannon swiveled in his saddle and looked at the half dozen Indians who had ridden out from behind the hills.

"Best we just set here a spell and don't you be pointing that gun at anyone," MacLeod said. "Those bows they're holding are ready. They can shoot an arrow quicker than you can point that fowling piece."

Two Indians walked ahead. MacLeod touched the gelding's flanks and followed.

The camp was spread out on both sides of the stream. The Indian in the lead stopped beside a small fire burning in front of the largest shelter. Half a dozen Indians rose as the group approached. Another, an old man wearing a patterned piece of cloth over his shoulders, remained seated. Age had worked itself into the creases of the man's mahogany-colored skin. His gray-white hair hung ragged to his waist, his bent and swollen hands resembling claws. Yet, his eyes appeared clear, watching MacLeod as he approached. MacLeod spoke to him in Spanish, figuring at least one of the Indians was probably a runaway. The old man answered.

"He says the Spanish call him Jesus," MacLeod said. He does not know why. He says he is *Lakisamni*."

Concannon shook his head. "Another Jesus. Seems a lot of them around. Did he say what happened at his village?"

"He said the soldiers came, and he sat and spoke with them. They were hungry and he told the women to feed them. Then the soldiers took out their guns and started to gather the women and children. They told him they were taking them back to the mission because they had run away. He said they took his new wife. Also claims he knows nothing about the ones we're looking for."

"What about the bodies we saw?" Concannon asked.

MacLeod spoke to the old man again, then said to Concannon, "The men were angry because many of the women were not from the missions, and their husbands wanted to fight. Someone shot an arrow and all the guns were barking and everybody who the soldiers were not keeping ran away. Says he misses his new wife. She was very young and kept him warm at night. She could not cook but that did not matter."

"I'll bet," Concannon said. "I could use one myself these last few nights. You saying he knows nothing about those we're looking for?"

"I believe he's lying, but I can't see killing more Indians to find out." MacLeod looked up at the darkening sky. "Best we get back across the river while we can. Maybe I can think of something."

MacLeod woke to cold feet. He pulled his knees up to his chest and tucked his head deeper into his blanket. The cold persisted. Finally, he threw the blanket aside and began gathering dry branches from beneath the bushes and started a fire. He added half a dozen larger sticks before walking to the river for a pot of water. Across the river, the charred poles of the burnt-out village stood like sentinels guarding the bodies of the dead. He wondered if the old Indian would bring his people back and rebuild.

He put the last of the coffee in the pot to boil, then sat back on his heels. No reason to wake Concannon, he figured. He knew the man wanted to go back to San Diego. But if they went back, what would he tell her? That he found nothing? She couldn't blame him for not trying; he knew she wouldn't do that because that was the way she was. She would thank him for trying. She would say she understood. He threw another handful of sticks on the fire.

MacLeod poured himself a cup of coffee. The sun's rays crept down the sides of the low hills and worked their way toward him. He rose and walked out a ways, feeling the need to shake the night's cold from his bones and feel the sun's warmth, still wrestling with what he would say to Francesca.

He sipped his coffee for a quiet moment, then knew what he could do. Go to Monterey and send word to Father Fernández, and catch a ship for home from there. Fernández would find a way to get word to her. There was no reason to ride all the way back just to give her the bad news.

Concannon broke MacLeod's reverie, grumbling about what little coffee was left to go along with another breakfast of dried fish.

MacLeod walked back to the fire, where Concannon sat shivering, his blanket wrapped around his shoulders. As if he could read MacLeod's thoughts, the Irishman said, "You did your best. She can't be blaming you at all. You can't be blaming yourself, either."

"I hate to quit. It's a problem I have. Quitting's not in my nature."

For the third time, MacLeod's eyes followed the tracks left by the soldiers, leading up to the top of a low rise. He saw where they cut around another rise and headed toward a gap in the hills far to the north. He figured the soldiers came from one of the presidios in the northern part of Alta California. San Francisco or Monterey. The fathers hated to lose their converts. They hated to lose the free labor the converts provided, and allowing some to escape without punishment only encouraged others to try.

He wrapped his own blanket tighter around his shoulders and thought of the old man whose young wife had kept him warm. An idea began to form in his head. Foolish, probably, but still there was always the possibility. Something had been bouncing around in his head like a bird caught in a barn, and the answer had just come to him. That shawl the old man had wrapped around his shoulders. He thought it looked familiar. Rosalie was wearing it when Father Fernandez brought her into the room at the mission to take Diego. In fact, he had seen her wearing it when he stopped at the shelter near Pala.

Concannon grunted. "I see more trouble comin'. I think we should saddle our beasts and be on our way, 'fore you get yourself going on down another path leading nowhere."

"No, Irish, they're up there in that camp. I think I know a way I can get them back."

"How do you propose to pull off this miracle, you not being one to believe in miracles, I'm thinking?"

MacLeod grinned. "I'll trade for them."

"And what, in all kindness to your intelligence, do we have to trade?"

"Nothing yet, but I will have. I need your help, though. I need you to stay here. With the river rising, I doubt anyone from the camp will come across. I'm going to be riding long and hard and can't be having you hold me up."

Concannon threw his hands in the air. "Here? And if you get yourself shot, what you suppose I should be doing? Give me the sea and the stars, and I be knowing where I be, but here, there's nothing."

"You'll manage. I'm going to get the old man's wife back, and I need to catch those troops who took her. Then I'll trade."

Within an hour he was ready to go. Concannon had not stopped complaining about being left out in the wilderness alone.

The tracks worked their way into a westward-slanting canyon and through high meadows before dropping down to a well-used trail. MacLeod pushed the gelding hard. Thankfully the troops appeared to be in no hurry to return to wherever they came from.

He reached their camp the next night, an hour after the moon reached its apex. He found two guards posted on the fringes of the camp sleeping and slipped past them. The camp contained only one tent, the rest of the troops scattered among the trees.

MacLeod spotted an old woman tied to a tree near the tent. He figured she was one of the captives and crept past the dying fire to reach her. He untied her and asked her where the other captives were. She told him the chief's wife was inside the tent. MacLeod gestured for her to find horses. then moved to the rear of the ten. He slashed it open, finding a young Indian women entwined with the other occupant. He placed a hand over her mouth and dragged her from the tent. She struggled to break free, and MacLeod got the idea she had no intention of going back to her husband.

He slipped back into the tent, and gagged and hog-tied the man who he figured was the officer in charge of the troops. The man struggled, so MacLeod slapped him on the head with his pistol. If the man died from the blow, it would serve him right after the massacre at the Indian camp.

As MacLeod led his small party back to the camp by the river, the Irishman's wide grim revealed his obvious relief. Concannon pointed at the young Indian woman, who was bound to her horse. "You sure this is the right one?"

MacLeod nodded as he slid to the ground. "Yep, she's the one, but I think she had something else in mind than going back to her husband. She tried to turn back a couple of times till I tied her to the saddle." He untied her hands and pulled her from her horse, turning her over to the old woman.

"What be her problem, if I might ask, you going to all the trouble to rescue her."

"Well now," MacLeod said. "It appears her, and whoever was in charge of the troops, had come to an agreement. Seems she preferred keeping him warm and not return to do likewise for her husband."

The weather turned sour, a fast-moving storm sweeping in from the west before they had a chance to cross the river. They huddled together beneath a shelter of branches to wait for the weather to change.

PACHECO RETURNS TO PALA

"I watch for him," the girl said.

Francesca stood up and arched her back. "Watch for who?"

"You know the one, the one you are also watching for."

"You are a silly girl," Francesca said. She had not realized she was being so obvious. But she watched the road also. She waited, praying whenever she heard horses approach.

Juana said, "It has been much time since he left. I do not think he will come back."

"He will come back, but you need to spend your time picking up wood for our fire. When you wake in the night and tell me it is cold, I will laugh at you." Francesca gathered her own stack of branches, afraid to admit that she too had begun to doubt his return.

The Indian girl grinned. "If he comes back, you can ask the priest to give you to him."

"You do not tell the priest you want someone to marry, and he gives them to you. Be busy little one or you will get no hot supper."

The girl picked up a piece of wood and drew a circle in the dirt. "But that is why I ran away."

Francesca frowned. Juana had avoided telling her why she left the mission in San Diego. "Why did you?"

"The old priest told me someone wanted to marry me. He said to bring my things and he would take me to my new husband. I ran away because I knew who wanted me. He was old and beat his other wife until she ran away. Then he wanted a new one for his babies."

"Then it is good we watch out for the soldiers still. You are fortunate they are so lazy or they would come and take you back. Now, take that wood to the house and come back. We will need more in case the rains return."

Yes, he had been gone a long time. Each day she watched the road, hoping for his return. Every night she went to bed with disappointment, to dream of what was not possible. She could never tell him the truth. The truth would drive him away forever.

A shrill cry pierced the thick woods. Francesca dropped her load of sticks and ran down the path the Indian girl had taken. It could have come from no one else. Then she saw the girl racing toward her.

"Soldiers come, soldiers at the house, I will hide," she said. She raced past Francesca.

Francesca grabbed her by the arm. "Juana, listen. Tell me what you saw. Are you sure they were soldiers?"

The girl struggled to pull away. "I saw the horses. It must be them."

"Could it have been the *Americano* returning?"

Juana shook her head. "No, I would know his horse and there were others, too."

"Stay here. I will go."

Francesca approached the house and saw the horses by the corral, but not the men. Then she heard laughter as she rounded the corner of the house. Four soldiers stood smoking and talking while one held the reins of a fifth horse. She tried to keep the panic from her voice. "What is it you want?"

"Señora, we have come to visit with you, are you not happy?" one said. The others laughed.

"What is it you want?"

"Oh, Señora, simply to visit, I guess. You will need to speak with the sergeant, I think."

Then it struck her. Who did the other horse belong to? She swung around and saw the door to her house ajar. She knew she secured it before she and Juana went searching for wood. She rushed to the door and flung it open.

"Ah, there you are. I did not want to have to go and look for you," Sergeant Pacheco said.

She felt her knees weaken. "What is it you want? You are in my house."

"I do not need your permission. Who is it you will report this to, your *Americano?* Where is he? I do not see him anywhere."

Pacheco turned his back and continued searching through her clothing, and the few pieces of pottery and dishes she had managed to gather. She thought about the pistol, but she had hidden it outside, under a loose roof tile, when she discovered Juana playing with it. Could she back out and retrieve it. But what would she do with it, since four of his men waited outside. "There is nothing here for you to steal, please leave."

Pacheco overturned the hair mattress on the wooden bed frame and turned back to her. "They say you have an Indian here with you. Where is this Indian?"

Had they come for Juana? Is that why they were here? But Pacheco came from the pueblo in los Ángeles, not San Diego.

"There is no one else here, as you can see. The one who was here has run away."

Pacheco looked around the small room and grinned. "So, then we will be alone."

Francesca backed away when he took a step toward her, but he brushed past her and went to the door, ordering the troops to return to the mission and wait there. She saw her only chance would be to slip past him and make it into the woods to hide. The woods and thickets along the stream led up into rough, steep mountains. and they would have a hard time following on their horses. Seldom had she seen the soldiers, or any of the men, go anywhere they could not ride.

Pacheco turned back, grinning. "Now you will learn what it is a man can do for you. I imagine the *Americano* had his turn, yes, but he is not one like me."

She backed away, hoping to draw him away from the door, but he moved forward, reaching out for her. When he stumbled on an overturned chair, she darted under his arm toward the open door.

Pacheco's long arm reached out and caught the back of her dress, ripping it off her shoulders and causing her to fall to the dirt floor.

She screamed, covering her nakedness while attempting to crawl away from him.

"You will like this, I know. You will say, Sergeant Pacheco, when will you return? I think so." He jerked her arms away from her breasts. "It will be better than the *Americano*, I promise."

"Please, you cannot do this, I will go to the priests and tell them what you have done."

Pacheco laughed again. "And who will they believe, you who had this *Americano* living here with you, who is not within the Church, or an officer in the employment of the Republic of Mexico?"

"He did not live here. He and the other one with him repaired this house, that is all," she said.

Pacheco pulled her to her feet and stripped off the torn dress, running his hands down her body.

Francesca backed away, clasping her arms around herself. He followed, fumbling at his pants as he backed her toward the overturned bed.

"You will like this, so do not try to run." Pacheco pulled his sword from his belt and thrust the point into the skin of her stomach.

Francesca looked down and saw a thin trickle of blood run down into the mound of hair at her groin. She took another step back, feeling for something to use as a weapon. If only she had kept the gun in the house.

Pacheco flung the sword into the corner, his face flushed, his breath coming in gasps as he released the ties of his pants. He reached down, touching his hardness, using the other hand to pull her toward him.

No, she told herself, I will not let it happen again. She had one chance. She would only need a few seconds to slip past him and run. She took a hesitant step toward him, her arms outstretched, accepting.

"See, I told you, you would like this," Pacheco said, kicking aside the blankets on the floor and going to his knees in front of her.

Francesca clawed at his face with both hands, tearing furrows of skin from his cheeks, one finger entering the corner of his eye as her hands slashed down his face.

Pacheco screamed, his hands flying to his face as Francesca bolted past him. She felt his strength as his hand seized her shoulder and pulled her down to the floor.

Pacheco rolled her onto her back, pulled her legs apart, and thrust his body toward her. She saw his face, twisted in pain, one eyeball twisted in its socket. She felt his hardness at her legs and tried twisting away. He struck her face with his open hand, momentarily stunning her. He parted her legs again, sweat rolling off his face, unaware of the damage to his eye as lust overcame the pain.

Francesca reached up to claw at his face again, an instant before she heard the crack of a pistol.

She heard the grunt from Pacheco, then she felt his body shudder and fall forward onto her. She gritted her teeth, pushing at the smothering weight until it slid to the side. She crawled out from under him and pushed herself up onto her knees, her hands trembling as she combed the dirt floor for pieces of her dress, then she saw the blood running down between her breasts.

A plaintive cry startled Francesca. She turned toward the open door. Juana knelt on the dirt floor, still clutching the smoking pistol in both hands.

"Oh, little one, what have you done?" Francesca said.

"He was going to hurt you, the same as the others wanted to do to me."

Ignoring her nakedness, Francesca rose and took the young girl in her arms. She held her for a moment before remembering the blood on her chest.

A quick inspection revealed that the blood was not hers. She covered herself with a blanket and knelt to inspect Pacheco, turning him over onto his back. He groaned.

"Juana, quickly, bring me water, he is still alive."

The girl hurried back with a jug of water. Francesca peeled back the sergeant's shirt to reveal the gaping wound in his shoulder. She found her dress, tore off a piece, and began bathing the wound, thinking about what she would tell the others when they discovered him. She pulled his hands away from his face and saw the damage her nails had caused, and gasped when she saw what was left of his eye.

Juana knelt beside her, keening and crying out that she had killed him and they would come for her.

Francesca knew it was true. Nothing would save an Indian who killed a *gente de razon,* especially a military officer. They would hang Juana. She had to save her, somehow.

"Listen to me child," she said, taking the weeping girl in her arms. "Run to the priest and tell him. You will tell him I shot a man, and you will tell him he is not dead. He must come at once."

Juana nodded. "I will say I killed him?"

"No, you will say the señora shot this man, do you understand?"

"But you did not."

"Juana, do you remember the man, last year, the one who killed his wife because she went with one of the soldiers? Do you remember what they did with him?"

The girl nodded. "They put a rope around his neck. They left him in a tree for many days."

"Yes, and they will do that to you if you tell them you shot the sergeant."

"Will they put the rope around your neck?"

Francesca wasn't sure what they would do to her, but she doubted they would hang her if Pacheco died. "No, little one. Now hurry and bring the priest back. Go now."

The pistol lay in the dirt by the door. She picked it up and placed it on the bench, then sorted through her things for clothing to cover herself. She felt a calmness replace the earlier panic. Still, would she have been better off letting him have her? Would he have left then, having satisfied himself? But, would she then have another child, and what if he came back, the *Americano*, what would she tell him?"

The soldiers arrived first, their horses kicking up clods of dirt as they raced toward her on the narrow road. The four he had sent back to the mission pushed past her into the house, their voices rising in anger at the scene in the room.

Juana hurried toward her, dragging the old priest by the hand. It was good the priest was visiting the little mission, otherwise he would have to be brought all the way from San Luis Rey. She saw it was the older of the two priests. He crouched before her, his hands on his knees, attempting to catch his breath. Francesca worried the run might have killed him. Finally, he straightened, crossed himself, and entered the house.

She waited, hearing the voices shouting out in confusion and anger, filling the air with their threats. She knew what they thought of her. She knew each one of them desired her. She saw it in their eyes when they passed, the licking of the lips, the hands twisting the front of their pants.

Two of the soldiers burst from the house and lumbered over to the corral. They cut the leather straps holding the gate to the fence and returned, carrying the gate between them.

Francesca waited, Juana sitting at her feet, running her fingers through the dirt. Voices inside the house whined with indecision before she heard that of the old priest taking charge. But what if the one looking for her Catalina returned and she was not here? Who would tell him where to find her? Would anyone here know where they had taken her? What if he had found Catalina, then could not find her.

The Indian girl pulled on her dress. "Señora, why you weep? Will they take you away?"

Francesca rubbed the tears away. "Yes, they will take me somewhere. I do not know where."

"Where will I go then?"

"I do not know, Juana. You must look for someplace you will be safe. I will speak with the old priest for you. Maybe he will allow you to remain with me."

She heard loud shouts from the men in the house and the groans of the wounded man. She hoped he would not die.

The four mission guards carried the body of Pacheco past her on the makeshift stretcher, the old priest trailing behind, his wooden sandals kicking up puffs of dust.

The late afternoon breeze rustled the leaves in the trees. She waited, still sitting on the rock outside her house with the pistol at her feet, waiting for someone to return for her. They would soon realize they had left her behind.

With nothing to do until they came, she thought of the Americano again. She thought about the river, about standing in the knee-deep water and wringing out her long hair while she turned to face him, and him watching.

She felt relieved that no one could see her blush.

THE LOST CONTRACTS

Gaston Dupré waited patiently while Luis Antonio Argüello, acting governor of Alta California, busied himself with the papers littering the table. Dupré knew it would take a while for the man to discern what had been put before him to sign. Where did they find these men they sent to govern this country? From what he had seen this vast expanse of land offered enormous possibility, if in the hands of the proper people. It appeared there was no one in Mexico who saw this. He had told others of the news he brought from

Europe. Spain was in the process of losing her empire. Her days of glory were over. Was this not the opportunity for France to once again step forward and regain her proper place in the world by taking control of this young country? The American president could be dealt with after the fact.

The young girl slipped passed him again, running her fingers across the top of his back. He sensed she wanted to be noticed. He wondered if she was a favorite of the governor's, one of the many he had around him.

Governor Argüello raised his head. "Ah, Señor Dupré, there you are." He reached out to grab the young Indian girl as she passed. She twisted out of his grasp and trotted off. "They are all children, these young ones, even when they are no longer children. What would they do without us? If I do not keep them near, I am afraid they will only entice my soldiers. I hope I have not kept you waiting too long."

Dupré shook his head. "I have time to wait. I wish to speak with you about a thought I had, that is all."

"Then you will join me for dinner. It is rare I have the opportunity to speak with someone of your education and I would enjoy your company."

"I would be most honored to dine with the governor of this great country. I will certainly make note of it in my next dispatch to France. Perhaps it will reach the ears of those in power."

"That would be good of you, and you may pass along my most sincere wishes for their health and prosperity. You may also announce to them that I, as a leader in Alta California, wish for more opportunities for trade."

"Certainly, Governor," Dupré said.

Three young Indian girls made their way in bearing trays, giggling amongst themselves as they placed the food on the table. Dupré judged the youngest to be about fourteen or fifteen although with these aborigines he had difficulty guessing their ages. She appeared to be with child.

He waited for the man at the other end of the table to have his mug refilled before continuing. "I have heard little of matters in Mexico, Your Excellency. Has your independence been what was expected?"

The governor threw up his hands. "As a man of your education and title, I can be open with you when I say how difficult it is to governor here. Every ship that leaves my harbor for Mexico carries my dispatches. I ask for direction concerning these people in the north who build their fort on our land."

"You refer to the Russians?"

"Yes, I ask what to do about them. I receive no guidance. I ask for the pay for my soldiers to be sent. I ask them to direct these priests to open up their warehouses and feed my soldiers as it is their duty to do so. I hear nothing in return. But I do hear about the complaints the priests have made about the conduct of my men. What do they expect, I ask?"

Dupré stroked his mustache, sipping the foul wine and wishing to be back on board his own ship. "There is nothing you can do about this?"

The governor held up his hands. "What can I do? Every time I see a ship enter our harbor I expect a dispatch to say I have been replaced. But enough, you have a request you have said?"

"I need to obtain certain information that might help me, and in return your great country."

"Yes, of course, whatever is in my power."

"*C'est tres bien*. As you are aware I have been unable to obtain the skin of the otter with which I had hoped to fill my ship." Dupré's efforts to hire those experienced in hunting otter had been fruitless. Mexico had forbidden the licensing of any more hunters.

"Yes, these Russians I spoke of. They have cleared our ocean of these animals and paid us not a peso for it. That is why we are attempting to put a stop to it. But, Señor Dupré, why is it you have not engaged yourself in our hide trade? I see others doing so, and I ask myself why it is this man of excellent title with an empty ship does not avail himself of this opportunity. I have heard that others from foreign ports will soon arrive."

Dupré could not believe the offer being placed before him without his asking. With that offer, the governor would feel the obligation to help since he had proposed the idea. "I had thought this magnificent opportunity was beyond my reach. I was told your missions had already signed contracts to supply others."

"Oh, that is only partially true. Some of the missions have done so, and others have chosen to trade with those they wish."

"The Englishman, I have heard he has signed up a number of them?"

"I have heard this also. I received something saying he had hired an *Americano* to work for him."

Dupré bristled at hearing about MacLeod. He well remembered the two occasions they met, and the threats that passed between them. "I heard something of this. Has he not found by now this child he claims to have lost?"

"Not to my knowledge."

"In my country we would not have let one such as him wander about. Would it not be better putting him out of your country? I do not wish to pass on information I am not certain of, but I have heard he may have relayed certain information about your country to people of importance in America."

The governor paled at the insinuation. "What type of information would this be?"

Dupré wiped his mouth while contemplating how best to damage the man. He shrugged. "I, of course, cannot be sure but I assume it is of matters pertaining to the possibilities available in this great country of yours."

With a sweep of his hand, the governor sent the servants out of the room. "This news is not good. We are not prepared for defending ourselves, although we would do so down to the last man. However, there was another incident you may not have heard of in which this man may be of help. A group of *gentiles* down in the south raided a village and captured some of our people. One is my sister's child. I have promised her I would do all in my power to bring him back. Unfortunately, I have received word from the commander of the San Diego Presidio that his troops returned without success. He said they fought numerous battles with these savages but were forced to retreat when their powder ran out."

Dupré smiled. "I met your man when I was in San Diego. I believe his name is Martín. I though him incompetent, but how does this affect the American we were speaking of?" Dupré did not mention the fact that the soldiers he saw in San Diego were slovenly laggards who probably would not know how to fight.

"Yes, well, this captain in San Diego has sent me a dispatch informing me he has given this *Americano* permission to go in search of these children."

Dupré laughed. "And how is it possible he would succeed where your troops have not?"

"In this dispatch," the governor said, "Captain Martín has noted that this man appears to have a history of dealing with Indians."

The statement brought back to Dupré the two instances when they met, and the words that had passed between them. So the man has scuffled with ignorant savages. It did not prepare him to stand and face a pistol at twenty paces, especially if it were in the hands of someone with his own experience.

Governor Argüello continued. "Of course he will fail, but I owed my sister this one last attempt. As soon as he returns from the area of the *tules* I will revoke his passport and send him home."

"I believe that would be a very wise decision, Governor. Now you have spoken of these hides you wish to trade. What are these contracts you speak of?"

"They guarantee you three years of trade with each mission priest who signs them. You promise to pay a certain price for the skins and the fat, for the length of the contract. Here let me show you."

The governor called one of the servants over and sent him out of the room. The man returned a few minutes later with a small wooden box. The governor dismissed the servant, then removed a bundle of papers from the box and passed them over to Dupré. "These contracts with the English firm of *Macala y Arnel* were left at the mission of San Gabriel. They were sent up to me by one of my young officers, a Corporal Rodríguez, who found them."

Dupré sipped from his cup while contemplating the information.

"I think if you could offer the same price as the Englishman, you could fill your ship and go home. A little trade with France would be good for us," Argüello said.

The governor drained his cup, then pulled another paper from the box and unfolded it. "Ah, yes, this is what I mean about having to make all the decisions. This officer of mine from down there in the south, Pacheco. He is only doing his duty and this woman shoots him. Where she got this pistol no one seems to know. She is lucky she did not kill him, but now I must decide what to do with her."

"Is this woman one of your converted Indians?"

"No, she is a widow, I am told, but I am also told she has caused many problems with my soldiers. I am sure you know what I mean."

While Dupré reviewed the information the governor had given him about the hides, the servants cleared the table and placed mugs of brandy in front of them. "So, you believe I will have no trouble convincing these priests to sign contracts with me?"

"You are of the same Church, the Englishman is not, and has not become a citizen of the Republic of Mexico."

Dupré had a sudden inspiration. "I understand these priests are all from Spain. They are surely homesick for news. I spent some time there before we sailed for America. Perhaps they would like to hear the news of their land."

Argüello slammed his hand on the table. "You see? Already you have two steps over this Englishman. Between us we could take over this whole trade."

If he decided this dirty, odorous way of making his fortune was what he decided to do, it would not be with a partner. "This woman you speak of, the one who shot your officer. What will you do with her?"

"I have not decided. I will send the information to Mexico. Perhaps they will tell me what is best. In the meantime, I have sent orders to have her shipped up here. She will be taken to San Carlos Borromeo de Carmelo, a few miles from here, until it is decided."

"You have no jail you could put her in? Is it not possible she would escape?"

The governor laughed. "And go where? There is no one who will take her. No, she will remain there. It will give these priests something to do besides complain. You know the priest that was causing all the problems. I don't know what you might have heard, but he was said to steal children. What was his name again? Yes, Father Ignacio Pérez. I understand he came here with an Indian woman who carried a child. The man wanted to take it to Mexico."

"Where did he obtain this child?"

Argüello held his mug out for more brandy. "I do not know this. No, somewhere in the south maybe. Where he picked it up no one can tell me."

Had not the governor mentioned earlier that the American searched for a child a priest took? Had he not considered this? Dupré thought about the possibilities. Could this be an opportunity being handed to him? If this child the governor spoke of was, indeed, that of the American, what could he do with this information? He chuckled.

"Do you remember what happened to the child?" he asked. "Did this priest you speak of take it with him?"

For a moment it appeared the governor had fallen asleep. Then his head jerked up and he pushed himself to his feet, swaying momentarily. "I do not remember. Possibly I had it sent off to the Father President to deal with, but I cannot be certain."

"This Father President you speak of, where is he?"

"You know the place, in the north, San José de Guadalupe."

A NEW RUMOR

As MacLeod, Concannon, and the Indian woman rode into the center of the thatched huts, the women and children ran up to touch the rescued woman. Smoke from fires smoldering beneath racks of drying fish rose up into the overhanging branches shielding the village.

As before the chief squatted in front of his hut, the woolen shawl still wrapped around his neck, and waited for his young wife to be brought to him. When she arrived, she dismounted, brushed past him, and strode into the hut without a word.

"I think there will be a spell of trouble tonight, especially if the old man feels the need of a little comfort," Concannon said.

"I doubt she'll stay long. But it's not our worry any longer. Sooner we take care of business the better."

MacLeod and Concannon joined the chief at the fire and asked again about Rosalie and the two children. The man shook his head and told them to try the next village.

"Seems his memory's a mite in need of reminding. You have a plan for this?" Concannon said.

MacLeod pushed himself to his feet. "You might consider rounding up our horses, Irish. I think we may be leaving in a hurry. Take my rifle with you when you go. And while you're at it round us up a couple of extras horses."

Concannon rose and stretched. He picked up the fowling piece and started toward the trees where they had left the stock.

MacLeod, casually drawing his knife, walked around the fire to where the chief sat between two others. He dropped to his knees, wrapped an arm around the old man's neck, and placed the knife at his throat. He knew the other men at the fire were runaways and understood Spanish. MacLeod lifted the old man to his feet, then backed away from the fire. "I figure it'll be dark soon. I want the people I'm after to be brought here before that fire dies, or the old man's head will be lying in the ashes."

He backed up, dragging the chief with him, until he reached the horses. He said to the Irishman, "Keep an eye on the biggest one by the fire. I think he'll be the one to give the orders. If he makes a move this way, shoot him."

A brief conference followed. MacLeod's observation proved correct, and the big Indian sent two others racing up the creek toward the far end of the camp.

MacLeod recognized Rosalie as soon as he saw her hurrying toward them, carrying a child in her arms and holding the hand of a boy of about seven. She appeared to know they were being rescued and ran toward MacLeod.

Rosalie placed little Catalina on the ground and brought the other child forward.

"He is the one they took also," she said. "He has been good to the little one. He has helped me carry her at times."

Concannon brought four horses forward and MacLeod passed the old chief over to him. "Tie him on his horse and keep your gun on him," MacLeod said.

Concannon pointed at the boy. "And this one?"

"I'm sure the governor will be most generous with us for rescuing his sister's boy. We'll be taking him."

When they reached the river, they turned the old man loose and continued up into the mountain pass.

Anxious to return the children, MacLeod pushed the group hard. On the third day, they came to the road that would take them to San Diego and turned south.

The boy said his name was Antonio and proved adept at taking care of the stock and helping with the nightly chores. He had taken to riding alongside Concannon, much to the delight of the Irishman.

With the sun nearing the tops of the mountain range in the west, they saw buildings in a field. "You'd think they could have found some place better for a mission," Concannon said.

A couple of acres of poor-looking soil near the mission buildings were enclosed by rows fifteen-foot cactus plants. MacLeod found the priest arguing with his Indian *alcalde*. Apparently, half a dozen neophytes had run off the night before.

MacLeod waited until the stoop-shouldered Franciscan sent the Indian on his way. Before MacLeod could speak he said, "I have not seen you here before. Are you from Monterey?"

"No, we're from the south. I've been searching for some children the Indians took."

"Yes," the priest said. He crossed himself and led MacLeod to a stone bench beside the stained adobe wall of the church. "It is always the children who suffer most. I have been here since I was assigned by the Father Prefect, and I have seen this suffering. From which of God's missions have you come?"

"Been to quite a few, though the first was San Gabriel. What's the name of this place?"

"It is called Nuestra Señora de la Soledad."

MacLeod nodded. "Our Lady of Solitude. Pretty name."

"Yes, when Father Pérez passed this way, he said he had been there with Father Fernández, but I could not get him to speak of it."

MacLeod felt the knot form in his stomach at the mention of the priest. "Father Pérez. He stopped here?"

Yes, he came one afternoon with a woman carrying a child. He said he wished to save it for the Church. I felt it odd."

"Father, you saying this Pérez had a child with him?"

The priest nodded, then said. "He said he had two but one went to live with Our Lord at San Miguel. The other one he said would need much prayer. He said the parents were heretics."

No, it's not possible, MacLeod thought. Why was he been tortured like this? Yet, he couldn't leave the question unasked. "Father, was the child a boy or a girl?"

"It was a boy, of course, since he hoped to return to our college in Mexico with it."

MacLeod felt his chest tighten. "Father, when I was at San Miguel, they told me the story of Father Pérez, but they said he had only brought one child, the one that died. I saw the grave."

A sad smile creased the priest's sun-weathered face. "That was what he told them. He did not want them to take the other away from him."

MacLeod collapsed onto the bench. Could Diego be alive? If so, where is he now? Did Father Pérez take the boy with him to Mexico?

MacLeod could only shake his head. He walked toward the end of the mission buildings to think about what the priest said. If they were sending Pérez back to Mexico, where would he go to catch a ship? And would he have travelled to see the Father President first?

After MacLeod told the story of the taking of young Diego from San Gabriel by Father Pérez, the old priest took MacLeod's arm. For a moment, he hobbled along beside MacLeod, complaining about the situation at the Soledad mission, and the hardships they encountered with the poor soil and lack of timber for building construction. Then he gripped MacLeod's arm. "This child you say our brother has taken. If he is your son, I pray you will recover him in time, but the instructions Father Pérez received from the Father President were very explicit. He was not to go on to San José de Guadalupe. The first ship available was to take him to San Blas, were he would go by land to Mexico City. I am sure Father Pérez has already left Alta California."

MacLeod found Concannon in the mission kitchen with Rosalie and the children. "Change of plans, Irish. We're going to Monterey." He knew Francesca waited for news, and the young boy's mother also waited, but he had to take the two days to find out.

He saw it beside the road, about a mile ahead and framed by lifeless mountains, a pretty sandstone mission church with a star shaped window between the bell towers. Behind it rows of thatched adobe and stick huts marked the Indian village. A vaquero tending a cattle in an adjacent field told MacLeod it was called San Carlos Borromeo de Carmelo.

They continued down the road toward Monterey, the seat of power in Alta California, where all foreign ships were required to pay their duties before sailing up and down the coast to trade.

The Presidio of Monterey consisted of a series of long adobe warehouses built on top of a slope some distance from the water's edge. The town sat below the military establishment. The neat, whitewashed houses with red-tiled roofs washed clean by the recent rains were far different from the drabness of San Diego. Closer to the shoreline, two uniformed guards leaned against the wall of a large single-storied adobe building.

MacLeod approached an old man sweeping the dirt from the space between the two dozing guards and asked the man for directions to Macala & Arnel. The man pointed to a smaller building a few doors down. Two *carretas* piled high with flint hides stood alongside the building, and an Indian leaned against one of the wooden wheels.

Macleod told Concannon and Rosalie to wait outside and entered the warehouse. Rough wooden shelves balanced on kegs acted as a counter. A few men and women milled about, inspecting stacks of goods and bolts of material. Barrels, with open tops displaying various goods, sat side by side on the dirt floor, leaving little room between them. Hartnell was bent over the counter, making notes in a journal. A young boy waited at his side.

Hartnell looked up as MacLeod approached. "Well now, William," Hartnell said with a wide grin. "I've had it in mind to ask about your whereabouts. Soon as I finish up here, we can talk."

"I've people outside need attending, Mr. Hartnell. I'll be needing a place for them to stay."

"Of course." The Englishman called out to someone in the back of the warehouse, then led MacLeod through a narrow doorway into a small room, where he sat on the corner of a hewn-plank table.

"By god, William, I am surprised to see you. Last I heard, this fellow comes tearing into town and demands the governor organize a party to go after you. Claimed you abducted a woman he was returning to a mission. Problem was, he couldn't explain how the troops he had with him couldn't do the job."

A moment later a young man stuck his head in the door. Hartnell put his hand on his shoulder and brought him into the room. "This is Mariano Vallejo. I hired him to help clerk here at the store. I have been helping him and a couple of his cousins learn English. However, he will be leaving me shortly. I'm afraid he has joined the military as a cadet in the Monterey Company.

Hartnell told Mariano to fetch someone to look after the woman and children, then sent him off and turned to face MacLeod. "Now tell me how you come to be here?"

MacLeod pulled an empty keg over and sat down. "Mr. Hartnell, it's a long story. Starts with an Indian raid in the south."

"Heard something about that raid," Hartnell said. "You're speaking of the one that took our governor's kin? Everyone's heard about that, and the failure to rescue him."

"Yep, that's the one. Took another child, too. Well, they're both outside your door right now."

"Who?"

"The ones the Indians took."

Hartnell's jaw dropped. "How did you manage that? Why, it was told here that the troops fought pitched battles with those Indians out in the *tules*. We heard a hundred Indians were slain before the troops had to pull back for lack of ammunition."

MacLeod laughed. "Those they sent out from San Diego never even got close to the Indian camp before they hightailed it. It was another bunch from up here in the north that raided an Indian village in the *tules* looking for runaways. They killed a passel of innocent Indians and took an old chief's young wife in the bargain. Happens that's the Indian camp that had the captives we were looking for. We never fired a shot. Took some bargaining, but you can see it for yourself."

"By god, this will set the town talking," Hartnell said.

"Mr. Hartnell, you remember the story about my son."

"Of course. That's the reason I was able to hire you, and I'm mighty glad I did."

"Yes, sir, he's the one. Can't recall how much I might have told you, but I followed him up as far as San Miguel Arcángel. A padre there remembered him and said the child he had with him died. They showed me the grave. But now I discover that damned priest had two children and told them at that Soledad mission he took one away from a heathen. That would be me, I expect."

Hartnell held out his hands. "That sounds like the young fellow might still be here somewhere. What else were you told?"

"Only that this Pérez fellow received instructions to come here immediately for a ship to Mexico. I need to find out if he took Diego with him or not. I figure if anybody would know, it would be the governor. That's why I came here. I figure to speak with him and find out for sure."

"I can help arrange that," Hartnell replied.

"There's something else, Mr. Hartnell. I left the signed contracts at San Gabriel. Somehow they were misplaced, though I have other thoughts."

"That's unfortunate. However, since the price I'm offering will remain the same, there should be no problem. We can ask them to sign another."

"I'm obliged to you for your understanding," MacLeod said. "Perhaps when you have a moment we can balance our accounts. I'm hoping I haven't overdrawn with all my purchases. This rumor about my son has put a knot in my traces so to speak. Can't figure on taking the first ship home until I find out for sure."

"Home is it?" Hartnell said, signing a document one of his clerks brought to him. "I was rather hoping you'd find a reason to stay. This country has a future, though with who I'm not certain."

"Appreciate your concern, but I've about had enough of these people and their church thinking. Poor damned Indians haven't any choice in their lives once they fall for the chatter of these here priests. Soon as they sign on, they're prisoners and slaves."

"Won't last, William. Can't. If you would stick around awhile, you'd see for yourself. Doubt it'll be good for the Indians though. Everyone lining up to grab what they can."

"This mission system they set up was supposed to last no more than ten years," Hartnell continued. "Here it is, nigh on sixty-five years since Father Serra founded San Diego de Alcalá, and they're no closer to bringing these Indians into their way of thinking than they were the first year."

"Do they believe what they're doing is for these Indians? I saw some pretty harsh treatment of the people by these fathers."

"Oh, some have been accused of being too harsh in their punishments," Hartnell said. "Most of them have been at their assigned posts for years and are pretty set in their ways. Some of them can see what's coming. There's been talk of breaking up the missions for some time now. But as to what you're talking about, I think they truly believe in what they're doing. I think they believe strict adherence to their teachings is the only way to civilize the neophytes. In a way, I feel sorry for the Indians though. In the end they'll have forgotten how to live the old way, and I doubt they can live the new way, once they're free of the mission yoke."

MacLeod remembered the villages he visited in the *tulares* and along the river. "I saw a lot of runaways. Some didn't look all too healthy. Come to think of it, there were a good deal of fresh graves at some of the missions I visited."

"Disease," Hartnell said. "They don't speak about it much, but I've heard some of our sicknesses have hit the Indians pretty hard. They don't appear to have the ability to recover once they catch it. Measles is one of them. And it's not spoken of, but the soldiers bring their diseases with them and pass them on to the Indian women. You'll see the results in the children if you look closely enough."

The young clerk returned, bringing an old Mexican woman. Hartnell told her about the woman and children outside and said he would send supplies over for cooking.

MacLeod scratched himself, thinking a hot bath would be where he wanted to start, soon as he found a place to stay for a night or two. "First thing is find out what the priest did with the child he had. Hopefully, find out pretty quick because I have a little one out front needs to be taken back to her mother."

"That's understandable. I can't imagine what she must be going through." Hartnell slid off the desk and stepped around a puddle of mud on his floor. "You know, a man could make himself a fine business here if he could build himself a mill to saw lumber. There's not a home or warehouse here that wouldn't stand in line to buy sawn planks for their floors. Could even build themselves two-storied houses. Now wouldn't that be something."

"Why hasn't someone done so already?" MacLeod asked.

"You said so yourself. No one wants to work. Ride their horses, gamble, drink. Every house has at least one or more Indian servants to do the work. Some have a servant for each child, plus more to take care of their animals, washing, cooking, just about everything."

Concannon stuck his head in the door. "Begging your pardon, but I've been a talking with the soldiers here and found a place to stay. So I'm off to find myself a little shore leave so to speak."

MacLeod thanked him, explaining to Hartnell where the Irishman had come from.

"Well, William, whatever happens with that youngster of yours, you'll be staying with me for now, and no argument. Our governor's away at present. No telling when he'll be back."

3 4

Three months later, a rumor surfaced that the governor and his party would return within a week. Almost daily MacLeod paced the dirt streets between the houses of Monterey, chastising himself for not having returned to the south with Francesca's child. He couldn't bring himself to visit the anguish she must be suffering. At first heavy rains swamped the land, making the rivers impassable. People said the governor would surely return as soon as the weather cleared. MacLeod sought out a ship sailing south, but none visited

Monterey, most lying in snug harbors waiting for the new *matanza* to fill their holds with hides and tallow.

All of December seemed like a celebration of some sort. Christmas they called *Las Posada*, followed about two weeks later by another to honor the arrival of the three wise men. MacLeod remembered the Frenchmen, Charbonneau and Belanger, referring to this event as *petite noel.*

MacLeod discovered that his passport had expired, and Hartnell laughed when MacLeod, still purple with rage, told him about being marched to the presidio to speak with the comandante about this flagrant violation.

"Well, William, your troubles should be resolved soon," Hartnell said. "Word reached me this morning that our Most Excellent Governor will return shortly. In fact he's planning on attending the wedding of a relative in a couple of days. I can think of no better way to present you to him than to attend the wedding. I'm positive he'll find time to speak to you once he discovers it was you who rescued his nephew."

Macleod had stopped by Hartnell's warehouse to purchase some clothing, and Hartnell continued. "By the way, I doubt you knew but Vicente Montero, from the Pueblo de los Angeles, has moved up to Monterey. I'm surprised you haven't run into him already."

"The Monteros?" MacLeod said.

"Yes, you remember him. The wife also. You must remember her, William, else I'll believe you're a might daft. Tall, very beautiful, was going to . . .?"

Did he remember Marisol Montero? How could anyone forget her? He also remembered thinking he would be better off if he never met her again.

"By god, that's right, I had forgotten," MacLeod replied, feigning ignorance. "Of course, the Frenchman was paying her a great deal of attention if I recall. But Doñ Montero spoke up for me with the *alcalde major* in los Ángeles. Helped me obtain papers so I could work for you."

"Anyway, she's back," Hartnell said. I heard that she lost the child on the voyage. They'll be at the wedding."

THE WEDDING
APRIL 1824

Four days later, MacLeod learned the rumors were true, the governor would attend the wedding, which had been postponed a number of times to await his return. The following morning, after soaking in a wooden tub for an hour the night before, and painfully scraping off the months of whiskers, MacLeod followed Hartnell's black mare out onto the cart path. The rancho of the bride's father lay twenty miles out of Monterey, a land grant given to a soldier who had come up to Monterey with Father Junípero Serra fifty years before, and passed on to his sons.

The day's trip took on a party atmosphere as they joined up with *carretas,* men and woman on horseback, some riding double, and crude wagons taking families and their servants to the festivities to take place the following day. After spending the weeks chasing through the *tulares,* in search of Catalina and Rosalie, MacLeod appreciated the opportunity to speak with Hartnell about lighter matters. The Englishman's knowledge of Alta California was superior to most, having travelled up and down the coast buying hides and tallow. MacLeod learned of the continual bitterness between those in the south, and those in the north. Some of it he had heard at Vicente Montero's as well.

They followed the line of guests into an open courtyard. The main house stood under a dozen aged elms and black oak trees, their canopy of branches offering a quarter acre of shade. Blankets had been spread on the ground under the trees and people wandered about, meeting friends they had not seen since the last celebration.

Several men came forward to greet Hartnell and eyed MacLeod when he was introduced as the American gentleman who had rescued the children.

He and Hartnell walked around the edge of an area lined with rough plank tables piled high with food. People filled wooden bowls from pots of steaming stew and held their cups out for the mission wine being poured from leather bags. The wedding would not take place until the following morning, when the elderly Franciscan priest from San Carlos Borromeo Carmelo would arrive to perform the ceremony.

MacLeod searched among the small groups but failed to see the woman from San Diego, wondering if she would remember their brief encounter.

Many of the men found space in the shade of the trees to sit and gamble, playing a game MacLeod was not familiar with. Others rode their horses, draped with the silver trappings MacLeod had seen on the horses of the wealthier families in New Mexico. He could never understand how a large family could live in a small, one-room, adobe house, with a *tule*-cover roof, yet the man of the house would spend whatever he could make from the sale of his few hides for rich decorations for himself and his horse.

Long before the night's celebration ended, MacLeod had found a spot far from the noise and wrapped himself in his blankets to sleep. The next day, he would speak with the governor.

Cheers rang out at mid-morning as the crowd of partiers welcomed the arrival of the groom and his family. At that point, all that was needed was for the priest to marry the couple and begin three or four more days of celebrating.

The governor and his party rode in at noon and were quickly surrounded by the families of both the bride and groom. Hartnell explained that the governor was an uncle of the young groom.

The bride soon made her way toward the spot beneath the oaks chosen for the ceremony. Indian musicians announced her arrival, and the young groom, dressed in heavily embroidered silk and linen vest and pantaloons, his soft buckskin boots new for the occasion, was brought forward to meet his bride.

MacLeod stood at the back of the crowd, while Hartnell waited with others he knew from Monterey. A hush fell over the gathering as the young bride was brought forward under a canopy of silk to meet her husband-to-be.

MacLeod watched the people turn to see the bride as she made her way toward the front. Then he saw the woman. She sat on the grass across from him, her husband standing behind her. But standing beside Vicente Montero was the Frenchman, Gaston Dupré.

It surprised MacLeod to see the Frenchman with them. How could Vicente Montero be unaware of the attention Dupré paid to his wife? MacLeod recalled his brief conversation her, in San Diego. She understood Dupré's infatuation for her and admitted her relief that her ship would sail the following morning, and she would be away from him. Had things taken a different road, MacLeod wondered. Had Dupré's persistence paid off, and she accepted his presence? From the few words he had exchanged with her, MacLeod couldn't bring himself to believe it. Or was Vicente Montero willing to accept Dupré's flirtation with his wife, for fear of being called upon to defend himself?

MacLeod watched the three, feeling his hatred rise at the sight of the man. But how could he question her, when it was no business of his?

The ceremony over, the bride and groom made their way through the crowd of friends and family, eager to impart their best wishes on the new couple.

"Ah, there you are," Hartnell said as he joined MacLeod. "I think this would be a good time to meet the governor. In fact, I understand he has been inquiring about you."

Hartnell led MacLeod through the crowd to where the governor stood with his aide and secretary. Dupré had shouldered his way through those circling the governor and stood by the governor's side.

Hartnell offered his hand to the governor and introduced MacLeod. "Your Excellency, this is the American, William MacLeod, who rescued the young man. He has been asking to meet you."

"This is the man I owe so much to," the governor said. He reached out and gripped MacLeod by the shoulders. "I cannot wait to dispatch a ship to San Diego to return the boy to my sister. I cannot believe such a day. You rescue this member of my family and another marries the beautiful daughter of my good friend."

MacLeod bowed his head, acknowledging the governor. "Thank you, Your Excellency. I doubt he's been harmed by his captivity."

"I am sure he will be in fine health. Now, you must tell me how I may be of service in return."

"Thank you. There is something I wish to speak with you about."

"Yes, yes," the governor said, pointing to a thin-faced man at his side. "You will see my secretary here, and he will see you get an appointment to come so we can discuss this more."

The governor half turned, adding, "And this is Señor Dupré. From that French ship you see in my harbor. Perhaps you can help him with some questions he might have, since I am to believe he will soon be involved in the trade of skins and fat, like yourself."

Gaston Dupré glanced at MacLeod and smirked.

MacLeod couldn't pass up the opportunity. "Monsieur Dupré, I was under the impression you considered the trade beneath you. You were more interested in a quick profit in otter skins?"

Dupré stood with his hands behind his back watching Marisol Montero walk across the grass, then turned to MacLeod. "A full hold in my ship is not beneath me. You are mistaken in what I meant. However, I can understand your lack of knowledge in such things."

MacLeod clenched his hands at his side. "My understanding of the trade is sufficient to ensure full holds for any ships that my employer commissions. You do understand about the contracts that missions sign?"

A cold smile creased Dupré's narrow face. "*Mais certainement*, these contracts are available to all. In fact, I have already obtained some that were left unguarded, you might say. The governor has voided them. He has offered me the opportunity to replace them with those of my own. I believe I have I have a guarantee from some in the south already."

At that moment, MacLeod was certain of what had happened to his contracts. That damned thieving Corporal Rodríguez. "Looks to me like I'll be dealing with a skunk."

Dupré's eyes flared. "Be aware, American, I will ignore your insult this time due to your obvious lack of breeding. Do not challenge me again, or I will be forced to request satisfaction. Because you were able to rescue these people from savages do not think I am as easy as they."

"Well now, that's good to know. I hadn't realized you were such an expert in the fighting ability of Indians. Perhaps someday we'll need to find out," MacLeod said.

He found a quiet spot to let his temper cool off. He would have to let Hartwell know that the stolen contracts were in Dupré's possession, damning himself for not taking better care of them.

The guests began to gather for the dance. The musicians moved into the open as the wedding couple walked to the center of the tree-lined enclosure. The music began and the couple stepped to the lively beat of the *Jarabe Tapatío.* Soon other couples joined them, the women wearing a wide selection of colored skirts and blouses, thought to be accurate copies of the latest European fashions.

Watching the couples, MacLeod had the impression the men had taken great care in putting together their own attire, from the heavily embroidered satin vests to the gold buttons adorning their breeches. All wore the wide-brimmed *sombreros* even he had begun wearing.

He listened to the music, watching the dancers perform their ritual moves: the women, heads tilted to one side, their hands holding their long skirts to show their feet and the delicate steps they took. The men danced with their hands behind their backs, knees bent, and their feet stepping out and tapping the ground in keeping with the music.

Across the dance area, MacLeod saw Dupré again push himself in among those surrounding Marisol Montero and lean over to whisper something in her ear. Whatever it was, she declined the invitation, leading her train of admirers away from the sulking Frenchman.

Macleod moved to one of the tables and filled a mug with thick *champurrado*, a chocolate drink the Mexicans loved. A small group of the wedding guests gathered near the Indian cooks and watched a steer rotate over burning oak coals, to be served with bowls of *puchero* and *enchiladas*. Other tables overflowed with olives from San Diego, pastries and other sweets brought in on the ships from the Sandwich Islands.

She appeared at his side without him noticing her approach. She laid a hand on MacLeod's arm and leaned in to whisper, "Señor, we met in San Diego, do you remember me?"

MacLeod was taken back. "Of course, Señora Montero. I doubt there is a man in Alta California who would admit to forgetting you, once they were introduced, but I offer my sympathies. I have heard that you suffered the loss of your child."

"Yes, but there is always hope of another, is there not?" she said, somewhat casually as the musicians prepared to play another dance tune.

Dupré had followed, and stood off to the side, attempting to attract her attention. MacLeod watched the man take another step forward.

Marisol squeezed MacLeod's arm. "You will ask me to dance the *contradanza*, please."

MacLeod looked at her without speaking. Marisol's eyes laughed. "Do not be afraid. It is not difficult, and I will teach you. But first you must ask me before Señor Dupré does. Quickly now."

"I have faced wild Indians, raging waters, and charging buffalo with less fear than asking you to dance, Señora Montero. But if I were to pass up this opportunity to dance with you, I would regret it forever. Señora Montero, would you do me the honor of this dance?"

Marisol curtsied. "Yes. And now that you have asked me, I must tell you that I have never asked a man to dance with me before. I do not know in your country whether a married woman may ask another man to dance."

"Can't say as I know about that, but I guess it doesn't matter none now since it's done."

Marisol again laid her hand on his arm. "I hope I have not been too brazen. I do apologize if I have," she said. "Now, walk out among the others with me, and when the music begins you will follow what I do," she said. She drew a thin fan from the sleeve of her dress and opened it.

MacLeod studied the others who stood with their partners, waiting to begin. A guitar strummed. Marisol dipped in a slight curtsey and took his hand as the couples held clasped hands, raised their arms above their heads, and began walking in a circle.

"I will leave you for a moment, please do not go away," she teased, as she joined the other women in their group of four couples and circled together while the men stood and waited for their partners come around again.

Soon MacLeod found himself following along with ease, his eyes never leaving the slender, dark-haired beauty who caught the eyes of every man she passed. Then the dance changed, the couples in front joining hands and allowing the next in line to duck down and go beneath their arms.

She gripped his hand and moved in close to his side, looking up at him with laughing eyes. MacLeod hoped the music would continue for the rest of the afternoon. Would he ask her to dance again?

Marisol answered the question herself. "I should not have asked you to dance, but I did not want to be forced to say no to Señor Dupré again. It is not good for me to dance like this with someone other than my husband."

The music died and the women fanned themselves, then walked to the side to refresh themselves. Marisol took his arm. "Walk with me over to my husband. I am sure he would like to speak to you again."

Dupré glared at him as they approached. He said something to Vicente Montero, then pushed his way through the men gathered nearby and stalked off. MacLeod wondered what they had been discussing, seeing a troubled look on Montero's face.

Vicente Montero took Marisol by the arm and followed Dupré without acknowledging MacLeod's presence. Marisol looked over her shoulder and bit her lip.

What had the Frenchman said that turned Montero against him, MacLeod wondered. Only then, watching them walk away, did

MacLeod realize he had not told her about the rumor that Diego might still live.

A RENDEZVOUS

MacLeod paced beneath the trees in the small secluded grove while he awaited her arrival, still clutching the note in his hand. He had read it a dozen times since the girl had bumped into him. He read the words in the note again, warning him to keep their meeting a secret. The girl called out to him and beckoned him to follow her.

He found Marisol standing in the shade, her back to him, and her long hair hanging in a single thick braid below her waist, so different from the way she had pinned it up with a silver comb for the dance. She turned as he approached, her eyes searching behind him for anyone who may have followed.

"Señora Montero," Macleod said, bowing at the waist.

She held her hand out to him. "Please, we do not need to be so formal. Today you will call me Marisol and I will call you Guillermo."

MacLeod grinned. "And tomorrow, what will I call you?"

She tilted her head to the side. "I do not think we will meet again. My husband has said we will leave after siesta."

"Señor Hartnell said you and your husband now live in Monterey. Would it not be possible that we meet again?"

"Please, listen to me. I cannot remain here alone with you. If someone were to see us, it would be very disrespectful for my husband. I could not believe the way he treated you last night. However, I believe it was something that man Dupré has said. My husband is very intelligent, but he is very weak in many ways. He is in love with the attention this Frenchman has given him. I am afraid his esteem grows greatly with the flattering, especially when he us asked his opinions about the government of Alta California and Mexico."

MacLeod frowned. "I can't figure it out. What could Dupré have said? He knows so little about me."

"He said things he claims he has heard about you and the mother of your son. He said he has heard it questioned how it is that she died and you did not. He asked what you have to hide. He is a dangerous man. You must guard your words and actions when you meet."

MacLeod waited for her to finish, captivated by her presence. Her warning, though, caused him to turn and walk away to contemplate the significance of Dupré's lies.

She came up behind him and placed her hand on his shoulder. "Please listen to me on this. I cannot help but believe I may also be the cause of his hatred for you."

"Why do you allow him to be at your side? It is as if you desire him to be with you. What is it he wants from you?"

She laughed, shaking her head. "Oh, Guillermo, he wants what every man wants. He wants me. But do not worry. He cannot sway me. He will soon leave our country and have nothing of me but his desires."

"Have you spoken of this to your husband?"

Marisol turned her back and walked farther under the trees, before answering. "You must understand. I worry this man might turn his anger on my husband if I were to turn him away. My husband loves me greatly. I would not be here in this beautiful country without him."

"Are you not from Alta California?"

"Please do not ask me to explain too many things about me. I am not what you see."

"I'm afraid I don't understand," MacLeod said.

"Perhaps someday I will tell you, but maybe not. We have so little time before I must return. I wish to know something of you. Will you take a few moments and tell me about this child you rescued? There must be a good reason for you to go to such an effort."

A smile lit his face, remembering the scene in the little room at the mission with Diego suckling at Francesca's breast. "The mother of this girl-child I found took my son and cared for him when I arrived here. My son was near death. She had her own to feed. She was a widow, her husband was a soldier but those at the mission drove her out."

Marisol looked puzzled. "I do not understand. Why would they drive her away from a mission?"

"They did. They said she caused problems with the soldiers. It seemed the soldiers believed that, since she was a young widow, she would not turn away from their advances. Father Fernández at San Gabriel took her in."

"The poor woman," Marisol said. "And then her child also is taken. I feel for her. You have rescued her child but she does not know this. Why are you still here and not taking the child back to her?"

MacLeod felt the burden of guilt and the need to explain. "I know how she must be suffering, but I have heard a rumor about my son that I had to follow. I was told that he may yet live. Almost too much to believe after all these months, but I have to check."

Marisol gasped. "How can that be? What have you heard?"

"Something a priest said about this Father Pérez who took him. Said he had a child with him when he passed, a boy about the right age."

"That would be wonderful. How are you going to go about finding out if this is true?"

"It's why I came here instead of taking the girl back to her mother. I know she's waiting to hear, but I have to speak with the governor. I can't leave until I find out."

Marisol's fingers caressed his arm. "I understand. To have a child that is yours must be a love that cannot be explained to someone who has none."

"I'm sorry," MacLeod said. "I should not have mentioned it. But there is hope for yourself, is there not. There will be other children?"

Her face fell as tears ran down her cheeks. She turned her back to him and walked a few feet away. "I have told no one this. I trust you to also tell no one."

"Of course," McLeod said, wondering what she could mean.

"I admire my husband very much. Part of this weakness he has comes from a secret knowledge we share. We cannot have children."

MacLeod mumbled, "I'm sorry. Was this because of the one you lost?"

"No, my husband is unable to produce children. He is unable to perform this act. The child that was lost was one we offered to purchase from a woman in Lima."

It took a moment for her words to sink in. He held his hands out. "I know little of such thing. Did you know this when you married?"

"Yes, but the life he offered me was one I could not refuse. I would not be alive today if he had not taken me away from the life I was living."

"What are you saying?" MacLeod asked. He wanted to put his arms around her and comfort her.

Marisol seemed to sense his intensions. She backed away and held up her hands. "I am not the young woman dressed in this finery you see here. You must take my word and not ask any more of it. We have little time left. Will you walk beside me and tell me of the mother of your child. What was her name?"

"Maria."

"Tell me how you met."

MacLeod told her about the death of his trapping partners and of Maria being sold to the Mescalero Apache, Romero, by her promised husband. He told her about his own escape and search that led him to the slave trade camp where the Apache had brought her to sell. He told how the women refused to accept her back into their civilized lives. Marisol listened without a word until he finished.

"That is a terrible story. How did you manage to rescue her from this Indian?"

"Afraid I had to kill him," MacLeod said, recalling the moment he buried his knife in the Indian's belly.

"And the man who sold her to this Indian. What happened to him?"

"I turned him over to an Indian tribe whose children the man stole."

"And they killed him?"

"Oh yes, but not right away. They promised to make his death last a long time."

"Were you not afraid, to travel over a strange country with people looking for you?"

"Afraid most of the time, never knowing who my friend was and who wanted to kill me. But, I had made her a promise."

They walked some distance before she said, "You killed this man to save her. Was it hard to do this?"

"It's always hard to kill someone. Even if they're only Indians. The other ones I had to kill, too. It's hard when I think about it now. They're people like us, only in different ways."

She stopped again and looked at him. "You are different, Guillermo. You are a hard man, not soft like all the others who talk of their desires to wage wars but do nothing. In a way, I worry for you."

"Worry about me, why is that?"

"I do not think you can change. I think you will always be a hard man, even to those who would love you. I know now why you do not take my warnings about Señor Dupré seriously. He has killed men, too, and he does not like you."

"I guess he has a problem then. If he's saying all these things to scare me, it won't work."

The Indian girl ran toward them, pointing back over her shoulder. "They come, they come," she cried.

Marisol took her by the shoulders and shook her. "Who is coming?"

The girl shrugged.

He heard the sound of horses approaching and knew it would only be a few minutes until they arrived. He felt her hand again on his arm and turned to put his hands on her waist, drawing her closer. He couldn't bear the thought of not seeing her again.

For a moment they stood locked in an embrace, before she gently pushed him away. "Guillermo, it can never be. You are the first man I have wanted to hold me like this, but it is forbidden. I am married, and soon you will return to your own country. What would I do if we were discovered? Go to this woman whose child you have rescued. She needs you. Think no more of me, please. If you are again in Monterey, do not look for me."

Before he could say more, she turned and took the Indian girl by the arm with one hand and held up her long skirt with the other. Together they ran toward the approaching riders.

MacLeod stepped back into the trees and out of sight, and watched her leave. Would he ever see her again, he wondered.

MacLeod brushed past the guard at the door, remembering to duck his head. Twice he had smacked the low doorway, which hadn't improved his attitude any, this being the fourth day he had come to arrange an audience with the governor.

The willow-thin man sitting behind a low table buried his head in a ledger when he saw who it was.

"You suppose he might decide to come in today?"

The man shrugged. "I do not know, Señor, he does not tell me this. He is a very busy man."

"Is he here in Monterey?"

"Oh, I do not know this either. He does not tell me."

MacLeod propped his rifle against the wall, placed his hands on the table and leaned toward the man. "Tell me what you know. I spoke with him four days ago, and delivered his young nephew to him. He told me to see you and make an appointment to speak with him on a matter that happens to be very important to me. I'm here to make an appointment. When do you want me to return?"

The man shuffled through a stack of papers as if looking for the governor's schedule, then answered MacLeod with a thin smile. "I cannot make this appointment until I see Our Excellency. Then I will send for you immediately."

"You mean that's it? How can you get anything done if the only man who can make decisions can't be found?" MacLeod said.

He grabbed his rife and stormed out of the office, making a determined effort to knock the door off its iron hinges by slamming it shut behind him. The pair of guards, having heard the exchange, found a moment to walk to the far side of the whitewashed adobe building.

MacLeod mounted his horse and kicked him harder than necessary, sending the big gelding racing out of the presidio compound and down the rutted road toward the town. With every stride the horse took, MacLeod cursed the governor and all the indecisive officials who attended him.

He brought the horse to a skidding halt in front of Hartnell's young clerk, Vallejo, who stood in the middle of the track frantically waving his arms but readying himself to leap out of the way of the charging horse.

"Mariano, isn't it?" MacLeod said.

"*Si*, and Señor Hartnell wishes you to come. He said it is most important."

"Well hop up here and we'll go and see what it's about," MacLeod said. He reached down to grasp the young man's hand and swung him up onto the back of the saddle.

When they arrived at the warehouse, Hartnell had a handful of women with him, inspecting a bolt of cloth. He waved to MacLeod. "Be right there, William. Have a seat in my office."

Hartnell appeared a few moments later accompanied by a man dressed in sea-going gear who whipped off his hat and held it in front of him. "This is Señor Torres, off that ship that arrived this morning. They came up from San Diego. So happens I've used the man for a few things before, and he stopped by to find out if I had anything for him until they sail again. Brings quite a tale with him."

MacLeod paid little attention to what Hartnell said. "Do you know that fool up there who is supposed to be running this country still hasn't shown up? It's been four days now, and the man who claims to be his secretary said he doesn't know where the governor is."

Hartnell seated himself and waved Torres to an empty chair. "Doesn't surprise me none. I heard he was too drunk to attend his own wedding. Had his brother stand in for him."

"I believe it," MacLeod said, standing up and pacing the narrow space in front of Hartnell. "I can't wait much longer. There's a woman waiting to hear about her child. I know better than most how she feels. But I hate to leave until I find out for sure whether that priest had my boy when he left. By god, if he did, I'll ride all the way to Mexico to find him."

Hartnell opened a drawer in his desk and took out a box of cigars, offering one to Torres. He bent over and lit a twig from the stove, held it out to Torres, then lit his own cigar while waiting for MacLeod to finish.

"Begging your pardon," MacLeod said. "I had to tell somebody."

"You finished?" Hartnell asked.

"Guess so."

"Well, Señor Torres here was telling me about this woman they brought up from San Diego as a prisoner. Seems she shot a soldier down there at the San Luis Rey mission."

"Well, I can understand that happening," MacLeod said. "Hard to figure where she would have gotten a gun."

Hartnell nodded and admired the ash on his cigar before continuing. "Now here's where it gets interesting. Seems this woman is the same one whose child was stolen by the Indians a few months back."

MacLeod sat open mouthed. It had to be her. He had given her the gun and showed her how to load and use it. But why would she shoot someone? Then it came to him what Hartnell had said. "She shot a soldier? Did she kill him?"

"No, I do not think so."

"Well, that's one good thing," Hartnell said. "Señor Torres, did you see the woman while she was on the ship?"

Torres grinned. "The first two days I see her, but the captain sent her below. The men would not work when she was there. Then we had bad storms and I did not see her again."

"But she's all right?"

This time Torres held his hands out and shrugged. "She is very sick. She could not walk. An Indian child tried to help her, but she also was too sick."

"I imagine she was suffering from seasickness," Hartnell said. "The ship was overdue. Word is they didn't know if they would ever round Point Conception. Some thought they would flounder."

MacLeod asked, "Where did they take her?"

"I think to the mission. They put her in a *carreta* and took her away. She could not walk."

"I'm going up there soon as I round up the old woman and the girl. You any idea what they might do with her?".

"Shootings are rare in this country," Hartnell replied. "Most of the confrontations amount to little more than bluster. I suppose Governor Argüello will have to send a dispatch to Mexico for advice. I can't see him making the decision."

"How long do you suppose that might take?" MacLeod asked.

Hartnell laughed. "Well now, seeing as those officials in Mexico are apt to pass the matter on up the line as far as it will go, I wouldn't expect an answer for twelve months or so, and then they may decide to ask for further information before they do. But you might consider speaking with the comandante at the presidio first. They might not let you see her without his permission."

"I'll do that right now," MacLeod said. "You mind if I use young Vallejo here to round up the old woman and girl?"

Hartnell shouted for his young clerk. "I'll send him right away. But keep in mind, William, the comandante is the brother of the man you humiliated when you rescued that Indian woman and took her back to her husband. Tread lightly and mind your temper."

MacLeod felt for once his life had changed. He found the comandante in his office. The man leaned his chin on his clasped hands while listening to MacLeod's request, then shuffled through the stack of parchments on his desk, pulling one out, then carefully restacking the other papers and placing them to one side.

MacLeod waited, rocking back and forth on his feet, while visualizing Francesca being carried to the mission. He muttered a curse in French, damning the man who ran his finger over the paper and mouthing the words as he read.

"This document here has only arrived on my desk this morning," the comandante said. "I have not had time to view its contents until now. It is a very serious charge against this woman. I see she has attempted to kill a devoted officer of our country. Now, what is it you are standing in front of me for?"

MacLeod cleared his throat. "Does it say who the woman shot?"

"Yes, yes, it says so right here," the comandante said, pointing to a line on the paper. "Her name is Francesca, that is all."

"Was it a Sergeant Pacheco she shot?"

"Yes, that is the name here also, Sergeant Pasqual Pacheco. You know of this officer?"

"I know him. Fact is I had a run in with him once before. This woman didn't want anything to do with him."

"Hmmm," the comandante muttered. "A run in. I do not understand this?"

"I told him to leave that woman alone. He had thoughts that she didn't share."

The comandante looked up at MacLeod. "I know who you are, *Americano*. They all speak of your rescuing these children from the Indians. Yes, the soldiers they sent could not do this, but you did. I would have done so also, but they did not ask me."

"I figure you would have, too, sir," MacLeod said.

The man slid the paper to the side of his desk. "You are always rescuing women, it appears? You say you warned this Sergeant Pacheco about bothering the woman. You took a woman away from my brother. Did you know that? His men are all laughing at what you did to him. And now you want something from me. Why should I do this for you?"

"Well, sir, I reckon you haven't much of a reason to. Righty sorry about your brother. I'd apologize if it would do any good," MacLeod said.

The comandante leaned back in his chair and smiled. "We must always do these things for women, must we not? This woman here," he said, pointing to the paper. "This Francesca with no other name, she is beautiful maybe?"

MacLeod nodded, thinking back to when he saw her standing naked in the river. "Yes, sir, she is that."

"I do not know anything about this Sergeant Pacheco. It is good she did not kill him. Maybe they let her go, but I do not know. My brother should not have taken this Indian woman away from her husband and do what he did to her. It is against the Church to do this, do you not think so?"

MacLeod wasn't sure were the conversation was leading but he figured it best to go along. "Sure is, least that's what the good book says."

"Well, I do not know anything about this book, but my brother is a fool. Now, I have much work to do. What is it you wish of me?"

MacLeod took a deep breath. "I heard they took the woman to the mission. Señor Hartnell said I would need your permission to visit her."

"Yes, of course. I would visit her, too, if she is beautiful, and I understand she has no husband. Yes, I would certainly visit her," he said. He picked up the document. "But I cannot do so without permission from the governor. Perhaps tomorrow, or maybe the day after when he returns."

The hell with permission, MacLeod muttered. He stomped out of the room, shaking his head and figuring he could talk his way past the priests.

Hartnell had already obtained a horse for Rosalie. The old woman's face was a mask of concern. It was obvious she had heard of Francesca's condition when they took her off the ship.

Recent rains had worked their yearly miracle on the land, turning the drab pastures and rolling hills into lush green blankets of green. A steady breeze off the ocean cleansed the air of the odors of stagnant pools of refuse.

The Mission of San Carlos Borromeo de Carmelo, the second mission in the chain of missions that ran through Alta California, was dedicated by Father Junipero Serra in 1770, according to what Hartnell had told him. Originally built beside the Monterey Presidio, the mission was moved a year later for the good of the neophytes.

The church looked strangely shaped to MacLeod, with one short tower domed and the other not. The star-shaped window above the arched doors was unlike any of the other missions he had visited. Hartnell had called it Moorish. The attached buildings containing the quarters of the single women and soldiers, along with the various shops and warehouses that formed the rest of the square. The few scattered trees provided little shade from the sun.

MacLeod stepped down from the saddle and tied his horse off on a fence post before taking Catalina out of Rosalie's arms.

Rosalie dismounted and spoke to an Indian woman sweeping the stone steps of the church, then took the child from MacLeod and hurried away.

MacLeod sat on the steps while the Indian woman trotted off to find one of the priests. He watched tiny swallows dart into the sky from their nests built on the wall below a narrow shelf beneath the roof, much like they did at San Juan Capistrano.

An elderly priest, gray bristles covering a deeply tanned face, emerged from the church door. MacLeod stood to greet him and explained his presence. The priest sighed and shook his head. It would not be possible to see the woman brought from the ship. In fact, the priest said, he would also need to turn away the woman who had carried the child past him a moment earlier. The paper that had come with the woman said she was to be kept as a prisoner. Therefore, only the governor himself could allow anyone to see her.

MacLeod cursed under his breath, mounted his horse, and rode around to the back of the enclosure. He peered past the gates and saw Rosalie arguing with a soldier who stood in front of a narrow doorway, brandishing a musket. She pushed his musket aside and entered the room, cradling Catalina in her arms.

The cry of joy from within the room told MacLeod everything he needed to know. He turned back toward town.

Dupré walked across the dirt road to the custom house and pointed up at the governor's house. "He returned last night. I spoke with him briefly and he assured me the mission priests are free to sign new contracts since the others were lost."

The French ship's captain argued. "But what do we have to offer since I was unable to find in Lima what it is they desire? They have no use for coin, of which we have little."

"How much coin do we have left?"
"I would need to count it. Soon they will want us to pay our debt.

We have only enough to cover what we have already purchased. We would need a full hold of these hides to pay for the voyage. Even then I do not know how they will be accepted in France."

The captain's raving fell on deaf ears. Dupré's thoughts returned to the report he had received the previous night. The Indian woman told him that Marisol Montero had slipped away after the wedding and met secretly with the American. Should he pass this along to her husband, or could he use it himself? He reviewed the plan he had come up with after meeting with the governor. The new killing season would begin in a few months, and he had much to do before then. But first he must convince this stupid man the trip could still be a success.

"The governor has given me a letter of introduction to those in charge at these missions. It assures us of having a favorable reception," Dupré said. "You will sail immediately for los Angeles and take Monsieur Montero with you. He is dissatisfied with the people here in Monterey. I will make an agreement with him for the loan of enough to provision the ship. Then sail to San Diego and procure a warehouse of some sort to collect and cure the hides."

"Very well, monsieur. I will arrange for the cabin to be ready for these people."

Dupré waved the captain away. He would need to speak with Vicente Montero as soon as possible and convince him that issuing a loan for the provisioning of the ship would be a profitable investment.

Other thoughts crowded Dupré's mind. He had little desire to ride the length of Alta California, arranging for the buying of hides, and having to spend needless hours listening to the complaints of the priests. And what if he ran into the American along the road. Why bother with the formal method of settling affairs. He could dispose of the problem immediately. He wondered how much more attentive Marisol Montero would be to his advances with the American out of the way.

Mariano Vallejo, Hartnell's young clerk and student, burst through the door of the storeroom and stood before Hartnell.

"What is it, young fellow? You look as if you've run a mile to tell me something."

The young clerk nodded his head vigorously, still attempting to catch his breath and speak. Finally he pointed toward the door and blurted out. "He is back."

"Who?" Hartnell said.

"Doñ Argüello, the governor. He is back."

MacLeod took Vallejo by the arm. "You saw him?"

Vallejo nodded. "Si, señor, he is there in his place now."

"I better go," MacLeod said. "He's liable to take off again, and there's no telling when I'd get another chance."

"I think you're right. But don't lose your temper, William. He reacts to flattery, not confrontation. Remember, he is only the acting governor, and rumor is the people in power in Mexico have appointed a new man for the position. It's only a rumor but there's not much for an ex acting governor to do in Alta California. The man will drink himself to death if he's replaced, I fear."

MacLeod grimaced. "I'll keep it in mind."

A crowd waited outside the governor's office. MacLeod pushed past the guard who attempted to block his entry.

"You will wait outside, please," the governor's secretary said. "His Excellency will see you in time."

"Afraid I can't wait. I've been trying to see him for weeks," MacLeod said.

The governor held up his hand when MacLeod approached. MacLeod waited for him to acknowledge his presence. When it didn't look as if he would, MacLeod said, "Your Excellency, I've come looking for the information I spoke to you about at the wedding, and about the woman that came up on the ship."

The governor sighed and reached for a cup holding down a pile of papers. After taking a drink, looked up at MacLeod, a frown creasing his forehead. "Information? What information is this?"

"Sir, I understand a priest, Father Pérez, came up here some months ago and was put on a ship to Mexico. They say he had a child with him and you wouldn't allow him to take it on the ship. Is that a fact?"

The man scratched his head. "Have you not asked me this before?"

"No, sir. I didn't get the chance when I saw you at the wedding."

"Pérez, Pérez. Yes, that fool. I received word from the Father President to see that he was put on the first ship returning to Mexico. As it happened, one was in the harbor waiting to leave."

"And he had a child with him he wanted to take?"

Argüello rubbed his temples. "This I do not remember. It was so long ago. I think I would have remembered if he had a child with him."

MacLeod stepped back from the table and sank onto a stool, his hopes shattered again. How many times would he be given false hopes? How many times would he dream of home and wait for the first ship returning to Boston, only to ride off to follow another rumor.

Argüello said, "You have done so much for me and my family. Is there not something else I could do for you?"

MacLeod glanced at the governor's secretary standing beside him. The man placed more papers on the table and awaited the governor's signature.

MacLeod pushed himself to his feet. "Yes, sir, there is something. I would like to visit the woman that was brought here for shooting a man down at San Luis Rey. Maybe you can tell me what it is you'll do with her."

The governor's fingers tapped the table. "What should I do with her? That is the question. It is possible it will not be up to me to decide. You have heard, maybe, that there is someone else coming up from Mexico to take this seat, since I am only an appointee"

"Only what Mr. Hartnell heard, same as you."

"Well then," Argüello said. "If you were to find this Sergeant Pacheco willing to forgive this señora, and you bring me this in his writing, and I am still in this position when you return, I will consider forgiving her, with a warning of course."

MacLeod left the governor to his worries and headed toward the mission. He didn't want to think about the boy right at that moment. That would come later. If he could find Sergeant Pacheco, he might be able to convince him to sign a paper, even if it was looking down the barrel of MacLeod's pistol.

The old priest who turned MacLeod away earlier stood on the steps of the church and read the note the governor's secretary had written. He tucked the note into the sleeve of his thread-bare robe and walked around the corner of the church, his bare feet sending up tiny clouds of dust. MacLeod followed him past a number of doors to the end of the long adobe building, where the priest indicated MacLeod should wait outside. The priest entered a narrow doorway and a moment later returned, followed by Rosalie.

MacLeod stepped forward. "I tried to come before, but they wouldn't let me see her. How is she?"

Rosalie Lorenzana tilted her head from side to side and held her hands apart. "She has little strength in her since she came from the ship. Now that she has the girl, I think she will try more."

"I want to see her. The governor said I could only come this one time."

"Let me have time to speak with her."

Rosalie went inside and came out a few minutes later, beckoning for him to join her.

A weak voice greeted MacLeod as he ducked under the shallow doorway. "You have come. I have waited to see you."

"Yes, ma'am. I heard what happened down there, and I'm mighty sorry," he said.

"You found my Catalina. I can never thank you for this. I do not know what they will do with me. They have said nothing."

"Did they not listen when you told them what happened?"

"The others, the soldiers, they said other things. They said I asked him to stay."

The Indian girl crawled up beside Francesca and buried her head under an arm. MacLeod had a thought, remembering when he taught Francesca how to load and fire the pistol. The girl, Juana was there.

"I spoke with the governor," MacLeod said. I tried to tell him about Sergeant Pacheco, but he wasn't in the mood to listen to reason. I'll try again, I promise." He wasn't about to mention the governor might release her if he got a statement from Pacheco. He had a feeling a meeting with Pacheco might leave one of them dead.

"I have little strength to talk. Why do you not tell me all you have been doing and I will listen."

MacLeod began with the search in the *tulle* country, how he and Concannon had brought the old chief's young wife back to him and traded for Catalina and the others. He was sure Rosalie had already told her, so he kept the story short, leaving out the rumors about Pérez.

She lay with her eyes closed, the shadow of a smile creasing her pale face. "And the wedding, tell me about the wedding. Rosalie has said many went."

"Yes, Mr. Hartnell said I would get the chance to speak to the governor since the other child the Indians took was his sister's." Then he told her about having met again the Frenchman, and Marisol asking him to dance.

Her face grew pale. MacLeod looked from Francesca to Rosalie, who showed her own concern.

A moment later Francesca spoke, her voice barely above a whisper. "This Señora Montero, I have heard some speak of her. Is she as beautiful as they say? You will tell me how she dressed?"

"Well," MacLeod said. "I'm not much on describing what womenfolk wear, but some said she brought her dress back from some place down in South America. It sure looked awful pretty. So pretty I was afraid to touch it when I danced."

"You have not said if she is beautiful or not," Francesca said, her eyes still closed.

"Yes, I guess she is. Most of the men there were wanting a dance with her. It appeared to upset some of the women folk."

"But you have said she asked you to dance?"

MacLeod grinned. "Yes, but only the one time. Her husband came for her and she didn't dance again."

"I am tired, I am happy you came, but you must go now and allow me to rest."

"Well, like I said, I'm not sure when I can visit again."

"Maybe when you are able to return I will be better and beautiful like your Doña Montero," Francesca said, voicing a tone with an edge to it MacLeod had not heard before.

Rosalie took his arm and pushed him out the door before he could respond. The priest stood waiting to escort him back to his horse.

40

"Who is she, this woman who he cannot stop talking about," Francesca cried. "What does she want from him, to ask him to dance with her? She is married, is she not?"

Rosalie wiped Francesca's forehead with a cloth and helped her to lie down again on the narrow, blanket-lined pallet.

"Why did he talk of her? Did he think I wanted to hear this?"

"You asked him about the wedding. He is a man and does not know how to care about what he says. You asked him about this woman."

"When you were with him, did he speak of her?"

Rosalie picked up a sleeping Catalina and gave her to Juana to care for, ignoring Francesca's question.

"He spoke of her, did he not, when you were with him? Tell me, Rosalie. I wish to know," she said.

"He said nothing. He is a man. Only he knows, and he was troubled."

"Troubled?"

Rosalie nodded. "At the mission of San Antonio, a priest spoke of that Father Pérez. He said he had a child with him. The señor thought it might be the child of his that was taken."

Francesca sat up. "And was it true? He would have told me if it were true."

"I do not know. He has been waiting to speak to the governor. That is all I know."

"He would have spoken of it if it were true," Francesca said.

"Think of other things," Rosalie said, "You must regain your strength, for your child. You must live for her and forget this man. He is a strange one. He came to the Indian village for us. The one with the hair that is red spoke of him and said he is someone who has killed other men. You must forget him, even though he has done these good things for you."

"No, I know him. He is good. We have both suffered things. Why does he play with me like this? Does he not see how I feel?"

Rosalie shook her head. "He will leave soon for his country. He is not of ours."

"No, I believe he will stay," Francesca said. She wondered what she could do to convince him to remain in Alta California.

Rosalie pulled the blanket over Francesca and the girl. "I saw the way the priests spoke with him. He is not of our Church. They are afraid of him and his ideas."

A soft breeze carried the scent of spring through the open window. The bells began their peal again, announcing the time for the midday meal. Francesca reached up to Juana and took Catalina in her arms. "He will not leave. I will change him. If he does not join the Church, he cannot be a citizen of our country. But if he will not do this, I will be with him without their approval."

"Your family will not allow this," Rosalie said. "They will stop you."

Francesca put Catalina on the bed beside her and sat up. "Look where I am because of my family. They sent me away with my child, they and the priests. Why should it bother me if he will not accept their ideas?" She knew her bitterness toward the Church and her family caused the old woman many hours of private grief, and for that she was sorry. Without Rosalie, Francesca knew she would not have lived.

Rosalie sent Juana to the kitchen to collect the midday meal. With the Indian girl gone, she asked. "And the child, you will tell him about her?"

Francesca gathered Catalina in her arms. "Of course, she is my child and my husband's. My husband is dead. That is all there is to tell."

G aston Dupré laughed at the easy in which he had accomplished his mission. The idea had come to him earlier, but not all ideas come to fruition without hard work or, in this instance, a stroke of luck. This time it had been a mere off-handed remark to the governor's secretary. Dupré had said he wished to inquire again what had taken place when the priest Pérez was placed on the ship for his return to Mexico. The secretary had informed him it was he, not the governor, who made the arrangements to place Pérez on a ship bound for Peru. The captain had agreed to put the man ashore at

San Blas, Mexico. Dupré had asked whether Pérez had attempted to take a small child back with him.

"Yes, but I would not allow it," the man said. "I gave it to a woman who had lost her own. She took it when she returned to her home in Branciforte, a few miles across the bay from Monterey."

It took him a day to find the woman's tiny adobe hut on the outskirts of the small pueblo. The woman had been reluctant to part with the boy until Dupré had given her enough to purchase a cow and a pair of sheep. Dupré had hired a woman in Monterey to take care for the child.

He rode down the dirt road, dodging *carretas* and young children playing in the street, until he came to the house of Vicente Montero. He also knew Vicente Montero had left that morning to arrange passage back to the Pueblo de los Ángeles.

The woman who responded to his hail returned to say the señora could not see him. Furious at her refusal, Dupré sent the woman to say he would not leave until the señora had spoken to him.

Dupré's heart leapt when he saw her. Her hair hung loose below her waist, her thin night clothing clung to her body. She motioned to the woman to stay.

"What is it you want, señor. You have been told my husband is not here. I cannot allow you to enter the house without his presence."

Dupré bowed from the waist and said, "*Pardon madame*, I do not wish to cause you concern. I am in need of a solution to a problem and I thought you might assist me."

"What problem could I possibly help you with? My husband will return soon and you can take up this problem with him."

Dupré held up his hands. "*Une moment s'il vous plait.* As you are aware, my ship travels the coast of Alta California. In these travels I meet with captains of ships from other places. One ship, whose captain I am very familiar with, has returned from the Sandwich Islands. On his most recent trip, he had the unfortunate circumstance of losing a passenger who appeared to have fallen from the ship during a storm. The man's wife was violently ill from the seas caused by the storm and died a few days later."

Marisol Montero's Indian servant came from the house and placed a robe over Marisol's shoulders, much to his displeasure. She wrapped it around her body and held it tightly, seeing where Dupré's attention was directed while he spoke.

Dupré removed a scented cloth from his sleeve and touched it to his forehead before continuing. "It is unfortunate that this man and his wife had a child who the captain was forced to turn over to the first woman who agreed to take it."

"That is most unfortunate, señor. However I do not see how I may assist you."

"I thought of you, *madame*, when I learned the woman could not keep the child. I know of your loss, and it was my hope I might lessen it by taking this child into your heart and your home."

"That is very kind of you, Señor Dupré. However, I do not think I can be of any help. As you know, we are returning to the Pueblo de los Ángeles and a child would be a burden."

Dupré felt his opportunity slipping away. He turned and motioned to the Indian woman who waited with the boy, and she brought him forward.

The boy walked up to Marisol and held his arms up to her. She knelt and picked him up as he began to cry.

Dupré let his breath out. He knew then she would forever be in his debt. Give her and the child time, and she would do anything to keep him as her own, including leaving her husband and returning to France with him.

Tears slid down her cheeks. "What is the child's name?" she asked.

Dupré shrugged. "I do not know. The man who gave him to me said nothing."

The servant girl put out her arms to take the boy, but Marisol shook her head. "I will call him Vittorio. Yes, that will be his name," she said. She held him at arm's length and gasped. "Look at him, he has eyes that are as blue as the sky. And you are sure of this story about the parents of this child?"

Dupré bowed. "Yes, I would not have agreed to take him if I had not known of your own loss. I hope I have pleased you, *Madame*. I am positive the boy will soon learn to love you as if you were the mother he has lost."

"Yes, señor, you have given me something I will live forever for. You may tell this captain when you see him again the child has a home."

Dupré stroked his mustache, pleased beyond his hopes at her response. He would need to see the American did not visit her again. There were ways to take care of the problem. All he needed was a reason that these stupid people would accept for what he had to do. Her robe opened with her caressing of the child, her breasts pushing out against the thin material of her nightdress. Dupré swallowed. He turned quickly and retreated to his horse, his loins swelling with lust.

A s the warm days of spring stretched into early summer, the temperature and the activity surrounding the missions increased. A new killing season approached. MacLeod stopped briefly at Santa Cruz before continuing south toward San Juan Bautista.

Hartnell had said no ships would be leaving the Pacific Coast with a full hold for months at best, and MacLeod figured he would use the time to chase down Pacheco. He would also work for Hartnell in order to travel the state with the proper passport.

The first sign that something was different in the minds of the priests came at San Antonio de Padua. A priest he had not met before came out from his quarters, followed by the Indian *alcalde*. The bloated figure in his woolen robe shook his head when MacLeod asked about their hides and tallow for the coming season. With further questioning, the priest reluctantly informed him they had received a better offer from a man who represented a French ship. MacLeod then knew Dupré had become active in his search for trade.

A week later, he saw a horse tied to a bush alongside the road, its rider attempting to covet what little shade the bush offered. MacLeod shifted his pistol to the front of his belt. Something about the figure looked familiar.

"If you've a mind to be looking for hides down the road a piece, I wouldn't spend your profits yet."

MacLeod grinned. "Last I heard of you, the governor was claiming you caused half his garrison to be in jail or too drunk to stand."

Concannon pushed himself to his feet. "Aye, and His Excellency, of all people, should be discussing those that drink."

"What are you doing here? It's a long way from Monterey."

"Well now, as you can imagine there were some who didn't value my presence, and when talk of putting me back at sea came up I thought you might use my vast experience. I heard you were down this way somewhere."

"Vast might be a little overdoing it," MacLeod said. "And what's your meaning about spending my profits?"

Concannon brushed the grass off his pants and climbed into the saddle. "You not being one of us Papists, it might be hard to understand, but these priests have few to speak with. So when a bright fellow like me sits with them over a glass of wine or two, they unload their souls. Their minds are poisoned, William. The Frenchman passed this way, not two days ago."

MacLeod untied his water pouch and handed it to Concannon, who took a long drink before handing it back. "And what has he been saying?"

"Oh, about you being a heretic that if left alone will preach your views to the Indians. That you have read some fellow by the name of Voltaire. This Frenchman related the views of this Voltaire about the Church, in case the priests were not aware. He told them the child you sought was of an incestuous relationship with this woman who you claim died."

"The lying dog!" MacLeod shouted. "He knows there's no way to counter these claims. He's free to say whatever is necessary to turn their minds. They live in these prisons with no contact with the rest of the world."

"True, but you must admit, William lad, it has its effect. I doubt you could buy a bag of tainted tallow. Oh, you have me forgetting. The Frenchman is offering a dollar and a half a hide."

"Damn. How's he paying them? The last I heard his credit was thinner then watered down soup, and I understand the ship has few things the missions want."

"Coin. He's offered the higher price in case the governor up and decides to write a new tax."

MacLeod remembered his discussion with Hartnell about the rumors that Dupré's credit had about run out. "If you're willing to ride along with me, I could use your help with these priests, you being a Papist and all, like you said."

All of Alta California worked on a type of credit system where a man's word held more worth than a letter of credit, and financial agreements seldom had time limits. There was little need for someone to go to a higher authority to collect on a loan. Coin of any kind was seldom available with most transactions. Even taxes were levied in the form of hides.

Anger at the duplicity of Dupré, and with little to lose, MacLeod and Concannon did their best to convince the profit-minded priests it would be in their best interests to ask for payment in coin on delivery of the hides and tallow.

MacLeod sent Concannon on to Santa Inés, one of the newest in the southern chain of missions. He figured to give the Irishman a day to convince those in charge that MacLeod's offer, though lower than the Frenchman's, would be guaranteed with the credit taken in goods directly off the John Begg & Co. ship.

He then rode through the rolling, oak-studded hills toward the little mission, hoping to run into the Irishman soon. He dozed in the saddle and came awake when the gelding snorted.

MacLeod reined the horse to a stop and surveyed the road ahead, where it crossed a stream whose sides were thick with willow and berry bush. He pulled the pack mule up alongside and slid the rifle out from under its lashings, resting it across the front of his saddle. He had a feeling something had spooked the horse.

At the bottom of the shallow gulch, the road turned and disappeared behind a wall of willow and a small grove of cottonwood trees. MacLeod remembered the spot, having camped beneath the trees once when passing through. He tapped the horse's sides with his heels and walked him forward, his thumb resting on the hammer of the rifle.

Half a dozen saddled horses stood among the trees. MacLeod recognized the black Concannon had been riding.

He waited while the gelding danced, eager to move forward. MacLeod walked him ahead a dozen steps and halted again, searching both sides of the road for those he knew waited. He lifted the rifle off the front of his saddle, thumbing back the hammer and shifting it to his left hand, then drawing his pistol with his right.

From the shadows, figures emerged, five in all, and spread out to block the road. MacLeod recognized Sergeant Pacheco immediately, even with the patch over one eye. "Well, Sergeant, I believe we've met a time or two. Need to have a word with you but first, where's the man belongs to that horse?"

Pacheco smiled and moved a step closer to his own horse. MacLeod could see the butt of a musket peeking out from a leather scabbard.

"Wouldn't go there, if I was you, Sergeant. Maybe you should move over among the others where I can keep an eye on you. Can't believe my luck finding you out here like this. Thought I'd have to go searching for you."

Pacheco grinned. "There are five of us and only one of you."

"Yep, seems you got that part right. I would just as soon shoot you right where you stand. I warned you about going near that woman, but you wouldn't listen. Now she's sitting up there in Monterey waiting for your sheep-headed governor to decide what to do with her, while you're walking around acting like nothing happened."

Pacheco rocked on his feet. MacLeod could tell the man was trying to figure a way out. "Let's try again, Sergeant. Where's the man that belongs to that horse?"

Pacheco pointed with his chin toward the trees. "He is over there."

"Well, you send one of your men over to bring him out. If he has to drag him out, you're a dead man, Pacheco."

The sergeant dispatched two of his men, who trotted into the trees and brought a hatless Concannon out, his hands tied behind his back.

"'Bout time you showed up. Thought I'd have to bunk with these bilge rats tonight."

"Cut him loose," MacLeod ordered. "Irish, why not saunter over to that tree. I believe I see your scattergun leaning against it."

Concannon grinned, pushing aside one of the troopers and collecting his gun.

"Is it charged?" MacLeod asked.

"Oh, I do believe it's ready. You want I should use it on one of them?"

"No, I want to talk to this one first. Keep the others in a knot. In fact, take them over and sit them in the shade. This may take a spell."

MacLeod slid out of his saddle, keeping Pacheco covered with his pistol. "Sergeant, we need to come to an agreement here."

Pacheco's grin contained no warmth. "This agreement you speak of. What is it? I do not think you know what you are doing. What you are doing is punishable by immediate arrest. I think you know what our jails are like, too."

"Like I said, that woman who's up there in Monterey did nothing except defend herself. I'm willing to overlook what you did this one time. On one condition."

Pacheco laughed. "Condition. You are giving me conditions?"

"In case you haven't noticed, I have the gun," MacLeod said. "And, to tell you the truth, I have a mind to use it on you. So, if you want to ride out of here on your own horse and not strapped to the back of it, it's really pretty simple. I reach in the bag hanging on my saddle and pull out a piece of paper and a pen, along with ink jar. You write a note to your governor dropping all charges against the woman."

"You are a fool. The woman attempted to kill me."

"I wish she had, but there's nothing I can do about it now. You do what I want or I'll kill you. You wronged a fine woman. Now is your chance to right that wrong, at least a part of it. Problem is, Sergeant, I can't leave those four men of yours as witnesses. Afraid I'd be forced to kill them also."

"You would kill five men over this woman who has probably been with many men?"

MacLeod raised the cocked pistol. Pacheco's eyes widened as he stared down the muzzle, only a few feet away.

MacLeod's voice quivered. "You are approaching your death mighty quickly, Sergeant. You ever see a man die been gut-shot? It's not an easy way to die. Takes a right long time. You'll be crying, begging me to finish the job, 'cause you know there's no hope. That woman's got a right to be left alone. All she's guilty of is denying you."

"Very well," Pacheco said through clenched teeth. "I will sign this agreement you speak of. I doubt the governor will accept it."

"That's my worry." A thought crossed MacLeod's mind. "You can write, I hope?"

Pacheco laid the paper on his saddle and scrawled the words MacLeod dictated, then signed it with a flourish. He handed it over to MacLeod without taking his eyes off the muzzle of the pistol.

MacLeod held the paper in his hand until the ink had dried before tucking it under his shirt. "Irish, why don't you drive the horses up the road a ways, and then take everyone's boots. Figure to let these here soldiers think about the bad things they've done while walking back to wherever they came from."

Pacheco spit in the dirt and wiped his mouth with the back of his hand. "You know, *Americano,* after all of this, it will be difficult for you to remain in Alta California. I think it is good what you do for this woman. I should have thought of this. Without that paper you have, she would remain locked away in that mission, or perhaps sent to Mexico. Now she will be free again and you will be gone from our country."

"That's a possibility, Sergeant."

Pacheco sneered. "I will have her, *Americano*. I do not believe you will shoot me now. When you are gone, she will be alone, and she will be mine. And if you are not gone when I see you again, I will kill you surely as you're standing there right now."

43

MacLeod and Concannon herded the soldiers into the trees, then turned their horses loose and drove the animals up the road.

Sometime later Concannon said, "What is it you're planning to do? It's easy to see you're disturbed."

"I'm thinking you can handle the rest of the missions, if you're of a mind. You're just as good at countering the lies spread by the Frenchman as I am, probably more, seeing they view me with an evil eye, being that these narrow-minded people consider me a heathen. Think you want the job?"

Concannon rode for a while without answering, but that wasn't new. They often rode miles carrying on a conversation of few words. "And what will you be doing?"

"I need to get this letter to the governor soon as possible. I hate to see Francesca all cooped up in that little room, and you never know in this country. They could change governors, and I'd have to start all over again."

"And then, William, what are your plans. Will I be running into you again?"

MacLeod rubbed the dust out of his eyes. "I think I've pretty much worn out my welcome here. I'll tell Mr. Hartnell you'll be working the missions south from here. I'm sure he'll deal with you squarely. Me, I'm not sure what I'll do."

"And the Frenchman," Concannon said quietly. "What's to be done about him?"

"Oh, I think we've caused enough of them to wonder about whether they'll get paid for their hides. He'll have a hard time filling his ship."

"I doubt you can find a ship for a spell. Maybe see you before you leave," Concannon said.

MacLeod tipped his hat. "Hope so. Good luck to you, Irish."

The early morning fog had just begun to lift when MacLeod rode down the dirt road toward the governor's office two weeks later. The governor's secretary took Pacheco's statement and said he would present it to the governor as soon as he arrived, if he did. Frustrated at yet more time wasted while waiting for the man to show up, MacLeod walked toward the harbor. A lone ship rocked gently in the placid waters of the bay, its masts still obscured in the thinning fog. As the tide turned, it presented its stern to the beach. A limp American flag hung at the fantail.

He heard his name being called and turned to see the governor's secretary waving to him.

"Señor, come. He is here now."

Acting Governor Argüello paced behind his desk, reading the note MacLeod had brought. He looked a sight better than the last time MacLeod had seen him.

"Ah, Señor *Americano*, I see you have been busy in your efforts for this woman. I think I should like to meet her someday. "I will send this on the next ship to Mexico, and I am positive they will make this decision to tell me to release her."

MacLeod stood, stunned at what he heard. It would take months for a decision to be made, even in Mexico. He knew he must be careful with what he said. "Your Excellency, surely you have the power to turn her loose. After all, Alta California is an important part of Mexico, and you are the one chosen to be its governor. They would not have chosen you without believing you could manage the job."

"Perhaps you are right. Let me speak to my secretary and see what he thinks about this authority. Return later and I will tell you of my decision."

With time on his hands, MacLeod visited Hartnell.

"There you are. Just the man I wanted to see," Hartnell called out when he saw MacLeod enter the store. "I've someone anxious to have a word with you."

Captain Fanning rose from his chair and offered his hand. "William, lad. I was holding out hope I would find you about. Edward here tells me what a fine job you've been doing for him, and here I am trying to convince him to leave John Begg and Co. and sign on with me."

"Well, sir," MacLeod said with a grin. "I wish you luck. How was your voyage?"

"Fine, remarkably fine," Fanning said as he returned to his chair. "We rounded the cape in record time and didn't lose a single spar. I hope you've left some hides for me. I've been hearing how successful you are with signing up missions."

"Yes, but now there's a complication," MacLeod said. He pulled out a chair, sat down, and addressed both men. "Have you heard the Frenchman's offering a dollar-fifty a hide, and upping our offer on tallow also?"

Hartnell nodded. "Yes, I've heard, and for the life of me I don't know where he figures to get the money to pay. He owes money everywhere. He came to me for an advance so he could supply his ship and I turned him down. I'm already holding paper on him."

MacLeod then told of his decision to turn over his role to Concannon and wanted to collect what money he had due. "Concannon and I tried to talk to those in charge at the missions. Hope we convinced some of them to ask to see the coin first," he said. "We'll have to see if it did any good. By the way, I think the Irishman's gift of the gab might help some of them decide in our favor."

Fanning shook his head. "This country will be a sight better off when that Frenchman's gone. I ported down in Lima for water and fresh produce. Had a touch of scurvy in some of the crew. Heard he killed a man in a duel down there over some slight."

Hartnell grunted. "Well, he's made no effort to quell any rumors of past fracases. Like you said, the sooner he leaves the better, before he picks a fight with someone here."

"My god," Fanning said, rising from his chair and patting his pockets. "With all this talk, I about forgot why I so wanted to see you. I have a letter here from your mother."

MacLeod's face broke into a grin. "You saw her? She's well?"

"Well as could be expected," Fanning said. "Perhaps the letter will explain more."

The captain's tone worried MacLeod. "But she's well?"

"Yes, you can be assured of that. Looked healthy to me. Sat me down and made tea and had me tell her all about you."

MacLeod took the wrinkled letter from Fanning. "Not being impolite but I believe I'll read this now." He left the storeroom and sought a quiet place in the shade to read the first news from home since he left three years before. But how would he explain returning without a wife or child?

A youngster MacLeod had seen near the governor's office scampered toward him. "Please, señor, come. He wants you."

Macleod waited, the unopened letter in his hand. "Who does?"

"His Excellency said go find the Señor *Americano* and bring him to me. Come." The boy reached out and took MacLeod's hand.

Together they trotted back to the governor's office, where MacLeod stood, waiting for the governor to notice him.

After a moment Argüello raised his head. "Ah, yes. I see the boy has found you. I could have had my secretary tell you, but I wished to do so myself."

The governor walked over to the slit that represented a window in the adobe wall and clasped his hands behind his back. MacLeod rocked from one foot to the other, aware of the unread letter in his pocket, and perhaps about to hear more bad news. The governor seemed relaxed. MacLeod figured that the word of being replaced was confirmed as only a rumor, and he appeared to be taking a renewed interest in governing.

"Yes, what you have said about my authority. I have decided to release this woman."

Macleod's jaw dropped. "Yes, sir, that's good news. I mean that's great. Thank you. When will you do this?"

"My secretary there, he will issue the papers. Would you like to take it to her?"

"You bet. I'll go at once." MacLeod could picture Francesca's face when she heard the news.

"Good. You can wait for it if you wish, or come back later. I have another appointment and must leave." The governor leaned over the secretary's desk and signed a blank paper before striding out of the office.

"Thank you, Your Excellency. I believe I'll wait." He wondered if he could slip away to read his mother's letter first or wait for Francesca's papers. He figured if he waited around, the man would take care of it immediately, and why give the governor an opportunity to change his mind.

MacLeod waited, the effort for the secretary to put a few words on paper taking forever. Finally, the man finished writing and dusted the paper, then held it out and blew on it. He handed it to MacLeod with a flourish.

"I thank you, sir," MacLeod said, reaching for the document.

The man pulled it back. "A moment, please, señor. There is another thing I have meant to speak to you about."

MacLeod waited.

"Yes, it was a question you asked of His Excellency."

"Today?"

"No, no. It was many weeks ago, I think. You asked him about Father Pérez, and he said he was not here when the man left. Yes, that was it."

MacLeod couldn't breathe. "What about Pérez?"

"I was the one, acting for the governor of course, who put this man on the ship for Mexico."

"Did he have a child with him?" MacLeod asked, still unable to breathe deeply.

"Yes. I took the child from him and gave it to a woman who said she would care for it.

It took a moment for MacLeod to respond. "What happened to the woman and the child?"

"Oh, señor, she went to live in Branciforte Pueblo, but she does not have the child now. I remember this because someone else ask me these questions."

MacLeod shook his head, attempting to put a rein around this new information. The governor's secretary sat smiling up at him, and

MacLeod could barely form his next words. "Where is this child now, do you know?"

"I think Señor Dupré of that French ship took this child." The man shrugged. "I do not know why. Do you know of him?"

MacLeod could only stand with his mouth open. Questions jammed his head like too many logs floating down a river. What would Dupré want with the boy? Was it really Diego that he took? Where were they now, and how would he find them? He took a deep breath. He needed answers. First he needed to clarify what the man knew. He needed to back up a moment.

MacLeod leaned over and placed his hands on the man's desk. The secretary's eyes opened wide, and he shot a plea for help from the guard at the door. As the guard stepped forward, MacLeod turned, grasped him by the elbow and pushed him through the open doorway. He then slammed door shut, barred it, and turned back to the secretary.

"All right, now, I want to hear from you everything you know about Father Pérez and this child."

The governor's secretary stared a MacLeod for a moment, then puffed out his cheeks and said, "The priest comes here and I am told to see he leaves on this ship. That is all. I do not know where he receives this child, only I say he cannot take him on the ship."

"Was this child a boy?" Macleod held his breath, not daring to hope after all these months.

"Yes, a boy, but I do not know anything else," the man said with a shrug. "He was not a little child, he could walk, but he did not look too well."

MacLeod stepped back, wishing there was a chair nearby he could collapse into. *It has to be Diego, and he can walk now.*

He ignored the pounding at the door and continued with his interrogation. "You say the Frenchman took him? Do you know why?"

But before the secretary could answer, MacLeod knew why. It had begun months before, in San Diego. It had continued when they met again at the home of Vicente Montero, and the near confrontation at the wedding festivities when MacLeod had seen him with Marisol. What MacLeod remembered most was the look on the Frenchman's face when he had danced with her. There was no mistaking the hatred Dupré felt for him. Somehow Dupré had heard about Pérez and the child, and figured to punish MacLeod by taking the boy as well as offering higher prices for the hides and tallow.

The growing fury within overwhelmed MacLeod's joy over the news that Diego was alive. Alive, but in the hands of a desperate man who would go to any lengths to punish anyone who crossed him. A man who bragged about those he had shot for standing in his way. *Why has he not challenged me,* MacLeod wondered.

The pounding on the door continued. MacLeod needed time to think. He had not been far behind Dupré in the south, but that was some time ago. His only consolation was the knowledge that Dupré wouldn't sail until he had filled his ship's hold, but at the prices he was offering it might not take long.

Figuring there was little else the secretary could give him in the way of information, MacLeod picked up the document releasing Francesca and left the governor's office, shoving aside the bewildered guards. Somewhere in the south the Frenchman had spread his lies in order to fill his ship. But what would he do with the boy? Would he take him back to France with him? Or would he rid himself of the child at the first opportunity?

A shudder swept over MacLeod. Whatever punishment Dupré sought to bring down on MacLeod, he would want MacLeod to know about it. The days ahead held the outcome, whatever it was that Dupré had planned. Macleod folded the governor's release and tucked it away in the pocket of his shirt, his fingers brushing against the thin letter from his mother.

He found a quiet place beneath a tree close to the water's edge. Out in the bay, seals announced their presence, gulls floated over the water searching for food. His mother's words lay inside the paper. Home, and the farm his thoughts had drifted to when times became almost unbearable, the place where he hoped to take Diego. His hands shook as he broke the seal on the envelope.

His eyes swept over the words from start to finish, recording her excitement at the letter Captain Fanning had delivered. First, how overcome she was when she heard he was still alive and in Spanish America. Captain Fanning had explained about Mexico's independence from Spain and Alta California being a part of Mexico, although she understood little of what he said. Was it true she was a grandmother, and what about the child's mother?

MacLeod returned to the beginning. His mother wrote that she had read his letter to a women she had met. The woman had a cousin, a man of great importance in government, a senator from Missouri by the name of Thomas Hart Benton, who would be most anxious to hear of these things Macleod spoke about, especially about their type of government and the richness of the land and its possibilities.

But near the end of the letter came words that disturbed him the most, and explained the troubled look on Captain Fanning's face when he spoke of having tea with her. She had moved into Boston, with an aunt MacLeod had met but once. The farm had been sold to cover debts his stepfather had incurred, debts she knew nothing about until the sheriff had come to the farm one day to collect on loans taken out with the farm as collateral. His stepfather and the man's twin children left one day for a revival meeting at a nearby town and had never returned.

His mother closed the letter by telling him how much she wished to hear from him again. She would pray for him. At the bottom of the page she added that she had just received a hand-delivered note from Senator Benton asking her to have her son write to the senator about the goings on in California. She included his address.

MacLeod sat, the letter in his hand fluttering in the breeze, Francesca's release papers forgotten for the moment. He had no farm to return to. His mother hoped he might find a life in California rather than return to Boston, where nothing remained for him. Certainly, if he began corresponding with this senator, it would need to be kept in complete secrecy, with letters handled only by loyal American ships' captains.

He rose finally, his plans for the future having vanished in the few words in the letter. If he did go back, he would find the man who had put his mother in this position. Knowing of the penalty for what he might do, MacLeod wondered what a future in Alta California would be like. And what of this United States senator who wished to know about Mexican California? But he would have time to address this later. He mounted the gelding and rode toward the little mission of San Carlos de Carmelo, and Francesca. Then it would be time to find the Frenchman and, hopefully, Diego.

THE FRENCHMAN'S PROPOSITION

Gaston Dupré wanted to kill. At the moment anyone would do, since the source of his anger was not available. He had left the mission of San Gabriel Arcángel with the foolish priest's words ringing in his ears. There would be no hides or tallow without first producing the coin. All this because the American had spread the word he could not pay. And how many other missions would then request immediate payment before turning over their hides?

Dupré fingered the pistol tucked behind his belt. He thought about the hides and bags of tallow already stored in the hold of the ship, knowing the profits would not be enough to pay off his debts, or satisfy those in France awaiting the return of the ship. He seethed. It was not too late. If he could somehow blunt the accusations, he might still procure a full cargo, but how? He would try to see Vicente Montero, who had returned to los Ángeles. Perhaps he would loan him the money long enough to satisfy the priests.

The woman who answered the door of the small adobe dwelling informed him Doñ Montero was away. She shook her head when he asked to speak with Doña Montero, then closed the door on him.

Dupré started for his horse, then paused on hearing a child's laughter coming from the small garden behind the house, followed by the light tone of a woman's voice.

When he presented himself with a low bow, Marisol turned, a startled look on her face. "Señor Dupré. I am afraid my husband is not here to greet you."

"Then perhaps I may speak with you until he returns," he said.

"It would be better if you were to return at a later hour. I know my husband will be honored to speak with you again."

With all that had happened the last few days, Dupré decided to circumvent proper custom when speaking with an unattended married woman. His eyes fixated on the positioning of her arms, which had the effect of accentuating the fullness of her breasts.

The child called out and ran to her, the child of the man who threatened to destroy him and who had the eyes, if not the secret heart, of this woman. She took the little one by the shoulders and placed him in front of her.

"I see the boy is well."

"Yes, he has grown since you left him."

"And you wish to keep him?" He said it without thought.

Her face hardened. "Did you not tell me he had no other place to go? Are his parents not dead?"

Dupré chose not to answer, reviewing in his mind his best approach. "It matters not. You have him now and it is up to you what you do with him. I will be blunt. My ship will sail soon. I want you to come to France with me."

She stepped back. "How dare you offer me this proposal. What would I be in France, your sometimes whore?"

The bluntness of her words caused him to hesitate before he continued. "You would have so much more than this mud hovel. You would be my mistress, as are many women of name in France. It is no dishonor to be the mistress of someone of my name."

Marisol Montero threw back her head and laughed. "Call it what you want. I will never lower myself again, for you or any man."

Dupré narrowed his eyes, his words carried by the courtroom tone of an accusatory prosecutor. "Would you not do it for the other? The one you met secretly in Monterey?" He knew his words struck her heart. Then her face hardened again. Had he said too much?

"Who I walk with is of no concern of yours. You have no right to mention this that you know nothing about. The man you speak of would never offer me a position such as you have. He would not even take me in his arms for a moment, as much as I wanted this. You will never be such a man."

He flung his response at her. "What would he say if he knew the child he has searched for so long is now in your arms?"

Marisol gasped, gently turning the boy around and kneeling in front of him. Did she see MacLeod when she looked into the child's eyes, Dupré wondered. It did not matter. He would see that she would never be with the American.

She stood up and placed the child behind her. "Go. Fill your ship and return to your wife. I will tell no one of your indiscretions today."

Dupré stomped over to his horse but could not refrain from one last thrust. "Yes, I will fill the hold of my ship. But first I must dispel a blot on my honor put there by your American. He has made accusations which I must answer."

"Answer?" she said. She handed the child to an Indian servant. "And how do you answer these accusations if they are not false?"

From his saddle Dupré looked down. "By killing the source. That is how men of blood and honor answer. I have heard he has ridden to Monterey. I will sail from San Pedro in the morning and kill this man."

"No," Marisol cried. "He does not deserve this just because I will not go with you."

Dupré chuckled. "You wish to make me an offer perhaps?"

"An offer?"

"It appears you wish for me to accept these rumors that are being told by him. Why should I?"

"You cannot shoot a man for saying things that everyone is saying or thinking."

Dupré struggled to control his fears. "Everyone? Who else is saying this?"

Marisol lowered her head, then straightened. "It is being questioned. You have been here for some time. It is known you have had to borrow to remain. So what is it this man says that is untrue?"

He could not believe this woman would have so much knowledge of his struggles. Without a full ship he was ruined. The sickness in his stomach needed to be addressed. "They are false. As soon as I get to Monterey, I will end them."

"By killing this man you hate," she said. "That will solve your problems?"

Dupré mounted his horse. "He will question me no more. And you, you will get to keep his child. If he is dead, he will never come to take him from you. Do you not wish you had helped him make it?"

"No, you cannot do this. You hate him because you have seen me speak with him. Is there no way to stop you? I will beg if you ask." She sank to the ground, her body wracked with sobs.

Yes, there is a way, he thought. It would not solve his problems, but the voyage was long, and he would have her while it lasted. And perhaps he could find an answer during that time. He sat, waiting for her to answer her own question.

He watched her wipe the tears from her eyes and stand. He thrilled at the determination and hate he saw in her eyes. He knew before she spoke he would have her.

"I will come with you. I will hate you forever. Do not expect me to help you. I will lie in your bed. That is all I will ever do. For this you will not kill him."

Dupré nodded. "Get yourself ready. You need say nothing to your husband. I will let you know when we will leave."

She threw her head back. "And the child?"

"That is up to you. You can keep the bastard if you wish."

"If you break your word," she said, "I will kill you myself."

Dupré stroked his mustache and laughed. "Yes, I imagine you would. Get yourself ready. Perhaps you will like it."

FRANCESCA'S SECRET

The priest studied the order from the governor for some time before directing MacLeod to wait while he conferred with the ground in front of the mission door, his thoughts still occupied with the contents of the letter.

Moments later the heavy wooden door burst open and Francesca and Rosalie rushed out, followed by the young Indian girl, who carried Catalina. Francesca ran to MacLeod. "How did you do this? They say I am free. Is it true?"

"It's true. I watched the governor sign the paper himself."
"But how? They spoke of sending me to Mexico since they did not know what to do with me. And the man who was shot. What about him?"

"Well, Sergeant Pacheco and I came to an understanding about the shooting."

"He has forgiven me?"

MacLeod pondered that question a moment. There was no way he would tell her how Pacheco felt about having her free. "I wouldn't go that far. Let's say he was persuaded that it was the best thing to do."

"Persuaded, how?"

"That's better left alone. Now, I can arrange with Mr. Hartnell for a place for you all to stay." Francesca started to reply and MacLeod held up a hand. "I've something else to tell you. I think Diego's still alive."

Francesca stared at him for moment, then leapt into his arms. "That is the most wonderful thing I could hear." She then seemed to realize the intimacy of her gesture and stepped back.

Neither spoke for a few moments, then Francesca asked, "Where is he then?"

"I'm not sure where he is yet."

"Then Father Pérez did not take him?"

"Oh, he took him all right, but they wouldn't let him take him on the ship, so he was handed off to a woman lived up at a pueblo."

Francesca smiled. "Then why are you here? Why are you not going to the pueblo to get him? If it is not far."

"Well now, it's not that simple. Wish it were. Seems someone else came and took him."

Francesca frowned. "Why would someone do this thing? Do they not know you have looked for him?"

"This person knew, but he had other reasons for taking the boy."

Francesca shook her head. "I am sorry. I do not understand this. You have come and saved me from whatever they were going to do to me, and you should be looking for your son. Who is this person who took him, and what could be his reasons?"

"Oh, he has his reasons. Weren't the kind of reasons would make others do what he did, but some of these foreigners think different, I guess. Soon as I can get you settled, I'm going in search of him."

"Then you know who this person is?" Francesca said.

"Yes, ma'am. He's a Frenchman I've crossed paths with a time or two."

MacLeod frowned at the sudden stiffness in her face.

"This Frenchman you speak of. Has he a name?"

"Has a real highfalutin name he calls himself. Claims he's owner of a French trading ship that's trying to fill its hold with hides."

Francesca's eyes flashed. "Guillermo, tell me now. What is his name?"

"Dupré, Gaston Dupré. Calls himself Le Chevalier of something or other."

Rosalie gasped.

Francesca's hand went to her throat. She shook her head and backed away. "No, no, this cannot be true. You must be mistaken."

Rosalie leaned over to Francesca and said. "You must tell him."

"Francesca, tell me what? What is it Rosalie wants you to tell me?"

Tears ran down Francesca's cheeks. She wrapped her arms around her body and ran into the shelter of a large olive tree. Rosalie hurried after her.

MacLeod shuffled his feet in the dirt, wondering what he had said to make her burst into tears. He would need to arrange for horses to take the women back to town, then they could decide where they would go next. Whatever they decided, it had to be done quickly. He wanted to be on the road as soon as possible. Dupré was somewhere in the south, and that's where he wanted to be.

Rosalie scurried over. "Come, she must speak with you."

He followed the old woman to where Francesca stood, her arms still wrapped around her body. She turned away as he came around in front of her. "No, stay. I do not want you to see me."

"Why?"

"I will tell you, and then you must go. But you must make me a promise first. Will you do this for me?"

"That's a hard one to say without knowing what you want, but I'll try," MacLeod said.

"When you leave us here, you are going in search of the boy. You must promise me you will send someone else to speak with this man. You must not go to him yourself," she said.

"Why, Francesca? What is it about him? You don't even know him, and I wouldn't be worried about what you hear."

"Because he will kill you. Do you not know of him? He kills people who he does not like."

MacLeod stood, stunned. What could she know about Gaston Dupré? He noted the stiffness of her body as she spoke, this woman who had once stood beneath the fluttering shadows of a cottonwood tree, in the middle of a rushing stream, naked for him to see. But at that moment, she wouldn't face him. He didn't know how to take it. Was she angry at something he had said? He had gone to great lengths to have the charges against her dropped, he had built a house for her and little Catalina, and he had spent months searching for the girl. "How do you know these things?" he asked.

"I know of them. That is all you need to know."

"No." MacLeod stepped forward and took her by the shoulders. He turned her around to face him. "Look at me, Francesca. I need to know more. I need to know why you are acting like this. I need to know how you know this man."

She took his arms from her shoulders and pushed him away. "I will tell you a story. I do not want you to ask questions until I am finished. Listen to me now, and do not say anything."

He nodded his assent and waited to hear what she had to say.

"I think I should begin by telling you my name is Francesca Hidalgo. My family lives outside the Presidio of Santa Bárbara."

"I was there," MacLeod said, forgetting his promise to not interrupt. "I met a man by the name of Hidalgo, a Señor Salvador Hidalgo, I believe."

"Yes, he is my father."

"Can't believe it. Why—" He stopped when she held up her hand.

"No, do not ask questions. Listen instead. My father desires to be important. Unlike most, he went to school in Mexico. He reads books and writes letters to men of importance, and some write to him and ask for his guidance. He even says that Governor Argüello asks him sometimes in the matter of government."

MacLeod had already formed a dozen questions in his mind but dared not interrupt again.

Francesca paused and turned her back to him. "You must understand, young girls in families in our country are many times used to promote family influence and fortune. My family is already one of the wealthiest, so there was no need to marry me to someone who might help in this way. But my father wished to form unions with those who might encourage others to see him as a future leader of Alta California."

The news wasn't any different from what he had learned in New Mexico about fathers marrying off daughters. It was the reason Maria de Cordero, Diego's mother, and the woman he had buried beneath the rocks in the desert, had been kidnapped and sold to the Mescalero Apache, Romero. He waited while Francesca appeared to gather her thoughts.

"One day, this man, this Frenchman, Señor Dupré, was brought to our house and introduced to my father. As you can imagine, knowing what I have said of my father, he was greatly impressed by what the man said. My father could not contain his excitement when this foreign man, who said he owned the ship he came here on, said he has royal blood."

"Actually, his wife's family owns the ship. Least that's what I heard," MacLeod said.

"Wife," Francesca said, turning around. She laughed. "He did not speak of a wife. In fact, it was understood he was not married."

"No, you must be mistaken. I spoke with the captain of the ship."

Francesca held her hand up again. "No, I am not mistaken. I know this. I know this because it was thought he would ask my father for my hand."

"Your hand? You mean to marry you?"

"Yes, that is what I mean."

"You wanted to marry him?" MacLeod couldn't believe what he was hearing.

"No, I did not want to marry him. I hated the man, but that would not have mattered if my father thought he would gain importance by marrying me to him."

Macleod remembered the story Father Fernández had told him about Francesca being the young widow of a soldier who had died. "So, what happened? Did you run away and marry your husband instead against your father's wishes?"

She ignored his question and continued as if she was speaking only to herself. Her voice dropped to a whisper as she walked off a half dozen paces and leaned against the trunk of the massive olive tree.

"Each night he would come to our house to speak with my father. Sometimes he would come early and ask to walk with me. My mother, or my sister who is married and lived in the house also, would walk behind, so we would not be alone and it would be proper. The man would talk again and again of the things he had done. He would hurry his steps sometimes so that we would be ahead of the others, and then he would touch me," she said.

An uneasy feeling begin to encompass MacLeod. He did not interrupt as she continued speaking as if only to herself.

"One night he and my father had been drinking their wine. My mother and sisters were busy elsewhere. Señor Dupré asked me to walk with him. I told him it would not be proper. He said he wished to speak with me of something of great importance, and he assured me he had already spoken to my father about it."

MacLeod held his breath.

"We walked out into the field. He kept bumping into me as we walked. I tried to walk away but he followed. Then he stopped me and tried to pull me close to him. I pushed him away, but he was stronger than me. I fell down in the grass, and he fell on top of me. He pulled my dress up. I struggled but I could not get him off of me."

"He did this? Dupré? He forced himself on you?"

Francesca began to weep.

The gentle ocean breeze gusted momentarily, riffling the leaves of the olive tree. Across the plaza an Indian majordomo on his horse drove a group of men toward the fields.

"And your father? What did he do?" MacLeod asked.

"He said I had made this story up. He said Señor Dupré would not do this. He said I had dishonored my family and his name."

Having met the man, Salvador Hidalgo, MacLeod could not believe the attack would go unpunished. "What about Dupré? Did your father not confront him?"

Francesca gathered herself. "Yes, my father apologized to him for asking such a delicate question. Señor Dupré denied it, of course. He said it was a blot on his honor to even ask such a question. My father chose to accept this denial and blame me instead. In the morning, Señor Dupré was no longer there. My father said that he had returned to his ship. When it was learned I was with child, my father said I had gone with some other man and he sent me away."

MacLeod recalled the sudden change in Salvador Hidalgo's attitude when he had mentioned the Frenchman's name. He thought little of it at the time. But at that moment, he understood.

"Do you not see why my father did this? To believe my story he would have to confront Señor Dupré. And to confront him, he would have to fight him."

"So he did nothing," MacLeod said.

Francesca laughed. "Nothing? He sent me away to live with the priests who were to salvage my soul for my error."

Suddenly it dawned on MacLeod. "Catalina?"

"Yes, Catalina. She is the something good that came of this. He is the father of her."

"Does he know this?" MacLeod asked.

"No, how could he?"

MacLeod could think of no words to say.

She put her hands on his shoulders. "That is why I do not want you to go after this man. He will surely kill you as he has others. Is there nothing you can give him for your Diego?"

Give him, MacLeod thought. The idea turned his stomach. Then the vision of Dupré and Vicente Montero came to mind. Was the Frenchman attempting to do the same thing with Marisol? Certainly, for all his bluster, Vicente Montero would not fight. No, MacLeod concluded. If it had not happened already, he would not allow it to happen again. Someone had to stop him.

He took Francesca's hands from his shoulders and held them. "I'm sorry. I understand your concern, but I must find him. Diego is all I have left of my Maria. If Dupré still has him, I'm going to get him back."

Francesca bit her lip. "But surely he will kill you, too. I do not want you to die." She wrapped her arms around him and began to cry. "Stay here with me and Catalina. I will be good to you, and maybe someday you will forgive me for what he did to me."

"Francesca, you need no forgiveness from me. But I must go. I can't let him get away with it. He has my son, and he may be trying to do the same thing to another woman. I can't let that happen."

"This woman. Is this the woman you have spoken of? Do you love this woman?" she asked

MacLeod frowned. "No," he said. "She's married. He paused. "But I've watched Dupré with her, at the wedding, and before. Her husband won't stop him. He can't. Same as your father." But, remembering their last encounter, Francesca's question brought up a feeling he had tried hard to bury. What about Marisol Montero?

"Then I will go also," Francesca said.

"No. Mr. Hartnell will find a place for you to stay. When I get back, I can find you another place."

"Guillermo, there is nothing here for me. If you leave me, I will ride after you. Perhaps he will only hurt you, and you will need someone to care for you."

MacLeod held her at arm's length. Was he making a mistake putting her off? Had he not thought of her so many nights, lying in his blankets? Had the vision of her in the stream not haunted him? And what if he found Diego? What would he do after learning there was nothing to return to Boston for? Was Alta California his future? "I'm not even sure where Dupré is. They say he is in the south somewhere. I'll have to ride hard."

"You do not know these people as I do. They will tell me things they will not tell you. Do not leave me behind. I want to see this man punished as much as you do."

"But, Francesca—"

"No. You will give me another pistol. If he kills you, I will do the same to him."

After failing to convince Francesca to remain behind, MacLeod bought horses and a pair of mules from the mission, along with saddles and pack saddles. He also arranged for two vaqueros to accompany them as far as the next mission.

Leaving the vaqueros to gather the gear and supplies, MacLeod took Francesca, Rosalie, and Juana to Monterey to outfit them and obtain travel permits, which the governor happily signed. MacLeod planned to be on the road by dawn the next day, and everyone understood the days would be long and hard, with no stopping at the missions for anything except information or shelter in case of extreme weather. He figured it would take them ten days or so of hard riding to get to Santa Bárbara, and another three or four days from there to the pueblo at los Ángeles.

MacLeod found Hartnell behind the counter of his storeroom. Hartnell grinned and introduced himself to Francesca. "I see you have rescued the young woman."

"Yes, sir. The governor found the courage to release her after the man dropped his charges."

"So, now you're planning to take them all back to San Diego?"

Macleod realized he had not told Hartnell the new information about Diego. Quickly, he filled him in and the need to find Dupré.

"What have you heard?" MacLeod asked.

Hartnell rubbed his chin. "News is, he's been somewhat successful in purchasing hides. Haven't figured out how he's paying for them, but they say his ship is about full. Appears he got lucky and found a couple of missions with a store of hides left over from last year. They hadn't heard of his financial troubles. You'll need to ride hard if he's that close to sailing. I wouldn't waste a minute if I were you."

MacLeod took Hartnell's advice. They returned to the mission and directed the vaqueros to pack for a late-afternoon departure. By nightfall the party rode through the coastal mountains toward the Rio Salinas Valley, and the next morning they turned south toward Nuestra Señora de la Soledad, the bleakest of all the missions MacLeod had visited.

He pushed them hard, changing vaqueros at each mission, refusing to allow the group to take afternoon siestas, much to the disappointment of the vaqueros. When they stopped for the night, Rosalie would gather wood and start a fire, while Francesca searched the food bags for their evening meal, then cooked and wrapped extra tortillas for the next day. MacLeod fretted, always wanting to go a mile farther before stopping.

As the miles disappeared behind the hooves of the small cavalcade, MacLeod's sense of a possible upcoming loss intensified. How could he have gotten so close to finding Diego only to possibly lose him forever by a day or so?

Four days later, they bypassed the mission of Santa Iñes, rode through the narrow pass, and once again found themselves on the shore of the ocean. The next day they would be in Santa Bárbara. Would the French ship be in port? Would Francesca visit her family?

On inquiring, the comandante of the Santa Bárbara Presidio told MacLeod the priests at the mission complained that the French ship had sailed without paying for its supplies, and he had concerns about the notes he had received for their early hides.

MacLeod slammed his hand on the comandante's table. "Damn, the French ship sailed this morning?"

"No, it left when the tide went out yesterday. I know because I wanted to speak with them, but it was too late. I am hoping they come back so we can discuss this matter with the supplies that have not been paid for.

"I doubt you'll see them again," MacLeod said. He stormed out of the office and stood looking out to sea. Would the ship catch a good wind that would deliver them to San Pedro, if that's where they intended to stop next? Or was the ship's hold already full?

Francesca had no desire to see her family until the matter with Dupré was dealt with. Spending only enough time to purchase supplies, MacLeod led the group back to the road.

He figured three days to make it to los Ángeles and the harbor at San Pedro. He pushed the vaqueros hard to keep the party together. Francesca and Rosalie, and the Indian girl, Juana, never complained though he knew they were close to exhaustion. It had slipped out one night, as they talked around the campfire, that Juana had been the one to pull the trigger and shoot Pacheco. Francesca explained her fear that they would shoot or hang Juana for the crime, regardless of Pacheco's attempted rape of Francesca.

After two days, MacLeod's patience snapped. He instructed the vaqueros to bring the party to the pueblo in los Ángeles, and he would meet them there, despite Francesca's plea that they could keep up. He would ride directly to the harbor in case the ship had already ported.

Late the following afternoon, MacLeod topped a low rise and looked down on an empty harbor. No ships lay at anchor and no sails could be seen approaching or leaving the tranquil waters. Figuring he was too late, MacLeod reined the sweat-soaked dun onto the narrow track leading to the pueblo.

The next morning, MacLeod stood outside a small adobe building, waiting for the *alcalde mayore*. Four hours later, the man rode into the dusty plaza and dismounted, handing his horse to an Indian servant.

"Doñ Castañeda," MacLeod said, removing his hat and bowing his head. "I am seeking information."

The *alcalde* rubbed his chin and frowned, then held up a finger and smiled. "Yes, the *Americano* who refused to leave our country or obtain the proper papers. You have come for papers this time?"

MacLeod handed over the passport the governor's secretary had prepared before they left Monterey. The man examined it briefly.

"So, what is it this time you want of me?"

"I'm inquiring about the French ship. Has it arrived from Monterey?"

"Please, come into my office where we can speak privately."

MacLeod didn't like the cloud of anger that draped the *alcalde*'s face. The man seated himself behind his table and pushed the stack of papers aside. "Why do you ask this?"

"Needed to see a man who is on it."

"And this man is?" Castañeda asked.

"His name's Dupré. He says he's the owner of the ship, but I've heard otherwise."

The last statement caused Casteñada to sit back in his chair. "This you have heard, from whom, please?"

"Folks up in Monterey, other ships' captains and such. Anyway, what I wanted to know is whether the ship came in, and if it did when did it sail?"

"The ship sailed yesterday with the evening tide, I believe. I did not see it go, of course, but that was its intention. Why do you need to know this?"

MacLeod ignored the question. With a fair wind, the ship could make San Diego in a day. He needed two days of hard riding. He started to leave the office, then asked, "Was he alone when he left, do you know?"

"No. I know this because he took a woman with him."

"A woman. Do you know who it was?"

"Her husband you know. He is Doñ Vicente Montero, and she is his wife. Doñ Montero came to me and asked me to stop the ship from sailing. I asked him how I should do that."

MacLeod couldn't believe it. A day late and somehow Dupré had convinced Marisol to go with him. How could she do this?

Casteñada continued while looking out his window, across the courtyard. "It is strange, because some time ago I have heard she lost this child she was to have, but she had one with her when they went to the ship."

MacLeod leaned on the desk, his heart pounding. "A boy, about two years old or so?"

"Yes," the man said, as he sat back down. "I thought it strange that she should go on this ship, but I did not know she had not told her husband."

So he still had Diego, and Marisol as well. But did she know whose child she had? "I need your help, sir. I believe that child with her is my son. If they're going to put in at San Diego, I still have a chance to catch them."

"What is it I can do?"

"Horses. I need a couple of good, fresh horses. Mine's been ridden hard the last few days."

The *alcalde mayore* agreed, and MacLeod also made arrangements with the man to supply Francesca and Rosalie with horses and supplies when they arrived. Then he raced out of the los Ángeles pueblo at a gallop, leading an extra horse. He figured he could reach San Diego by late the next night if nothing went wrong. The ship would certainly remain in San Diego for a day or more. He needed it to remain for two or three days for him to catch it.

The first storm of the season swept in from the west. MacLeod's immediate thoughts were for the safety of the ship. By early afternoon, the Rio Santa Anna overflowed its banks, forcing MacLeod to follow its course north, trying to find a spot to ford the churning waters. He cursed the weather gods at every bend in the river.

He worked his way along the banks of the river until he came to the narrow canyon without finding a place to ford. Night found him encamped ten miles above the road that led south, at a spot he figured would offer the best opportunity to cross in the morning, if the rains didn't begin again.

The rain began again the next morning, but MacLeod swam the horses across at first light and pounded down the muddy road, passing the mission at San Luis Rey and the narrow trail that led up to Pala. He still had a hard day's ride before he would make San Diego.

Hours later, an exhausted MacLeod peered out across the plaza of the San Diego Presidio at an empty harbor. Not a ship lay at anchor in the sheltered bay. He slid to the ground and clung to the saddle for support.

He found Captain Martín behind his cluttered desk. The captain told MacLeod the ship had not arrived. As MacLeod had learned in his time in New Mexico, and in Alta California, a favorite saying was *tal vez mañana*, perhaps tomorrow.

Captain Martín also had some information MacLeod might like to hear. There was someone here also who he would meet, his friend, the one with the orange hair.

MacLeod walked over to one of the adobe buildings alongside the officers' quarters. An obviously drunk Concannon answered his knock, a blanket thrown over his shoulders.

Two hours later they sat on the ground in the shade of the adobe. Concannon had heard nothing about the Frenchman for weeks, although hides promised to *Macala and Arnel* were mysteriously not available when Concannon arrived to arrange delivery. MacLeod had begun to steel himself against the possibility the French ship's hold had been topped off in San Pedro. At that very moment, the ship could be surging southward, toward the cape, with his son and Marisol Montero on board.

THE CHALLENGE

He camped on the bluffs overlooking the harbor and spent hours standing on the point, watching for any sign of a ship. Had the storm pushed them out to sea and left them beating their way back toward the safe harbor at San Diego? Hope faded as another day passed. Concannon had come to sit with him, but not to talk. Nothing needed to pass between them.

The following day, they were watching the gulls fishing when a man rode a heavily lathered horse off the road and toward their camp; two other riders followed. The man halted and waited for the others to catch up.

It wasn't until one of the vaqueros helped the swaying figure out of the saddle and placed her on the ground that MacLeod recognized Francesca. He rushed forward, lifting her head up and helping her drink from his water jug. Then he laid her on the ground and covered her with a blanket.

MacLeod spoke with the men while she slept. She had arrived at the pueblo in los Ángeles four days after he left and refused to leave Castañeda's office until he had hired two men to accompany her to San Diego. They laughed, explaining to MacLeod how she had driven them for three days to get to San Diego. MacLeod rewarded the men and had them check with Captain Martín before returning to their homes.

Sometime later Concannon hailed from the bluffs. "A ship from the north."

MacLeod ran to where Concannon sat. Far out against the blue of the sky he saw the first flicker of white. He stood transfixed. His hand shielding his eyes from the lowering sun as the ship came about and began working its way toward the bay. For an hour he watched, pacing the strip of land above the cliffs.

Finally, there was no mistaking the lines of the ship, or the flag that dipped at the mast and received the salute from the presidio. Dupré had arrived in San Diego. MacLeod's only thought was whether Diego was within reach. Was this the end of his search?

Francesca pulled him away and turned him around. "It is them, is it not? What will you do?"

"I guess it depends on what he does. If he has Diego, all he needs do is put him ashore. There's no need for it to go further."

"And if he doesn't?"

MacLeod watched the boat from the French ship being lowered into the water. Two men climbed down and sat in the boat with the captain's crew. "Then I guess I'll kill him, or he'll kill me. One way or the other, it'll be over."

"And the woman?" Francesca said. "Doñ Castañeda has said she is there also. What will you do about her?"

"I reckon that's up to her. Not sure why she's here with him. It's the boy I'll have."

MacLeod swung into the saddle. He wanted to be there when they beached the longboat. He could see no need for putting off the confrontation. He kneed the horse onto the road, toward the beach below.

Dupré stepped out of the boat and waded the last few steps to the shore. MacLeod knew Dupré had seen him. The cold reptilian-like mask that was the Frenchman's face told MacLeod all he needed to know. There would be no compromise.

"You have my son," MacLeod called out, attempting to keep his words from displaying the fury building inside him. "If you'll have the boat return to the ship and bring him here, this can be over. Some have asked me to put it behind me."

Dupré attempted to push past, but MacLeod stepped in front of him. "You can take care of your business with the captain as soon as you have the boy brought ashore."

"You fool," Dupré said. "You do not know what you are doing. Take your hand away from me now, or I will be forced to respond."

"You're not going anywhere until you send the boat back for the boy."

"I have no desire to kill you. Do you not know who I am? You have been told, I know this, and yet you choose to stand there and confront me. Dupré swatted MacLeod's arm away and brushed past him.

Before he had taken two strides MacLeod grabbed Dupré by the shoulder and spun him around. "The boy. Now," MacLeod said.

Dupré's face flamed in anger. He reached out and slapped MacLeod's face.

MacLeod dropped Dupré's arm and stepped back, stunned at the Frenchman's act. He rocked back on his heels, then drove his fist onto Dupré's jaw, knocking the Frenchman sprawling in the wet sand. Dupré rolled over and wobbled to his feet, rubbing his jaw while holding onto the ship's captain for support. *"I will kill you for this,"* he managed to say through a jaw that was swelling rapidly.

"Guess you have the right to try," MacLeod said. He dropped a hand to the butt of his pistol. "Your captain there has a pistol on him. I'm mighty sure he'd let you borrow it."

Dupré shook his head. "I demand satisfaction for this insult. I do not fight like one of your wild Indians. You will meet me here tomorrow morning, or your bastard will suffer."

The shock of the insult froze MacLeod for a moment. Then he dove at Dupré, but found himself locked in the arms of Concannon, who pulled him away as the French captain pulled his pistol and pointed it at MacLeod's chest.

"This will be done the proper way, as gentlemen, *monsieur*," the captain said.

"Gentleman, hell," MacLeod said. "No reason why we can't do it right here and now. And for your information, captain, that man is no gentleman. He is a lying, thieving coward."

"We will return in the morning, one hour after the sun rises." The captain took Dupré by the arm and helped him into the longboat.

"What the hell's he talking about," MacLeod asked. "What's wrong with right now?"

"That's the way the way these Frenchie's do it," Concannon said. "They call it dueling. Saw one in Portsmouth once."

"Dueling?" MacLeod said.

"Aye, they stand there and walk away from each other, then turn and shoot. Each man gets one shot."

"You heard him, Irish," MacLeod said. "He admitted he has my son on that ship. I have a mind to swim out there tonight and get the boy."

Francesca slid from her saddle and ran forward. She wrapped her arms around MacLeod, her cheek pressed to his chest.

MacLeod felt her body tremble with her sobs. He put his arms around her. "It appears people take it for granted he'll kill me. Could be I have other ideas. I guess we'll find out for sure tomorrow morning. This whole thing has been a long time coming. It's about over. Leastwise, it will be tomorrow."

49

MacLeod sat in the sand on the narrow beach below the presidio, his back against the side of an upended boat. Across the bay, the French ship turned slowly as the tide changed. Would he live to see the tide change again, he wondered. And if he didn't, what would happen to Diego? Would Dupré take him to France? If so, Diego would never know the story of his mother's struggle to survive, and their perilous journey to Alta California that cost her her life? Then the image he couldn't shake, Marisol

Montero with Dupré. What had caused this sudden change in her attitude toward the Frenchman?

The light of a new day began to creep across the water as the sun rose behind him. His last day, Or the Frenchman's. How many times had he heard of the Frenchman taking out his anger by challenging men who questioned him? Was Dupré so sure of his imminent success? Was he that good? Or was he also contemplating his possible injury, or even death?

MacLeod pulled his knees up to his chest. It had just dawned on him that the stories spread about Dupré's reputation never questioned the ability of those he killed. Dupré had no idea how good MacLeod might be with a pistol. MacLeod remembered his fight with the Apache, Romero, and the Indian's reaction when he realized he faced someone who knew how to fight with a knife. MacLeod had taunted the Indian, causing him to make a mistake that cost him his life. Could he do it again?"

He heard the scuffling of boots in the sand and turned as Concannon sat beside him.

"A beautiful morning, lad. A good day for a killing."

"You have a way with words, Irish."

Concannon pulled a small jug from his pocket and took a drink. "Do you know anything about what you're supposed to do?"

"Shoot him or he shoots me. Pretty simple."

"Oh, but it's the ceremony these high brows go through to make it look respectable," Concannon said. "You can't just shoot one another. You have to do it according to rules."

"What rules?"

"The Frenchie's captain there will explain it all to you."

"You ever see one of these here duels?"

"Aye, when I was a lad. A woman a man thought was his, chose another. They decided to have one of these duels, winner take the woman."

"What happened?"

"One died, one was wounded, and the woman, being an Irish lass, chose someone else. Speaking of women, what about the woman Francesca? Have you thought what will happen to her if the Frenchman kills you?"

"Trying not to consider that possibility, but I suppose I should. I'll leave it in your hands. Talk to William Hartnell. You can trust him. Tell him I want everything owed me to go to her."

Concannon pointed to the ship in the harbor. "They're lowering the boat. Looks as if they'll be on time, anyway."

MacLeod grunted. "Wants to get this over with and get out before the tide hems them in again. Or their creditors show up."

One last thing," Concannon said. "I've heard it said most men fire too quickly. They fail to take the time to aim proper like."

MacLeod watched as people passed through the ship's side and made their way down to the longboat. It was too far to determine how many, but one appeared to carry a bundle in its arms. His heart fluttered. Could it be his son?

He rose from the sand as the boat approached the beach. Dupré and the captain sat in the back of the boat, facing the shore. MacLeod could not see the faces of the other passengers.

"I will speak with this Frenchman. Perhaps he will listen this morning, though I doubt he has the sense of a loon."

"No, he won't be changing his mind. He can't. It's me he wants. It's between him and me. Might have been different if he hadn't taken Diego. Now it's too late to turn back."

Francesca walked across the wet sand and stood as his side. Rosalie had ridden in the night before with Catalina, and they waited above the beach.

Francesca took him by the arm. "What will you do when it's over, if nothing happens to you? If you do not return to your home, I would like for you to live with Catalina and me, and your son, too, of course."

MacLeod turned and looked at her. "You asking if I'd marry you?"

Francesca said nothing as the boat touched the sand, then said. "No, you do not have to marry me. Not after what he did to me. They would not marry us anyway. Others I know live together. They do not talk about it because of the church, but they do."

He watched Dupré help someone step from the boat to the sand. MacLeod knew before the figure turned it was Marisol. Why had she come to see this? Then she placed the bundle she held on the sand.

MacLeod caught his breath as he watched his son reach up and take Marisol's hand and walk toward him. *My god, how he has grown.* He fought the urge to rush forward and sweep the child up in his arms. Would he live long enough to do so?

Concannon moved past him toward the approaching party. "I'll have a talk with the captain. He won't know me, but he will know

I'm from the sea as is he. You be putting the boy out of your mind. Put it on the Frenchman, nowhere else. Kill him, and you can spend the rest of your life with your son."

MacLeod pushed himself to his feet. "Well, I reckon it was all due to come to this eventually."

"Who is the woman with them?" Francesca asked.

"That's Doña Montero."

"She is very beautiful, but why is she here? And why is she with your son?"

"I'm afraid you would have to ask her that question."

MacLeod watched Concannon converse with the captain of the French ship. The captain held a wooden box and lifted the lid. MacLeod could see the pistols nestled barrel to butt in the box. He wondered what was wrong with the pistol Dupré always carried. Then his eyes settled on Marisol's face.

She held Diego in front of her. She turned from watching the men speak and looked at MacLeod, then lowered her eyes to the sand at her feet. He was certain he had seen her body tremble with a sob.

Dupré spoke up, pointing to a smooth strand of beach, up against a stand of pine trees. Concannon nodded and came back to MacLeod.

"Wants to do it over there. Figures it can't be seen from the fort, so nobody's apt to interrupt. All right with you?"

MacLeod nodded. "Good a place as any. Let's go."

BLOOD IN THE SAND

The receding tide had left a hard-packed surface to walk on. MacLeod and Francesca walked behind the others, neither speaking. Dupré had yet to acknowledge MacLeod, which made him wonder if the Frenchman was as confident of victory as he made out.

Dupré and the ship's captain came to a halt and turned. MacLeod and Francesca stopped a few feet away. Dupré's face fell.

"Do you not recognize me, Señor Dupré? Or have you forgot me already?" Francesca asked.

"Am I supposed to know you?" Dupré said. He began unbuttoning his coat without looking at Francesca.

"Why do you turn away? Is it embarrassing to see me again, after what you did to me? Look at me."

Dupré shrugged and spoke with the ship's captain. "You will have this woman taken away. I do not know what she speaks of. Then we can get this incident over with and return to the ship."

MacLeod spoke up. "Well, Frenchie, I have a feeling your captain will be returning to his ship alone. You made any decision where you want your body left? I hate to think about you poisoning the fish if they dump you at sea."

"Fool," Dupré said. "What experience do you have of defending honor? You have so little of it."

"Never had to defend it. Had to kill a bunch to defend my life. You think that's any different? Course we weren't standing like fools in front of each other at the time."

The first shadow of doubt crossed the Frenchman's face. Then Francesca spoke up again.

"Do not ignore me, señor. Does the woman with you know what you did to me?" She spoke over her shoulder and Rosalie came forward with Catalina. "Would you like to see the result of your attack on me?"

Marisol gasped. "What is she saying? Is this true?"

Dupré spoke again to the ship's captain. "I do not need these false accusation at this time. I will deal with her later. Proceed with the instruction. I have already wasted too much time on this."

Concannon approached the ship's captain, who still held the box containing the pistols. "My friend knows nothing of your dueling customs. His experience with such things has usually come about in more of a hurry, dealing with charging Indians and such. You best be explaining your rules to him."

The man stepped forward with the box and spoke to Concannon. "Of course. However, it is also my duty, on behalf of *Monsieur* Dupré, to allow your man to apologize and save his life. Monsieur Dupré will forget the insult and the attack on him."

MacLeod bit off a curse. "And my son, what about him?"

The French captain looked over his shoulder at Dupré before saying, "Your son will live in France and receive a fine education, more than can be provided here."

"Well, you tell that dandy he'll have to kill me first."

"Very well," the captain said. He spoke to Dupré who came forward, his face a mask of rage.

MacLeod took a step closer and smiled, forcing Dupré to step back.

The captain held out the open box with the matched set of long-barreled pistols. "*Monsieur* Dupré has offered you the first choice of the pistols. You may watch while I load them and then chose one."

MacLeod reached over and took one of the pistols from the case. He held it out at arm's length and sighted down the barrel before returning it to the case. "I think I'd feel a sight more at ease with my own," he said. He pulled his pistol from his belt and held it out for the man to inspect.

Dupré laughed.

"But *monsieur*, these are the finest examples of French gun making. They are a perfect set. You cannot find ones more accurate than these," the captain said.

"How far apart we talking about with this fight?" MacLeod asked.

"The distance is twenty paces."

MacLeod stared into Dupré's eyes. He wanted to see his reaction. "Well, shoot, with this here sixty-caliber Bates of London I can knock a squirrel off a branch at forty paces. Why would I need one I never tried before? Besides, the bigger ball in my pistol carries a sight more punch than these."

Dupré swallowed.

"Well, Dupré, you about ready to do this thing?" He turned to Concannon. "Best you take the women and children away. There's no need for them to be seeing the man die."

"No, Francesca said. I will stay. I will pray that you will live." She directed Rosalie to take Catalina away and moved off to the side.

MacLeod looked at Marisol, who still held Diego. She raised her head, tears streaking her cheeks.

The captain beckoned to both men to step forward. MacLeod had watched him load the pistol Dupré had chosen. Dupré held the long-barreled flintlock at his side, in his right hand.

"You feeling any remorse, Frenchie? Seems you have two women here you've damaged," MacLeod said, then grinned. "Hope you didn't have too many plans for Doña Montero there. She's not going anywhere with you 'cause you're going to hell in a minute."

MacLeod watched the rage return to Dupré's face. It was the reaction MacLeod hoped for. He knew Dupré would fire quickly, in fact he counted on it. "What happens if whoever shoots first misses?"

The other man must stand and wait. "If you try to run after you miss, it is my duty to shoot you," the captain said.

Concannon stepped up. "And I'll shoot the Frenchie if he tries, so no need you be worrying about having to shoot your employer."

"Won't be necessary," MacLeod said. "I never miss. Let's be doing this now."

The captain positioned them back-to-back and instructed them to walk away from each other ten paces. He would count them off. At the word of ten, they were then allowed to turn and fire. If both missed the duel was over.

MacLeod leaned back into Dupré, forcing the man to stumble slightly. He could almost feel the hatred in the Frenchman. MacLeod had no doubt Dupré was an excellent shot. But maybe rattled a bit he would rush his opportunity.

MacLeod heard Marisol gasp as the ship's captain began the count.

The heavy flintlock in MacLeod's hand lay along his right leg, his finger caressing the trigger as he paced off the count. He had no doubt that Dupré would spin to his right, he would have done the same thing.

The French captain's voice rose as he neared the end of the count. MacLeod's mind froze on the image he expected to encounter when he turned. He wiped away the vision of the woman and Diego. Only the next few seconds mattered.

As the word ten fell from the captain's mouth, MacLeod bent his knee and spun to his right, sweeping his own pistol through a long arc, figuring Dupré would rush his aim and not expect a contrary move. MacLeod felt the ball from Dupré's pistol cut a thin furrow across his back as he finished his turn, his own pistol leveled at the center of the Frenchman's chest.

Francesca gasped as she realized MacLeod still stood.

Dupré held his pistol at arm's length, frozen, his face a mask of fear.

MacLeod straightened up and centered the end of the thick barrel of the gun, the heavy, .60 caliber lead ball seated against the powder, waiting for the spark. A ball that at this distance would blow through the Frenchman's chest.

MacLeod thought of what he was about to do. If he killed the Frenchman, as was inevitable at this distance, Marisol would remain in Alta California. If he only wounded Dupré, would Marisol leave with him? Would it be better for both of them if she did? And what about Diego, if Dupré lived. What would this duel have solved? No, he couldn't kill a man standing twenty paces away, even though the man had tried to kill him.

He shifted the barrel off Dupré's chest and aligned it with his shooting arm. His finger began to apply pressure to the trigger.

The seconds it took for MacLeod to come to his decision broke Dupré's. He began a turn away from the line of fire as the crack of MacLeod's pistol split the air.

MacLeod's ball punched through Dupré's chest. He crumbled to the sand, the spent pistol falling from his hand.

The ship's captain rushed to Dupré and examined him. "*Vous avez tué Monsieur. Il est morte.* MacLeod shook his head in disbelief. It had not been what he intended. He looked across to where Marisol stood. She dropped to her knees in the sand, took Diego's face in her hands, and spoke to him.

He felt the pistol being eased out of his hand.

Concannon stood at his side. "If he had not moved, he would not be dead, William. It was not a killing, if that's bothering you. For myself, I would have gladly killed him."

MacLeod's voice sounded hollow. "He should have stood. I only wanted to break his shooting arm."

Francesca ran to him and wrapped her arms around him. He held her a moment, then eased her away. "I got to speak to them over there. I need that man to do something."

The ship's captain rose from examining Dupré as MacLeod approached.

"Didn't have to end this way, sir, but now that it's done, there's something I would like you to do, if it's possible. I suppose you're going home now, but if you could run up the coast a day or two and take the lady back to her home."

"*Oui,* I can do that. She did not want to come with him. He made her. I did not have the power to stop him."

Marisol rose to her feet and took Diego by the hand. She led him over to where MacLeod and Francesca stood. "It will be difficult for you to understand. I believed the story he told me about the child's parents. I believed your son was dead. I did not want to think otherwise. Then when he told me what he had done, he said he would kill the boy, and you, unless I went with him. The boy did not deserve to die because of the man's hatred for you. It does not matter about me."

MacLeod dropped to his knees and held his son at arm's length. The boy had matured over the months. The blue eyes in a face that showed his mother's beauty. His search had come to an end. He had his son back.

Francesca picked Diego up and held him in her arms.

MacLeod stood up. "Señora Montero, the captain of the ship has agreed to take you home. I hope Doñ Montero will understand why you did it. I can never thank you enough."

A tear ran down her cheek as she watched Francesca clutch Diego to her chest. "He is so very beautiful. Perhaps someday you will bring him to me so I may see him again. Yes, Vicente will understand when I explain. If I had told my husband about Señor Dupré's attention, Vicente would have been forced to fight him. I could not allow that to happen."

Neither moved, then Marisol continued. "Is this the woman you helped rescue from the mission, the one who shot the soldier?"

"Yes, this is Francesca Hidalgo. She saved Diego's life when I first came here. Now you both have. He owes you much."

"You are very beautiful, Francesca. For what the man did to you, he deserved to die. I hope your life will be better now."

She stepped up to MacLeod and kissed him on the cheek, whispering in his ear. "Marry her Guillermo, please, for both of us.

You know it is the only way. Goodbye." She turned and hurried toward the longboat.

MacLeod reached down and took Francesca's free hand. "What you said before, about the Church not marrying us because I won't join them. Well, I've been thinking about that. Your father is a friend of the governor. Your father owes you for what he did to you. The governor owes me for rescuing his nephew. That makes two of them, and I hear the governor has the right to give out grants of land. Not to me, but he can to you. Maybe we could start a life of our own, here. We have a custom in America. The captain of an American ship can marry people. Captain Fanning will be in a port nearby soon. He can marry us."

MacLeod reached over and took the sleeping boy in his arms as they watched a boatman help Marisol into the boat. She turned and looked back at them before seating herself.

"And when you are with me, Guillermo, will you also be thinking of her?"

"No, she will return to her home now. She will always be a friend for what she did, but we will raise Diego and Catalina and begin a life here," MacLeod said. He watched the sailors load Dupré's body in the boat and push it off the sand. Marisol's last words rang in his ear, *"Please, for both of us."*

Yes, Marisol, he thought. For both our sakes, it would be better if we didn't meet again.

ACKNOWLEDGEMENTS

I thank my close family and friends for their patience while I researched and wrote this tale. The grass doesn't always get cut, the car needs washing, and the to-do list grows longer while the words slowly accumulate on the page.

Again, I need to thank Larry Edwards (larryedwards.com) for his invaluable help, and Tiffany Lynne (graypublishingservices.com) for the cover and interior design of this book.

OTHER BOOKS BY
E. PAUL BERGERON

TWO CAN PLAY
Available at: Amazon

The blood of ancient warriors courses through his veins.

A woman is dead.

A child is taken.

Only his own death would quell the hatred they feel for him. Can Gray escape his past and quench his bitter memories, or will others die to pay for his mistakes. He must answer the question. Does he flee, or fight? But he has sworn an oath to never kill again.

From the Blackfoot reservation in the north, to the barren lands of the Tonto O'odham in Arizona, this story takes the twists and turns that keep Gray alive. Because the man who deals in powdered death holds the key, and only Gray's death will open the lock.

*****

IN THE SHADOW OF VARGAS
BOOK ONE OF A LAND IN TURMOIL SERIES
Available at: Amazon

When William MacLeod, a member of an American fur trapping party, is forced into Spanish New Mexico to seek help for a wounded companion, he finds love and soon encounters a vengeance that will test his power to fulfill the promises he made.

Maria de Cordero, the beautiful daughter of a wealthy hacienda owner, is promised in marriage to another. That is until she makes the fateful mistake of falling in love with the young American. However, when her secret visit to MacLeod's jail cell is discovered, the man who lustfully awaits their marriage, Miguel Griego, captain of the governor's own militia, seeks his revenge against the insult to his name.

Can MacLeod find a way to escape, and save Maria from what her family believes is a fate worse than death?

ABOUT THE AUTHOR

You can contact E Paul Bergeron at: edpbergeron@cs.com

As I remember it, life began on top of a load of furniture in a sleigh drawn by a team of horses on a bitterly cold day. My mother was walking alongside in the snow when the moment arrived. She claims it was Valentine's Day, and of all people, she should know.

I attended a one-room schoolhouse outside of the French Canadian town of Mascouche, Quebec, and later in the metropolis of Montreal. At some point, an overworked schoolteacher wrote a note home to my mother to say that someday I would be a writer. The rest of the family laughed.

I spent long winter afternoons and nights reading, and acquired a love of history. I never realized the depth of this love until, years later, I stood on a street corner in old Montreal and read the inscription etched on a brass plaque attached to the cornerstone of a grey, brick building. It read simply, "Hudson's Bay Company." There stood the company synonymous with intrigue and adventure, and, being of French and Scottish heritage, the people behind those adventures were my ancestors. They were the French voyageurs, or coureur de bois, who traversed the mountains and forests, and paddled the streams and rivers, and the Scots who sent them out in search of the fur pelts, which led to the exploration of the North American continent.

I was sixteen when my father found an old farmhouse, badly in need of repair in West Bolton, Quebec. There I spent a year among people who would become lifelong friends. But my father passed away before he realized his vision for the house.

My mother took us back to Montreal, and I soon left school to find a job to help support the family. Then a Christmas phone call came from California, and the invitation to come west took us to North Hollywood, with palm trees and salt sea air--and word that I was too young to work. I returned to school.

I stood in the quad of North Hollywood High with a recent import from Australia, gazing at the parking lot and wondering how the school could have so many teachers. The Aussie informed me that it was the students' parking lot. Life had certainly changed.

I soon discovered California's lofty Sierra Nevada Mountains and streams filled with wild trout holding below the riffles, as if waiting for the dry fly attached to the end of my line. However, those towering, snow-capped peaks beckoned, and I could not care less if the trout were hungry. Life was wonderful.

With the early beginning of a writing life, and being married to an artist, our two beautiful daughters grew up in a home filled with artistic expression. Later, we moved down the coast to a town in Orange County, until it was time to sell a business and find a place to begin the work put on hold for so many years.

We settled in Hayden Lake, Idaho, with a beautiful home a few miles from the shores of Lake Coeur d'Alene. Now I load my Surly Long Haul Trucker bike on the back of the car and drive to the trail whose path winds its way along the Coeur d'Alene River. I find a spot beside a small lake to watch the ducks and geese feed among the lily pads, or sit in a small clearing beneath a canopy of leafy branches, and there work out the twists and turns of the stories I want to tell.

Visit him online at:

Website: http://www.epaulbergeron.com

Facebook: http://www.facebook.com/EPaulBergeron/

www.ingramcontent.com/pod-product-compliance
Lightning Source LLC
Chambersburg PA
CBHW060345260626
47160CB00006B/2208